In the Flesh

Sato could smell that Chloe had been in David's room. A combination of lily of the valley and musk permeated the air. Following the scent, he strode to his futon and threw back the covers. He expected to discover – who knew what – a snake? A cushion full of pins? Instead he found a scrap of lacy black and a note. He shook out the silk, which resolved itself as a pair of women's panties, and read the script: 'I can still taste you,' it said. 'Your firm resilience against my tongue, the flood of your salty strength. Perhaps you would allow another mouth, hungrier yet, to kiss your proud sword. Until then, sleep with these under your pillow and dream of me...'

The woman was a devil. There was no doubt.

By the same author:

Ménage
Cooking Up a Storm
The Top of Her Game
Velvet Glove

In the Flesh
Emma Holly

BLACK LACE

This book is a work of fiction.
In real life, make sure you practise safe, sane and consensual sex.

This edition published in 2007 by
Black Lace
Thames Wharf Studios
Rainville Rd
London W6 9HA

Copyright © Emma Holly 2007

The right of Emma Holly to be identified as the Author of the Work
has been asserted in accordance with the Copyright, Designs and
Patents Act 1988.

A catalogue record for this book is available from the British Library.

www.black-lace-books.com

Typeset by SetSystems Ltd, Saffron Walden, Essex

Printed and bound by Mackays of Chatham PLC

The paper used in this book is a natural, recyclable product made
from wood grown in sustainable forests. The manufacturing process
conforms to the regulations of the country of origin.

ISBN 978 0 352 34117 4

To Michele Hauf,
talented author and friend,
for believing.

Renunciation

The knowledge of what she'd done chased her from the club, chased her like the memory of Mary Alice Ryan's soft white throat. Her heels clattered across the car park. One slid on the gravel and her ankle turned, a stab of pain shooting up one tendon. She ignored it. She could see the car.

You're not to speak of this, her father would say. *It was just a bad dream.*

She battled against the driver-side lock, a sob tangling with her curses. Fucking thing.

The key turned and she flung herself inside the poison-green Ferrari, alarm bleating until she did the fucking seat belt. She gunned the engine; pulled on to the road with a squeal of rubber.

But she couldn't outrun the memories any more than she could outrun her fear of forgetting. *This never happened. Never happened.* Except it had. She'd meant to do it and it was done. She'd hurt David beyond forgiveness. She'd shown him what she was, what she'd always been, what he'd been too Sir Galahad-ish to see. She was who she was and now he could live with it, too.

She didn't think where she was going: just drove down the dark, winding road, past the Cumberland Farms shop and on to the highway.

She could go back to Atlantic City; perform again. She still had it. Everyone said she had it. She could feel the slick, cool pole between her hands, pressed against her barely covered sex. She could feel the eyes in the darkness; the hard-breathing, faceless men; the power she'd gather like a palmful of smoke. She shuddered at the memory of their sweaty fingers slipping bills under her G-string: fives and tens, twenties and hundreds. But she had money now, plenty of it. David didn't know the half of what she had. If she wanted, she could spend the rest of her life in bed. Alone.

She punched on the radio and let it blare through all six speakers. Mick wailed at her. He couldn't get no satisfaction. My man, she thought, her grin a snarl. She'd give David what he wanted. She'd give them all what they wanted. She'd be the whore everyone thought she was. The lights of the highway swept past her, sulphur-yellow brightness whooshing like the cars, like the short white dashes between the lanes. The tyres hummed on the surface of the road. *This never happened. Never happened.*

She clenched her jaw until her molars ached.

'It happened,' she said out loud, barely able to hear above the radio. 'Deal with it, bitch.'

The headlights came out of nowhere. For a millisecond they glinted on the old rain spots that bordered the windshield: diamonds and pearls. Then the glare blinded her. It was too bright, too close. She shifted down and jammed on the brake but she knew this was it. Her number had just been called.

'Fuck,' she said, surprisingly angry. Something big hit the car dead on, something huge. The shadow behind the headlights had an intolerable weight. Brakes squealed like tortured souls. As the world crumpled towards her in slow motion, shale-black shards of pain burst inside her skull.

'David,' she whimpered, but all that came out was *Day–*. The rest was swallowed by a cotton-wool fog. Her body disappeared.

I'm dead, she thought.

This never happened, said a familiar, acid voice.

But it wasn't her father's voice.

It was her own.

Seduction

1

Behind a pair of FBI-style sunglasses, Sato Takemori scanned the sea of reporters, alert to any threat. The sunglasses were a necessity. Throughout the lobby of Imakita International, flashbulbs popped like stars gone nova, their glare swallowed by the soaring, eighty-foot atrium. Huge banners hung behind the podium, behind the well-dressed, whip-thin figure of the speaker. These banners held screen shots of Imakita's most popular computer games: a medieval village from World Builder, a spaceship from Future Sim and, of course, the bodacious Laura Fleet from Fleet Streets I & II, their best-selling 1940s role-playing adventures.

Even Sato was not immune to Laura Fleet's appeal. Cartoon though she was, she was an Asian's dream of a Western woman: busty, bawdy, half dominatrix, half sex-kitten. But he could not afford to be distracted by fantasies. His master was speaking.

'This is a brave new world,' said David Imakita. Though his words were not deliberately humorous, the crowd chuckled. Sato was not surprised. His employer had a way about him in public, as if suffused with boyish glee. His private self was more complicated, but this *hyojo*, this public face, served him well. When the laughter died, David went on. 'Today Imakita, the largest publisher and developer of entertainment software in the world, joins forces with KL, the makers of the best gaming hardware. No longer will our designers have to make do with what's available, and hope it hasn't changed by the time our product is released. For the first time, we're in a position to maintain industry standards and to raise them. This represents a quantum leap forwards for both companies. In stability. In creativity. In potential for future growth. Our customers will reap the benefits and –' he twinkled '– so will our stockholders.'

The crowd laughed again. Sato watched them, weighing the sincerity of their smiles. He stood beside the skirted platform. His back was to the wall, his hands clasped loosely before him. Now and then he murmured orders to the tiny transponder on his lapel. The movement of his men through the lobby was discreet but visible. Six months had passed since David received the last death threat, but Sato had no intention of relaxing his guard. He tightened his left elbow. The compulsive gesture compressed his holster against his ribs. The weapon it held, a nine-millimetre semiautomatic, was as shiny as his ancestors' swords. His double-breasted jacket was specially tailored to hide the bulge, and to accommodate his physique. Though average in height, Sato's shoulders were massive, his belly big from his days in the sumo stable. He looked precisely what he was: hired muscle.

Sato did not care that ninety-nine per cent of the people in the room thought hired muscle was all he was. That was to be expected. How could spoiled Americans understand the love he bore his master? Or his utter dedication to *giri*, to duty. Their dogs would understand it better. Their dogs would understand his pride.

David Imakita had saved him from a life of mediocrity, had in truth saved his life. His gaze fell on his employer, tall as any *gaijin*, but far more elegant. From this angle, he could not see David's scar, a thumb-sized crescent beside his right eye. Sato did not know how David had earned it, but he was sure it was a badge of honour. He hoped Imakita's new partner had half David's integrity.

KL's CEO, a sweaty Korean with a face like a moon, stood beside David as he spoke. He nodded every few sentences, his grin broad and dazed as if he could not believe his good fortune. Though KL was a well-known firm, recent mismanagement had driven them to the brink of bankruptcy. Given David's ties to Japan, no one expected Imakita to look elsewhere for partners. But David was first and foremost a businessman. The Koreans had offered him a better deal.

Sato smiled to himself, an expression so subtle no one but he knew it was there. David Imakita was a businessman with a soft spot for the underdog. His Japanese associates didn't know it, but their dismissive attitudes towards the Koreans had cemented his decision.

Now David opened the floor for questions.

The reporter for the *Wall Street Journal* popped up from his chair. 'Mr Imakita, given KL's recent financial woes, what restructuring do you foresee needing to do and do you intend to keep present management in place?'

David folded his hands on the podium. 'I'm glad you asked that,' he said, as if the question were not a slap in his new partner's face. 'From Imakita's point of view, KL's greatest asset is its personnel. It is the human beings with whom we enter into this partnership, not the corporate structure. KL's management and I are reviewing whether any positions are redundant. If they are, I would feel privileged to move these individuals into other departments at Imakita. Our company is growing its employee base right now. I don't foresee that changing as a result of this merger.'

'That's very nice,' persisted the journalist, 'but how can Imakita afford to throw money into a black hole like KL Technologies?'

As if by wordless consensus, the rustle of notebooks and clothing stilled. In its place traffic sounds – the atonal music of midtown Manhattan – seeped through the lobby's tall arcs of glass. A single flashbulb went off. David smiled slowly, the expression narrowing his eyes. The power of the old shoguns shone from his lean, aristocratic face, power such as few Westerners could comprehend. They sensed it instinctively, however, and this was why they hushed. A burst of pride warmed Sato's chest. The reporter who had asked the question took an involuntary step back, almost tripping over his chair.

'Come back in a year,' David said softly, 'when KL's new graphics accelerator has emerged as the undisputed market leader. Then ask me if I've wasted my money.'

The room exploded with questions. What new graphics accelerator? When could they see a prototype? Why did he believe it would supplant current technology? David fielded the questions with aplomb, deferring to KL's CEO on technical issues, though he was knowledgeable on the subject himself. Each time he did, the Korean flushed with pleasure, his English becoming increasingly assured.

Sato nodded in approval. His master's diplomacy had earned him a friend. After today, his new partner would walk through fire for him. Which was, of course, precisely what David deserved.

Cold sweat bathed David's back by the time he stepped from the podium to the crowd. His jaw ached from smiling. Though he knew he was good at it, the public exercise of charm was trying to him, a mask he assumed for the sake of his audience. David might have been born in Chicago, but he'd been raised in a Japanese-style home. In his household, emotional restraint was the rule. He was *sansei*, third-generation Japanese-American. On days like this, he wondered how many generations full assimilation would require.

Now he shook the hands that shot towards him, accepted the pats on the back, and answered a last few questions. 'Great job,' the reporters who knew him said. 'Keep us up to date on the new graphics card.'

David spared a moment for all of them. In his business, the press could make or break a project, regardless of its intrinsic worth. Finally, he and Sato reached the blissful quiet of the back corridor. Shelley, David's petite blonde secretary, met them at the bank of lifts. His sigh of relief seemed to take her aback. 'Are you all right?' she asked, her Shirley Temple curls trembling with concern. 'You look pale.'

David straightened his sweat-chilled spine and smiled at her. 'Nothing an hour in a hot bath wouldn't cure.'

That startled her, too. A blush crept up her plump white cheek. Perhaps Sato was right about her having feelings for him. She handed him a small electronic slate. 'I thought you'd want your digital assistant. I input this afternoon's messages.'

'You're a gem,' he said. 'Why don't you head home? It's been a long week.'

'Thank you, sir.' Her eyes shone with gratitude, despite it being well past quitting time. The press conference had, as usual, run late.

She joined Sato and David in the lift. Three levels down they reached the underground garage. As the doors opened, the sound of a slap rang across the parking bay. Just outside, a man and woman stood. The woman, clearly the recipient of the blow, pressed her hand to her cheek and swore. David froze halfway over the threshold.

More than the violence had shocked him. The woman was a heart-stopper. She was slim and curved, her dress deep red lace over deep red satin: last year's Givenchy. David followed fashion the way some men followed art. This sleeveless sheath clung to her as if it had been sewn on to her body. The scalloped hem caught her mid thigh.

What a pair of legs, he thought. Wraparound legs. Her hair fell to the small of her back, a sheaf of polished mahogany, a shampoo ad. She reminded him of someone, though he couldn't put his finger on who.

'That's right,' the woman was saying, her hands planted on her hips, her incredible body vibrating with fury. 'Show me what a big man you are. Show me how much better you are than all the rest.'

'Bitch,' snarled her partner. He cocked his fist for another swing.

Before the man could strike, Sato grabbed him from behind. The woman didn't waste her chance. Immediately, she kneed her abuser in the groin. David winced as the man doubled over. Sato gaped in surprise but didn't let go. Apparently, one blow was not enough. With the fiercest laugh David had ever heard, the woman kicked the man's shins with her pointy-toed heels. Trapped by Sato's hold, robbed of breath by her first sally, the man could not defend himself.

David didn't approve of such behaviour, even from a woman.

'Hey,' he said, stepping between them.

This did not stop her, either. She attacked him instead. Her heel sent a spike of pain through his knee. Her nails arced towards his face. So determined was her assault, he had to hook his foot behind her leg to drop her. They fell to the cement with a mutual *whoof.* David was on top. As soon as the woman caught her breath, she went wild. Holding her was like trying to restrain a cornered animal. He could feel every muscle clench and fire beneath him. Slim though he was, he outweighed her by a good eighty pounds. He had a man's strength on his side, and Sato's training. She couldn't have dreamed she'd overpower him, but the futility of her efforts did not diminish them.

This woman was a fighter.

He cursed and got a tighter grip on her wrists.

'I'll call security,' Shelley quavered.

'No!' David and Sato barked, knowing better than she what a scandal this could cause.

'Get off,' the woman screamed, writhing like a cat who fears a bath. 'Get off, get off, get off!'

He slung his thigh over hers to still it. She growled low in her throat and pumped her hips upwards, desperate to throw him off. Her mound was surprisingly plump, a sheath of flesh cushioning her pubic bone. It crushed his balls against the root of his cock. The sensation was unexpectedly pleasurable. Heat suffused his groin, making him aware of a strong throb of blood between his legs. He was hard. She seemed to realise it just as he did. At once, she stopped struggling and stared. Her breasts heaved into the deep, square neckline of her dress. Her eyes were the colour of an autumn leaf. His erection, cradled precisely against her sex, pounded in the silence like a telltale heart. It was a miracle the others couldn't hear it.

One brow quirked behind her dark brown tangle of hair. 'Enjoying yourself?'

Her mocking drawl was a sharp contrast to her earlier hysteria. David flushed, but did not let her rile him. 'Have you got yourself under control?'

'Why, yes,' she said. 'I believe I have.'

He released her cautiously, the stiffness at his crotch making his movements awkward. Happily, she made no move to continue the fight. When she stood, her dress was rucked above her hips. David had a rather graphic side view of her lower torso. He should have looked away but couldn't seem to make himself. She wore sheer black thigh-highs topped with lace, and no panties. Her bottom was a sight to behold, each cheek firm and high and hollowed at the side where a muscle tensed inward. She tugged her hem down without the slightest sign of embarrassment.

'You're crazy,' panted the man David supposed was her boyfriend. He was staring, too. 'You need a fucking shrink.'

The woman pretended not to hear him. She readjusted her breasts inside her dress. Her bra was red.

'She's crazy,' the man repeated, his eyes going to David for support. His face was cadaver-thin. Every scrap of clothing he wore was black. He looked like a rocker or a druggie. He also looked familiar.

David stepped closer. 'Do I know you?'

The man shifted in Sato's hold. 'I'm Ian Quist. I'm composing the score for Alpha Raiders. I played it for your marketing department today.'

Ian Quist. He was the lead guitarist for a popular Boston band, not quite national but verging on it. He was good, David recalled. But that didn't mean he couldn't be replaced. 'Well,' he said. 'I think you had better leave before we reconsider our investment in you.'

The man complied with a muttered curse. David turned back to the woman. She was smacking her rear free of dust, facing away from him. Shelley performed the same service for his suit jacket. David barely noticed. He was too busy watching the woman jiggle.

'Are you OK?' Shelley whispered.

He squeezed her shoulder without looking at her. The woman's hair had fallen forwards over her shoulders. Her neck was exquisite, Audrey Hepburn-esque. He licked his upper lip. That neck demanded love bites. 'I'm fine,' he said. 'Go home. I'll see you on Monday.'

She departed with a birdlike twitter of worry. David waited, a formless tension squeezing his chest. The woman turned.

His breath caught in his throat. Every trace of emotion had been erased from her face. Her expression radiated the serenity of a Noh mask. He'd never seen features so perfect. Her lips were full, their edges delicate and defined. Her nose was straight and narrow, her brow high, her cheekbones dramatic. Her almond-shaped eyes seemed ineffably soft. He'd seen children without such flawless, blush-kissed skin. On skin like that, the fading slap mark seemed more decoration than wound.

She swiped her hand on her hip and extended it towards him. 'I suppose I should introduce myself. I'm Chloe Dubois.'

In a trance, David clasped her fingers. They were warm and dry. 'Pleased to meet you, Miss Dubois. Can we give you a lift somewhere?'

Her mouth twitched on one side. He supposed the offer seemed odd, considering they'd been wrestling on the floor a minute ago. She ducked her head, obscuring her smile while at the same time drawing his attention to it. The pose had a practised feel. Whatever flaws Miss Dubois possessed, insecurity towards men did not number among them.

'That would be very kind,' she said.

As usual, Sato slid behind the wheel of the silver-plum limousine. The passenger compartment was left to David and his guest. She took the leather banquette facing his. She did not stare at the muted Persian carpet, or the gold-plated door handles. Either she rode in cars like this every day, or she was very self-controlled. He suspected the latter. A bubble of amusement, giddy and fragile, expanded in his chest. This was surely the strangest encounter he'd ever had with a woman. He offered her a drink. He was thinking champagne; she accepted San Pellegrino. As she swallowed the imported water, he watched her throat move. Oh, that long, graceful throat. The rush hour traffic disappeared from his awareness, his cock expanding until his trousers drew taut across his hips.

He wondered precisely how he might seduce her, and how quickly.

'Good,' she said, and dropped the empty bottle into the lacquered trash slot. As she crossed her legs, the hiss of silk burned his ears. He remembered all the flesh her hosiery hadn't covered. A hand slid up those stockings, up those extraordinary legs, would find nothing but heat at the end of its journey.

But she was making her own inventory. Her gaze travelled over him, cool and inscrutable. Was she judging the cut of his suit, or the build of the body beneath? Perhaps both. Her perusal slowed where his erection distorted the front of his trousers. The back of his neck prickled. He had no doubt he was blushing.

This is ridiculous, he thought, and braced his forearms on his thighs. 'You look familiar,' he said.

She smiled and flicked her glossy hair behind her shoulders. 'I ought to. I'm your most famous employee.' She seemed to relish his confusion. Reaching forwards, she tapped his knee with one burgundy nail. The contact sent a zing to his strangled groin. 'Fleet Street? The case of the missing mummy?'

Light dawned through his testosterone fog. 'You're Laura Fleet?' She sat back, preening with satisfaction. David shook his head. 'I didn't know the designers used a real model.'

'Well, they did. And you've been paying me ever since.'

Something about that struck him as wrong, but he couldn't focus well enough to figure out what. He would unravel the mystery later, he decided – later, when she was gone. Not gone for ever, though. That wasn't what he wished at all.

Hers was not a salubrious neighbourhood. Trash blew in eddies along the cracked and weedy sidewalk. Graffiti marked the lower reaches of the undistinguished brick flats. A faint odour of urine hung in the air. Why a woman like her was living in a place like this, he could not imagine. Caution tightened his stomach as she swung her legs on to the kerb. One look at the teenage boys hanging at the corner – hoodlums, his mother would have said – convinced him Sato would have to guard the car.

Sato's samurai glower said what he thought of that.

'I'll be back soon,' David assured him and followed Chloe out.

His escort was not expected. Chloe threw an impatient look over her shoulder. 'My, aren't we the gentleman?' she said, but her sarcasm did not extend to demanding he leave.

Her progress up the stairs demolished his intent to remain alert. The clenching of her calf muscles, the peachy curve of her bottom, the willowy arc of her waist, all laid claim to his attention. He barely registered the stench of stale beer. At the third creaky landing, she slid her key into a lock and opened the door. 'Shit,' she said.

Adrenalin raced like wildfire over his nerves. His muscles tensed; his heart rate accelerated. Before he'd drawn another breath, David placed his body between hers and the apartment.

The place had been ransacked. Furniture, most of it secondhand, had been turned upside down, its cushions eviscerated. A dead goldfish lay in a puddle on the floorboards.

'My fish!' she said, sounding more angry than afraid.

He shoved her back into the hall. 'Stay here,' he ordered. 'I need to look around.'

She obeyed, though he heard her cursing as he checked for intruders. The search didn't take long. Her apartment consisted of a combined living and bedroom, a kitchen, and a bath. The kitchen floor was a sea of broken crockery. Everything in the place seemed to have been shattered or tossed from its home. Whoever had done this had made a thorough job of it.

Which ruled out Ian Quist. He wouldn't have had the time.

Brow furrowed, David retraced his path to the door. He knelt to examine the lock. 'No one seems to have forced this.'

Chloe waded into the chaos. 'Whoever it was probably bribed the caretaker. He's not exactly Mr Integrity.'

'Is anything missing?'

She lifted a brilliant Spanish shawl from the ruins of the pull-out sofa. The silk was miraculously unscathed. She folded it carefully and draped it over her arm. He noticed her lower lip was caught between her teeth, but this was the only sign of agitation she betrayed. 'No,' she said. 'Nothing's gone.'

'Do you know who did this?'

'Considering he's done it twice before, my guess is my ex-employer.' A flash of annoyance tightened the skin around her eyes. 'Crazy bastard. I told him I wouldn't work for him again if I was stony broke and starving.'

David tried to conceal how much this shocked him. What sort of life did this woman lead? He adjusted the knot of his tie. 'You can't stay here,' he said.

'No kidding.' She prodded the goldfish with the toe of her black suede shoe. The creature didn't twitch. 'Damn. I liked that fish.'

Her eyes glittered with what could have been tears or a trick of the light. An emotion David couldn't identify kicked his heartbeat up a notch. Whatever the feeling was, it was more intense than the adrenalin rush that had accompanied his search of the apartment. His skin crawled with it, wave after tingling wave. He stared at her. The afternoon light shone through the spotty windows, limning her figure, turning her dress the colour of living blood. She was as still as a painting: a peaceful *pietà* mourning the pathetic corpse of her pet.

This is why it happens, he thought with the corner of his brain that still worked. The curve of a cheekbone, a dress of a certain hue, the illusion of tears: this is why men make idiots of themselves.

'You can come home with me,' he heard himself say.

She didn't respond the way a normal woman would have. She didn't say: that's kind of you, but I'll call a friend, a hotel, my mother. Instead, she stared back at him, the same emotionless, measuring look she'd given him in the limo. Her gaze caught on his scar, causing the tightened skin to burn strangely for a moment. Her expression didn't change, but in her molten eyes something haunted lurked, the shadow of a shadow. Whatever test she'd administered, he seemed to have passed. 'All right,' she said. 'I'll see if the bastard left me enough to pack a bag.'

Sato's heart sank when he saw them both come down the stairs. David was carrying a large blue bag, the kind hockey players used to carry their equipment. It looked heavy. Sato popped the boot and got out of the car, not because he thought David needed help, but because he had to at least try to stop him.

'Are you crazy?' he hissed as soon as the hood blocked them from view. 'You do not even know this woman.'

David shrugged, uncharacteristically sheepish. 'Her flat was broken into. I can't let her stay here. Whoever it was might come back.'

'So take her to a hotel, or to a friend – assuming a woman like that has any.'

'She'll be safer with me,' David said, and slammed the boot.

Sato was sure he intended this as a dismissal. To question his superior further would have been improper.

He clenched his fists. The woman was inside the limo already, making herself at home. One last protest rasped his throat. 'She is trouble,' he said.

David stared at the nearest scrawl of graffiti. 'Believe me, old friend, I know.'

He slid into the car without another word, leaving his employee to follow. Sato swallowed a surge of anger at David's reckless disregard for his own safety. Who knew who this woman was? A dopehead. A murderer. An industrial spy!

He grimaced as he pushed his solid body behind the wheel. He knew one thing. He intended to watch this viper like a hawk.

As they pulled away, Chloe waved at the gang on the corner. The tallest of them, a handsome young man with a bandanna around his hair, grinned and gave her a thumbs up. His dark eyes admired her new ride.

David forced his eyebrows back where they belonged. That she might be friends with the hoodlums hadn't occurred to him.

An image flashed through his mind of the young black man taking her in the hall of her seedy building. He jammed her against a wall, his cock pumping between her legs, their arms spread in a mutual crucifixion of pleasure: black on white, bronze on cream. The fantasy was so vivid David could see the man's gold fillings gleam.

Suddenly hot, he shrugged out of his jacket and loosened his tie. They rode in silence until Sato turned on north 95. Chloe sat straighter. 'I assumed you lived in Manhattan,' she said.

'My main residence is in Vermont.' He schooled himself to stillness, his eyes holding hers. 'Is that a problem?'

She took a moment to think this over. 'I suppose not.'

'You don't have to stay with me. I can put you up at a hotel.'

She smoothed her palms down long, shapely thighs. Two fans of lashes hid her eyes. 'Do you expect me to sleep with you?'

She might have been asking if he preferred his steak rare or well done. She seemed to have nothing invested in his answer.

'No,' he said, but he was lying through his teeth.

2

Nothing could dim his awareness of her.

With the push of a lever, the pedestal that held David's computer whispered up from the floor. Chloe didn't bat an eye. He plugged his digital assistant into its slot and called up the day's messages. As he paged through them, he fought impatience. Some were urgent, but he couldn't keep his mind on business. Her stillness tugged at him. Gossamer thrills swept his skin, there and then not there, like spider's silk. She seduced him by doing nothing, by exuding her scent, by staring out the window like a geisha on a scroll.

She was a puzzle-box, a potentially dangerous one. But did that matter? He was David Imakita. He could afford to take risks. Perhaps he needed to. It had been months since he'd been with a woman. This deal with KL had swallowed all his time.

His cell phone trilled: an international call. No more than half aware of what he was saying, he responded automatically. Ironically, his Japanese had never been smoother. Yes, he'd be honoured to travel to Tokyo to reaffirm ties to old business friends. Next month? Yes, he understood how interested they were in his current venture. He would consult his schedule and get back to them. *Oya-sumi-nasai. Domo arigato.* Good night and thank you.

When he set the phone down, she was watching him. It felt like a victory.

'You were born in this country, weren't you?' she said, the first words she'd uttered in an hour. Her voice was husky. She must have strained her vocal cords. Despite her hoarseness, he had a hard time believing she was the same woman who'd screamed like a scalded cat and tried to scratch his eyes out.

'Well, were you?' she said.

He shook himself. 'I was born in Chicago. I studied Japanese as an adult. I thought it would be good for business.'

She turned to the window again, her curiosity sated. A memory snapped into his mind: his first interview, before he'd decided he'd rather work for himself. The manager, a cocky young Ken doll, had complimented him on his English. David was a *summa cum laude* Harvard business grad with a discernible Chicago accent. That idiot had acted as if David had just stepped out of a rice paddy. He was glad Chloe hadn't made the same mistake. Perhaps it was a small thing. Perhaps he was searching for reasons to like her: a woman who lived in a slum and had knock-down, drag-out fights with her boyfriends.

He studied her profile. She had beautiful olive skin, making him wonder about her background. He wasn't used to silence from Americans. Most required no prodding to talk about themselves. But she must have felt his attention. 'If you've got something to say,' she said, her tone milder than her words, 'spit it out.'

'I was wondering if you were an actress.' At her bark of laughter, an unwelcome heat suffused his face. 'I just thought, with a name like Chloe Dubois . . .'

She ran one finger around her plunging neckline, her smile crooked. 'I do lots of acting, though I'm not usually paid for it. I suppose you would say I'm a model.'

'And what would *you* say you were?'

Her teeth and eyes flashed in unison. 'Very quick, Mr Imakita. *I'd* say I'm a student of life.'

'Call me David,' he said.

A current moved between them: liquid, hot, a mingling of desire and respect. He knew she was reassessing him, deciding if he was worth her serious attention. 'Call me Chloe,' she said.

Her response gave him far more satisfaction than it should have.

They pulled up to his estate after dark, rolling past the iron gates and down the lane of tall boxwood hedges. Stars glittered in a deep, clear sky, always a shock after a week in the city. The staff had gone home for the night. Apart from the reflection of the heavens, no light shone in the twenty arched windows. The moon had set and Sato's security cameras ran on infra-red. As a result, the house was a looming weight: a pseudo ruin, like the twisted carcass of a tree preserved by a careful gardener. Missing stones softened its lines and gathered at its base in scattered cairns. This house had roots. This house belonged. Sometimes David could hardly believe it was his.

He rubbed his scar, the pad of his thumb circling beside his eye as he waited for the car to stop. When it did, he stepped out and offered Chloe his hand, his body tensing a moment before they touched. He expected her skin to be cool, but it was hot. The limo's air conditioning seemed not to have affected her.

A chorus of crickets blew towards them on a humid breeze. Chloe's hair fluttered. Her hand slipped away. She frowned at the crumbling stone walls. 'This place is falling down.'

David smiled. 'It only looks like it's falling down. The façade dates back to the Civil War. I bought the shell and built a new structure inside. Don't worry, though. It's secure.'

'As long as you're sure.' A smile coloured her voice.

She was teasing him. She couldn't have shocked him more if she'd bared her breast.

Sato stomped by, carrying her bag.

'Thank you,' Chloe called after him.

He grunted and shouldered the heavy door open.

David gestured her before him. 'Shall we?'

Auntie's household shrine, a small wooden structure with a pagoda-style roof, sat outside the door. A flame no bigger than his thumbnail flickered in the worn stone lantern. Any other night, David would have stopped to clap three times for the spirits. Tonight he merely nodded at the mossy, water-filled hollow. Chloe had enough to adjust to. At least, he told himself that's why he skipped the simple Shinto ritual.

'Shoes!' Sato barked, when she would have stepped through in her heels.

'Oh.' She looked around in confusion. 'I didn't know.'

David showed her the cleverly camouflaged shoe cabinet, then knelt to hold a pair of wooden slippers for her to step into. Unable to resist, he steadied her leg. Her ankle bone was strong but narrow enough to circle between his finger and thumb. Her hand settled on the back of his head. 'I feel like Cinderella,' she said, her voice coy.

He hadn't expect the flirtation and her words literally threw him off balance. His shoulder brushed her hip. She extended her hand to help him rise. As he took it, her fingers stroked his palm. The caress was subtle, but deliberate enough to send a ripple of sensation through his groin. He couldn't remember the last time he'd felt so drawn to a woman. Blood pounded through his veins in heavy surges. His cock was so hard it ached. Did she feel the same attraction or was she teasing him? A round paper lantern, a *chochin*, hung from the ceiling above them. Its subdued parchment glow did nothing to illuminate the emotion behind her eyes.

Then Auntie bustled out to greet them. Despite the hour, her kimono was immaculate, her eyes bright. 'Guests!' she exclaimed, clapping with the girlish enthusiasm that endeared her to everyone she met.

David kissed her wrinkled cheek. 'Just one, Auntie.' He touched Chloe's shoulder. 'Chloe Dubois, I'd like to introduce my honoured Auntie. She runs this house – and my life, when I let her. Auntie, this is Chloe Dubois. She's going to be staying for a while.'

'Pleased to meet you,' said Chloe. She seemed a little stiff, but not cold.

Auntie beamed and bowed. 'I'll prepare the green room,' she said, and scurried off to do so.

'Well,' said Chloe. 'She's certainly efficient.'

Sato spun to face her. 'She believes in doing her job well.'

'As do you, I'm sure.' She stared pointedly at her heavy bag.

Sato's jaw tightened. 'I'll take your things to your room.'

This time, she did not thank him. David fought a smile. He saw he'd have to keep these two in separate corners.

He led her on a tour of his house. The interior was Japanese, boasting *shoji* screens, airy spaces, and special alcoves for his *ikebana*. He preferred fresh to dried flowers, and the ones he'd arranged last weekend were decidedly tired. But such creations were meant to be fleeting. Aside from the faded arrangements, the predominant colours were ivory and brown and green. Rectangles were the predominant shape, repeated on half walls and woodwork, on ceiling beams and low, wide windows. The views of the garden lent the house its vibrance, and in the dark they weren't much to look at. He promised Chloe she'd see them in their glory tomorrow.

She smiled noncommittally, more fascinated by his dolls. She bent towards the last case, almost pressing her nose to the glass. 'I've never known a man who collected dolls before.'

'They're popular gifts. All mine are *kyo-ningyo*, display dolls from Kyoto. This one's kimono is a traditional costume from the Heian period. They're considered works of art. Just to look at. Not to play with.'

'They're beautiful. And they're perfectly safe in there, aren't they? No one can touch them.' Her voice had gone dreamy. He peered at her. She was stroking her neck and her face bore a strange, dazed expression. A second later, she shook herself and smiled. 'I don't suppose you could tell me where I can lay my weary head?'

'Certainly.' He hid his disappointment. 'I'll escort you to your room. Auntie will bring you a tray in case you're hungry.'

'Thank you,' she said, smothering a yawn. He knew he wouldn't seduce her tonight.

Because of his responsibility for David's safety, Sato lived in the main house. The rest of the staff, excepting Auntie, resided in the nearby village of Strathmore. Within the main house were two traditional Japanese baths: David's private bath on the fourth floor and the grotto bath on the first, not far from Sato's room.

Occasionally, David and Sato would soak together in the grotto. David, however, was not entirely comfortable with the concept of communal bathing, or perhaps he sensed Sato's own discomfort. In his homeland, Sato would not have given the practice a second thought. He enjoyed speaking informally with his employer, talking of business or other idle topics. Nonetheless, he was glad they did not bathe together often.

He did not want to jeopardise their friendship by making his feelings too clear. David was a man who walked a single sexual path. Sato suspected he had imbibed some of the Americans' unease for experimentation. Sato might wish it were not so, but he ignored David's inhibitions at his peril.

There was a chance his master would join him tonight. He might wish to smooth the tension that had risen between them because of the woman.

Regardless of whether he appeared, Sato would not be caught unprepared. In his room, before he donned his belted cotton robe, he dealt briskly with his arousal. He poured oil into each palm, took his rigid stalk in a two-handed grip, and proceeded to pull the hard, pliant flesh up and out, hand over hand. He had been erect for some time and the friction was a welcome relief. Softly, he sighed with pleasure.

Without his willing it, images drifted through his mind: David's hard belly, his shoulders, the way his leg muscles corded during their self-defence training. Sato had long since given up trying to banish these pictures. When his organ rose, they came. When it emptied, they would fade. He quickened the pace of his tugs and marginally increased the pressure. The head of his stalk made a sharp flipping sound as his oiled fingers snapped over it, faster, tighter. David's cock would make this sound. David's –

Sensation curled in his testicles. He saw his mouth descend to David's groin; imagined David's smooth, hard prick against his tongue. Then, as if the image were an erotic whip, Sato burst in a series of brief contractive pulses. His spine relaxed. His organ sagged. When he recovered his breath, he knelt and folded the towel he'd spread to protect the tatami mats. With the opposite side, he mopped his sweaty face and chest. A last string of seed dripped from his glans and he wiped that, too. He rose.

He felt heavy still. His penis dangled between his legs,

thicker than it should have been, more sensitive to the caress of the air. He suspected the woman was at fault. He'd been very aware of David's attraction to her; had probably known the second his master hardened as they wrestled on the floor of the garage.

Not that he faulted his master for this. The woman was as tempting as a ripe, red cherry, as spicy as Indian curry. If she had not had 'trouble' emblazoned across her forehead, Sato would have been tempted to pursue her himself.

His organ twitched weakly at the thought. He wondered if he should seek release again, but it would take longer this time. It seemed overindulgent, as well. A man of his position ought to exercise discipline. Should David turn up, the hot water would mute what was left of his desire.

The bathroom was empty when he arrived. As always, Sato paused to admire the raw granite walls from which the grotto took its name. Steam-loving ferns grew from hollows in the stones. The window, which overlooked the back garden, followed the irregular shape of the rocks that surrounded it. The floor was tiled in roughly dressed limestone and the huge hot tub, set flush with the floor, was rimmed in polished cedar. Sato activated the jets to heat the water, then soaped and rinsed himself under the separate tap.

He did not linger over the weighty flesh between his legs.

Clean and wet, he stepped into the tub with a sigh. The temperature was far from scalding, but it eased his tensions all the same. He rested his head on the rim, letting his feet float upwards through the bubbling currents. For now, his arousal was a pleasant state, undemanding, almost lulling. A man should be grateful, Sato thought, for a body that lived as fully as his. How many, after all, could say they enjoyed men and women equally? Life could be a banquet for one such as he. If his life was not a banquet at the moment, that was his choice.

Someone entered the room just as he was drifting into a pleasant dream. He opened his eyes. His belly clenched. The woman stood in the doorway. Her navy blue *yukata* matched his own. Auntie must have left her the robe. Auntie must have told her where to bathe.

She did not seem at all put off by his presence. Her smile was creamy. 'Well, look who's here.'

'I will leave,' he said, water sheeting off him as he rose.

'Don't be silly.' She stroked the front of her neck, a languid motion that drew his attention to its length. Did she know that, to his people, necks were as alluring as breasts? 'Japanese bathe together all the time, don't they? So there's nothing to be embarrassed about.'

Sato sank back under the water. 'David rarely uses this bath.'

Her smile deepened. Thickly lashed, her eyes were sleepy amber slits. Already the steam was flushing her cheeks. She looked like a woman who had just been fucked, or who wanted to be. 'Who says I want to bathe with David?'

The implication was, of course, that she wanted to bathe with him. Sato knew better. This sort of woman was a vulture for male attention, any male attention. The more the male resisted, the more she wished to conquer him. Her flirtation was not personal. It had nothing to do with him. 'Do as you please,' he said, and closed his eyes.

Her robe rustled as she removed it and hung it on a peg near the door. 'I wash before I get in, don't I?'

He was sure she knew the answer. 'Yes,' he grunted.

'Don't peek,' she said, archly mocking.

Irritated to the point of perversity, he opened his eyes.

She sat on the little wooden stool, soaping herself in three-quarter profile. Her body was everything a woman's should be: strong, curved, graceful. In that position, she even looked demure. And small. He doubted she stood an inch over five foot two. Her creamy, olive skin brought his tongue to dry lips. Her breasts made him fist his hands. Here was the lure of the *gaijin*. Her breasts were those of an old-fashioned pin-up girl. She reminded him of Marilyn Monroe or Betty Grable: an irresistible combination of innocence and sex. Her nipples were cinnamon pink.

Her eyes slid shut as she soaped between her legs. She had shaved her pubic hair to a thin, mink-black strip. Her labia curved together like the mouth of a conch shell, pink and ivory gloss. Her pearl was hidden in the lather.

He jerked his gaze away as soon as he realised he was looking for the tiny jewel. He was too late. The insistent throb of his cock told him the damage had been done. Her fingers delved deeper. 'Mm,' she said, a throaty hum. 'That feels nice.'

He frowned. 'You cannot lure me with such cheap, childish games.'

She opened her eyes and smiled. 'Can't I?'

Her approach was so obvious it should not have affected him. It did, though. It did. His breath came faster as she rinsed and stepped into the tub like Venus returning to the sea. A silver ring twinkled at her navel, then disappeared beneath the froth. She sat across from him. Water covered her to her neck. She wriggled. Her feet bumped his at the centre of the tub.

He would not demean himself by pulling back. The sad truth was, however, that he did not want to pull back. The brush of her toes sent a thrill of pleasure through his body. Chills swept across his shoulders, raising goose bumps despite the heat.

'Cold?' she suggested in a hushed, brandied tone.

He did not answer. She could seduce the Buddha with that voice, and never mind the rest of her.

With a convincing yawn, she stretched her arms and folded them behind her head. The upper slope of her breasts emerged from the water, flushed and shining. Her toes rasped the arch of his foot. He shivered again, his organ as hard as the granite wall behind him.

'So, Sato,' she said. 'Are you a karate master? Judo? Aikido?'

'Sumo,' he said, the word still Japanese in his mouth.

Her head tilted towards her shoulder, her expression curious. Most people were surprised to hear he'd studied sumo. They expected *sumitori* to be as big as elephants. 'Are there different weight classes?'

He did not wish to converse with her, but the habits of politeness were hard to throw off. He shook his head. 'It takes many years to grow as big as the *yokozuna*, the grand champions. The smaller wrestlers are quicker and more agile. That is how they defeat larger opponents.'

'I see.'

This time her smile was pleasant, intrigued. He felt obliged to disabuse her of the notion that he had been successful at the sport. 'I did not win many matches.'

She pursed her lips. Apparently, when she chose, her face could be very expressive. 'In that case, I presume you supplemented your skills before signing on as David's bodyguard?'

'I am an expert marksman, and fully trained in the latest security technology.'

'Good.' Her eyes sparkled with mischief. 'I feel much safer.'

His mouth jerked before he caught it. She had almost made him smile. No wonder David found her so appealing. The woman was a chameleon.

Now she clucked at him. 'Goodness, such a frown! With such a frown you could frighten little children.'

Too bad he could not frighten her. Before he could gather his wits, she tried another ploy. 'Oh, Sato,' she complained, rolling her head and rubbing the back of her neck. 'My muscles are so tight. Do you think you could massage the kinks out?'

'No,' he growled.

She laughed, not at all embarrassed. 'I thought the Japanese would do anything for a guest. I thought it was a point of honour.'

'Know all about us, do you?'

She simpered with a skill that made his unruly organ sting with pressure. 'I'm reasonably well read.'

'Hah, I'll bet you saw *Shogun* on TV.'

His words could not scratch her self-confidence. She tossed her hair. 'As a matter of fact, I did.' Suddenly she was rising, moving towards him through the churning water. 'Is that what you like, Sato? A demure, servile woman who puts her nose to the floor when you enter a room?'

She stepped between his legs. He hadn't been aware he'd spread them until she did. Her knees brushed his inner thighs. Her hands slid up his wet, hairless chest, then swirled around the shell of his ears. At once, the steam grew thicker. He could barely catch his breath. 'No,' she murmured. 'I don't think that's what you want. I think your fantasy is to be taken by a lusty, busty American whore.'

He gasped for air as her hands slid back under the water. He couldn't seem to make himself pull away. He felt like a *bunraku* puppet. She was pulling strings he hadn't known he had. Her nipples were pouted and rosy. As he watched, their centres crinkled and stood out. She wanted him. She was not like those other American woman who thought he was too fat or too foreign or who only slept with him because he carried a gun and was dangerous. She wanted him and, oh, she was exquisite. Surely there had never been another female so sensual.

Or did he believe this because she did?

She drew closer, strafing his body with hers. She was swan-light, swan-lovely. Their lips brushed. A growl echoed in his belly. His arm rose. Before he knew it, the cup of his palm cradled her delicate head. Her hair was silk, half wet, half dry. He pulled her mouth to his. Her lips parted. Their tongues met and stroked. Ah, she tasted of sake. Auntie must have taken a tray to her room. The taste of the liquor was familiar, the taste of her exquisitely unknown. She was an artist of feint and retreat, of attack and parry. His vision began to blur as if some huge *rikishi* had tossed him from the *dohyo* on his head. He wanted to lay her over the side of the tub and screw her senseless: no preliminaries, just a hard, long fuck.

Then her hands gathered together on his cock. They stroked up his straining shaft and caught the thick, gathered foreskin. Cleverly, swiftly, she moved it back and forth over his glans, massaging him with his own skin. Tiny stabs of feeling shot through the sensitive flesh. Her hands were sweeter than his. Surprisingly strong, incredibly deft, they wrung feelings from his rigid stalk he had not known existed. The pleasure was almost painful. His balls tightened.

'No,' he moaned, some portion of his brain recalling the danger. 'My master desires you. You are not for me.'

'Your master!' Her laugh was sharp and hoarse. 'Believe me, mister, I am your master now.'

Without warning, she plunged beneath the swirling water. Her mouth nuzzled his balls, then caught and held his shaft. He cursed to his Shinto gods. His hands gripped her slender shoulders.

But he could not bring himself to push away.

This woman must have sold her soul to a devil. In Japan, *sumitori* were akin to movie stars. Even bad *sumitori* had their followers. Many women had done this for him, but never had it felt like this. Hot flowers of ecstasy bloomed through his body, almost numbing in their power. She played his organ with her tongue, her lips, even the edge of her teeth. Again, she manipulated his foreskin over the bursting head, this time with the suction of her mouth. His groans echoed off the ceiling as she alternated between sucking him so strongly he thought she'd pull him free, and so delicately he had to strain for every sensation. She fluttered the tip of her tongue over his tiny slit. His toes curled so hard, their joints popped.

A minute passed, and still she did not rise. Her hair floated around his hips like a mermaid's tresses, waving with her movements. Her breasts bobbed between his thighs. She drew him to the verge of her throat and suckled in rhythm with his heart. His bones began to melt. Clearly, she had the lung capacity of a pearl diver. Part of him feared for her safety, but the rest thrilled to the effort she was making. What beautiful woman ever thought she had to work so hard? Not to mention the symbolic danger she was in. She was vulnerable to him. At any moment he might push her down and hold her under. Would she struggle if he tried? Would she bite him to win free? Confused images – violent, erotic, helpless – stuttered through his mind. He saw her and him and David; David taking her in front of him, making him watch, each thrust a blow to heart and body. The images heightened his excitement until every muscle drew taut with conflicting urges. He wanted it to go on for ever, but he could not bear another second.

Finally, she burst free, moaning for her first breath. When she'd caught her next, he gripped the sides of her face and kissed her hard. Their tongues lashed together, then away.

'Finish it,' he ordered, pressing her shoulders down.

She smiled, baring white, even teeth. 'My pleasure,' she said, her voice as fierce as his.

She sank beneath the water and took him in her mouth. His crisis was near. Already, the pressure of impending climax throbbed in his shaft. The ache was so intense it almost felt like an orgasm. She sucked steadily now, hands cupping and squeezing his scrotum. Her fingers seemed to push his seed closer to egress; seemed to gather and compress it. Her tongue was slicker than the surrounding water, her mouth hotter. He held his breath, trying to hold the unbearable anticipation a moment longer, a second, and then his climax burst beyond any control he could exert. Sensation streaked through his belly and groin. His vision darkened. His seed pulsed free. He heard a cry: the cry of a warrior slain by shuddering waves of pleasure.

His cry ended on a sigh. He went limp. Her mouth pulled free. Slowly, gracefully, she stood, smoothing her wet hair around her narrow skull. The motion lifted breasts that rose and fell with her breathing, their nipples shivering and sharp. He stared at the rosy points and wanted her all over again.

She seemed to know her victory required no words. She backed away, smiling her sleepy, mocking smile. She turned. Her progress up the steps was slow and swaying, almost ceremonial. Through bleary eyes he admired her heart-shaped bottom. Two deep dimples marked the top of her cleft, the left slightly higher than the right. She embodied the Buddhist principles of beauty: asymmetry, simplicity, austere sublimity. A *netsuke* master could not have carved her more enticingly.

'This will not happen again,' he said, with all the sternness he could muster.

She dropped her head in ironic acknowledgement, her amusement unshaken.

He had a feeling she did not believe him.

3

David's first thought on waking was Chloe. He rolled on to his back and smiled. She was here, in his house. Soon he would see her. The prospect pleased him immensely.

He smoothed his hands down his chest, pushing the sheet before them. As was usual for this hour, he had a strong erection. He played his fingers up his sex, enjoying the sharp, quicksilver sensations. He loved making love in the morning. Perhaps Chloe would, too. His smile broadened. He could be a presumptuous bastard but, in this case, he thought his confidence well placed. Chloe Dubois was as hot as sesame oil sputtering in a wok. Chances were, he'd have a hard time keeping up with her.

Not that he wouldn't enjoy trying.

He circled the cap of his penis with the third finger of his right hand, spreading a slippery flow of pre-ejaculate. His glans sat at an uptilted angle on his shaft, flaring and round. One of his lovers in college had called it cute. At the time, he hadn't appreciated the compliment, but he soon learned she had no complaints about what he could do with his 'little man'. Fortunately for him, she was the first of many Ivy Leaguers to make the discovery.

With a grin for the memory, he rolled to his knees and stepped naked from the futon. A wall of windows formed one side of his room. They'd been fashioned to mimic partitioned rice-paper screens, with dark slats of wood framing horizontal panes. He slid one unit aside and stepped on to the covered veranda. Outside, summer reigned. Though shaded, the air was warm. It beat softly against his naked skin, brushing his half-erection. With a guest in the house, he supposed he ought to dress, but the exposure gave him a wonderful sense of freedom.

Here, where he stood, the house bared its soul. The old stone shell fell away to reveal the modern interior. His rooms were on the fourth floor. One floor down, the roof jutted out to support a raked gravel garden. Beyond that, a sculpted landscape startled the eye with pleasure.

His gardener, Master Wu, had transformed forty acres of farmland into an elaborate Eastern paradise. In a few short weeks, the maples would blaze like flame. For now, though, all was green. Wooden bridges arched over winding streams, which spilled into pools that brimmed with lilies and carp. Miniature hills rolled where once the ground had been flat. Pines grew sideways, rocks grew moss, and the occasional stone lion gambolled up an artificial slope.

His practical Vermont neighbours called it Imakita's folly. Sometimes he did, too. This garden would never be a piece of home to him, because Japan had never been his home. His mother had seen to it that he was as American as apple pie. He would fit in, she vowed. Nothing like the camps would happen to him. All through his teens he'd dressed American, talked American, and eaten American. Only his face was foreign – and his spirit, which was neither here nor there. Sometimes the garden seemed as exotic to him as it did to his neighbours. This morning, however, in the brilliant August sunshine, with the scent of cedar in the air, it was simply beautiful.

He would lead Chloe through his wonderland today. He pictured her warm, dark colouring against the verdant backdrop. She would look lovely. He suspected that would be reason enough for her to enjoy the walk.

Amused, he descended the stairs to the raked Zen garden. He decided against dressing. The staff knew not to interrupt him and none of the neighbours had a clear line of sight. If Chloe wandered in, well, he imagined he'd survive the embarrassment. A cooling breeze swept his skin as he began the smooth, flowing movements of his T'ai Chi Ch'uan exercise. Life seemed full of pleasant possibilities.

Sato usually ate with his employer but this morning the security chief was nowhere to be found. David wondered if he'd heard what was on the menu.

Auntie had served a traditional Japanese breakfast: fish, white rice and miso soup. She knew David and Sato preferred bagels. This did not matter. To her, the arrival of a guest was a good excuse to 'do things right'. Luckily, the guest woke in time to enjoy it. Chloe took her chair as if she were sleepwalking. She wore a navy *yukata*, one of the belted cotton robes he kept on hand for guests. She must have rolled out of bed and come straight down. Her hair wasn't even combed. She still looked gorgeous. To David's surprise, she ate everything without comment, though she did wrinkle her nose at the green tea.

'Auntie,' he said softly.

As always, his housekeeper had knelt geisha-style beside the sliding door to the dining room. He'd never been able to break her of this habit. In her mind, this was how a good servant behaved. She beamed at him. 'Yes, David-san?'

'Could you scrounge a pot of espresso for Miss Dubois and myself? I think we could use a stronger dose of caffeine this morning.'

'Of course, David-san,' she said, as happily as if it had been her own idea. 'Right away.'

'Thanks,' Chloe said once she was gone. 'I'm useless without a good jolt.' She rubbed one hand over her cheek. Her skin was creased by sheet marks. He experienced an almost uncontrollable urge to lean over and lick them.

'Is the food all right?' he said.

She nodded, then laughed. It was a real laugh, half snort, half chuckle. 'I'll eat anything I don't have to cook myself.'

He smiled. Their eyes met in a moment of shared self-deprecation. 'I'm the same way,' he said. 'I almost starved when I moved off campus at school. If it hadn't been for my girlfriends, I think I would have.'

She lifted her miso and sipped it. 'Girlfriends, plural?'

'There were a few.' There were dozens, actually, but he wasn't going to admit that. 'I didn't, er, blossom until I hit college. I was making up for lost time.'

'Girls in high school thought you were a geek, eh?'

'A skinny geek who liked classical music and flower-arranging.'

'Bummer.' She wiped her mouth on her napkin, pressing the cloth to her smile. 'Bet they thought you were gay.'

'Gay or just very, very weird.' He let his laugh out, enjoying the way it warmed his chest. 'I couldn't impress anyone with the fact that *ikebana* was the traditional art of samurai. They said flower-arranging was for girls.'

'So why did you do it?'

'It was the only remotely Asian class at the community centre. And it was free. This funny Italian lady taught it, Mrs D'Onofrio. She was so Chicago. "Ya gotta combine da beautiful lines to make da beautiful form." But she knew her stuff. I was hooked after the first week.' He turned his teacup in a circle. 'My mother was horrified. She begged me to go out for baseball. "Just try, David, just try. Sports are good. Sports are American." My first game, the pitcher knocked me unconscious with a curve ball.'

Chloe reached across the table to touch his scar. His breath caught. 'Is that how you got this?'

'No,' he said, suddenly cold. 'That was an accident. A ... a cinder leaped out of a fire.'

'Oh,' she said, and pulled away.

He wanted to take back the lie, but then he thought: she doesn't need to hear my sob story. The truth wasn't that big a deal. He'd put it behind him. Still, his evasion cast a pall on their conversation. They ate in silence until Auntie returned with a tray of espresso and cream.

David poured a cup for Chloe and himself. 'Would you like to walk through the garden this morning?'

'Sure,' she said with a casual shrug.

I'm boring the hell out of her, he thought, feeling as awkward as he had with the popular girls in high school.

Then she lifted her head and smiled at him. Her honey-brown eyes were as warm as the August sun. 'I love gardens,' she said.

He could not tell if she was lying.

They walked down the stepping-stone path, over the mossy bridge, and into the twisted pine grove. The shade was a pleasant relief. Chloe wore a pale yellow sundress speckled with tiny flowers. She'd pulled her hair into a braid. Her lips were still sultry, and her eyes still seduced, but apart from that, she looked innocent. Now and then they bumped elbows. Chloe didn't seem to mind. In fact, he thought she walked a little closer. He wanted to hold her so badly his throat hurt. Sometimes being a gentleman was hell.

She noticed one of the motion detectors on the trees. 'We're not setting off alarms, are we?'

He took her elbow to guide her around a boulder. 'They're just for tracking purposes. In case we do have a break in.'

'Is there a reason for all this security, or are you paranoid?'

Her upper arm had stiffened. He rubbed it, then slid his hand down to twine with hers. That simple touch was enough to make him hard. 'There have been threats on my life.'

'Threats? As in more than one?' She stopped and faced him. 'Because of your business?'

'Not directly. I play hard, but I play fair. I doubt my competitors are desperate enough to want to harm me. Both incidents were stalking situations: two mixed-up people who fixated on me because I'm in the public eye, because I rose quickly and have things many people don't. For the most part, the security is to protect the valuables in the house and to ensure my privacy.'

'I imagine Sato likes to play it safe.'

'You imagine right.' Giving in to temptation, he stroked a strand of hair from her face. It clung to his finger like cornsilk. 'Please don't worry. Sato is good at what he does. You'll be safe here.'

'I feel safe.' The abstraction in her tone reminded him of the night before, when she'd admired the protective cases around his dolls. Was she thinking of the man who'd ransacked her apartment?

'Maybe you should give Sato a description of your former employer, so he can have his men keep a lookout.'

'I doubt he'd find me here. He's not smart enough.'

She seemed genuinely unconcerned. If that was the case, who did his security make her feel safe from? He opened his mouth to ask just as her hand pulled away.

'Oh, look.' She bounded ahead down the path. 'Butterflies!'

He followed her into a field of wildflowers, one of Master Wu's most artful creations. The waist-high grasses did indeed abound with butterflies. Nonetheless, he did not think that was why she'd raced ahead. She spun in a circle as he reached her, her face lifted, her dress twirling around her legs. She made an idyllic picture, but he could see she hadn't got much sleep. Dark hollows shadowed her eyes.

'Chloe.' She stopped spinning and smiled at him. It was hard to press when her face shone with happiness, but he forced himself to do it. Her safety demanded it. In any case, her happiness was probably feigned. 'Chloe, who are you really running from?'

Her expression went blank, then cold. 'Is telling my life story a condition for staying here?'

'I told you there were no conditions.'

'Good,' she said, and that was all.

They went on without speaking. Chloe walked a few steps ahead, but didn't try to leave him behind. When they reached the maples, her mood shifted again. She leapfrogged over a weathered stone lantern, then danced an impromptu can-can around a tree. Finally, she rested her back on the trunk and let the sleeve of her dress slip down her shoulder. She pressed one finger to her lower lip. 'You want me, don't you?' she said.

He recognised her actions for what they were. She was trying to force him into the role all her men had played, another slave to her charms, too besotted to ask questions she didn't want to answer. He rethought his strategy. Perhaps pursuing her was not a good idea. She would lose what little respect for him she had. On the other hand, he'd feel ridiculous pretending he didn't want her, even supposing she'd believe it.

'Yes, I want you,' he said. 'You're a very attractive woman.'

He didn't move. Their gazes held until a tinge of confusion entered hers. Slowly, he lifted his arm and stroked her cheek with the back of his fingers. Her skin was as soft and warm as a peach. Her mouth fell open. He stroked the inner curve of her lower lip. 'I'm not one of your marks, Chloe.'

The words were as gentle as he could make them.

When he thought they'd sunk in, he dropped his hand and walked away. He didn't turn to see if she was following, but his ears told him she was not.

She was on her best behaviour at dinner. He didn't know if this was her way of apologising, or if she was trying another tack. If she was, she'd chosen a good one. First, she refused to eat until Auntie joined them, a feat David had never managed. Then she got the housekeeper talking about her youth, keeping her sake cup topped up like an old hand at the courtesy. No one poured their own wine in Japan. That was the job of one's seat mate. David was beginning to think he'd underestimated Chloe's intelligence.

'You were a geisha?' she breathed. If her interest was feigned, she deserved an Academy Award.

Auntie bobbed her head, her eyes bright from the warm rice wine. '*Hai.* Yes. Once, this wrinkled old lady was the toast of Kyoto. No one was requested for so many parties as I. My *danna*, my patron, was an important politician. He kept my family safe during the war. Down to the last cousin.'

'And what was your art?'

'Hah!' Auntie slapped Chloe's thigh. 'You are not an ignorant American. You know what "geisha" means. A person of art. A person of culture.' She nodded to herself, answering some silent question, one that probably meant Chloe would be refused nothing for the duration of her stay. 'Miss Chloe, I'll tell you. Like many geisha of Gion, I was a dancer. In those days, that meant something, not like today when a geisha might as well be a bar hostess. Hmph.' She pushed her lips out in disapproval. 'Many hours we apprentices practised for the dances of spring, the *Miyako Odori*. And when we became geisha, still we practised every day.'

'Show us, Auntie,' David said. 'I'm sure you haven't forgotten the steps.'

Auntie covered her mouth and dissolved into giggles at the thought.

Chloe pressed her shoulder as gently as a child's. 'Please, Auntie. I've never seen a real geisha dance.'

'Yes,' Sato said. He sounded grumpy, probably because he didn't like agreeing with their guest. 'I have heard many speak of the famous Michiko of Gion. I would be honoured to see her perform.'

Auntie required a little more coaxing and one more tiny cup of sake, but finally she rose and shuffled to the end of the dining room where the scroll of cranes wading in the river hung on the wall. She assumed a pose, an invisible fan fluttering before her face. Sato hummed a song David had never heard before and she began to dance. David was delighted. Years fell from his housekeeper as she performed the stately, feminine steps. Her face glowed. Her eyes sparkled. He should have done this ages ago. He couldn't believe he never had.

When she finished – somewhere in the middle, David suspected – Chloe clapped enthusiastically. 'Yes, yes!' she chortled. 'I can see the beautiful Michiko of Gion. She is right before my eyes.'

After that, even Sato could not frown at her.

Sato grumbled under his breath as he checked security one last time before retiring. That woman thought she was clever, ingratiating herself with Auntie to get to David. She probably took one look at the Ming vases and decided to marry him.

Despicably, his knees weakened as he remembered the feel of her mouth on his penis, pulling him into her warmth, pulling him into paradise.

He growled at himself, an old curse from the sumo

stables. The man who watched the banks of cameras didn't understand the words but sat up straighter at the tone. He was a loyal employee, never drank on the job or gossiped in town. Sato slapped his shoulder. 'You are doing fine,' he said, his voice gruff. 'Keep up the good work.'

Sato had learned Americans liked this kind of talk.

When he reached his quarters, his senses went on full alert. She had been here. He could smell her: a combination of lily of the valley and musk. Following the scent, he strode to his futon and threw back the covers. He expected to discover – who knew what? – a snake, a cushion full of pins. Instead, he found a scrap of lacy black silk and a note. He shook out the silk, which resolved itself as a pair of woman's panties, very small, with nothing but a thong to cover the back. The note was written with black inkwash and a brush. The script was eccentric, to say the least. Fisting the panties in one hand, he deciphered the bold, slanting letters. At once, his cheeks began to heat.

'I can still taste you,' it said, 'your firm resilience against my tongue, the flood of your salty strength. I count the moments until I can taste you again. Perhaps you will allow another mouth, hungrier yet, to kiss your proud sword.

'Until then, sleep with these panties under your pillow and dream of me.

'P.S. I was thinking of you when I got them wet.'

Sato threw the underwear as far as he could, but they refused to flutter past the first tatami mat. The woman was a devil. He sniffed his fingers. Yes, her scent was all over them.

He groaned as a primitive, involuntary response caused his shaft to lift and swell. Yes, a devil. In the twenty-four hours since he'd met her, she had embedded herself under his skin. How would his master resist her when he was so much more trusting than Sato?

He wagged his head back and forth. He could not foresee this ending well.

After her triumph at dinner, David knew Chloe expected him to make some overture, if only a friendly one. Though she tried to hide it, she was taken aback when he said he had business to see to and excused himself.

He had decided he would not accede to her advances until her interest was truly piqued. A woman like her would only value what she had to fight for. In waiting, the advantage was his. He doubted her patience ran very deep; a good thing, considering how urgently he wanted her. He leaned back in his chair and smiled at the library's shelves. Yesterday's *Wall Street Journal* lay across the modern glass-topped desk. He hadn't read a word since he'd spread it there. She filled his mind: her dark hair shining in the sun, her laugh at dinner, the imagined curve of her breasts settling into his palm.

He chuckled to himself. He was enjoying this. He'd never played such games with a woman. He'd never guessed they could be so much fun. Just thinking about her was a joy.

But he'd been at it a while. In the time he'd sat there daydreaming, a thunderstorm had swept through the county. The last rumbles reminded him he wanted to open the windows and air the room. He pushed the sections apart and stepped on to the second-floor veranda. Lightning flashed in the distance, but here the rain had ended. The air smelled green and fresh and the wood was damp beneath his bare feet.

He looked to the right. He hadn't forgotten that the green room, where Auntie put Chloe, was two doors down from the library. No light glowed in her windows, but it was nearly midnight. Considering the circles he'd seen under her eyes, she probably had sleep to catch up on.

Without quite deciding to do it, he padded down the planks towards her room. Just to check on her, he told himself, to make sure she was comfortable. Some people couldn't adjust to futons. She might prefer a Western bed. If that was the case, he'd be happy to arrange a switch. His pulse tripped up a notch when he saw her sliding doors were open. Nothing prevented him from walking in.

Stop this, he thought, forcing himself to back away. Then he heard her cry out.

He nearly ran inside. She was sitting up in bed, breathing hard, her eyes moving wildly. A plain, worn T-shirt draped her trembling breasts. He found that surprising. But perhaps her former employer had torn her lingerie?

'Chloe?' he said, not certain she was awake.

She brought her fists to her temples and ground them into her skull. 'No, no, no,' she said in a high, tight voice. 'I'm not like Beth and Sharon. I'll never forget.'

He crouched by the edge of her futon. 'What won't you forget?'

She didn't seem to hear him, just pressed her knuckles harder into her flesh. He clasped her forearms, meaning to pull them down before she hurt herself. 'No,' she said, flailing at him. 'I have to save her. I have to save Mary Alice.'

'Hush,' he said, but she struggled harder. 'It's me, Chloe. It's David.'

She stilled. A smile crossed her face. 'I know David. He's the most beautiful man.'

He couldn't contain a chuckle. How infuriated she'd be to know she'd told him this! 'That's right,' he said. 'And don't you forget it.' He slipped his arms around her and laid her gently down. She sighed and snuggled into his chest. 'That's right. Just relax. You were having a bad dream but it's all over now.'

'Don't have bad dreams,' she mumbled. 'Never, never.'

He stroked her back until the final tremor left her body. Her weight was sweet in her arms, her breasts warm and soft. Reluctantly, he eased away. If Chloe had been awake, she wouldn't have wanted him here, not when she was vulnerable. More to the point, he probably wouldn't enjoy how she'd try to regain the upper hand.

He stood for a moment, watching her burrow deeper into the pillow. She seemed young in sleep, no more than a teenager. What nightmare had she been re-enacting? A conflict with an old boyfriend? Or something worse?

Something worse, he thought, his eyes narrowing. An old boyfriend couldn't account for the fear he sensed in her.

Bending one last time, he pulled the sheet to her waist and smoothed her hair over her shoulder. Could wounds like hers be healed? Could he help? And if he couldn't, would that stop him from wanting to? He pressed his lips together. She called to him, and the pull went deeper than any game. The more he learned, the harder it was to walk away. Some day he might have to, but tonight he would keep her in his prayers.

4

David's breath stalled in his lungs. Chloe stood on the rocky platform beneath the waterfall and tilted her head into the stream. Water cascaded over her shoulders, splashed from her plum-blossom nipples, and ran in glistening streams down her belly and legs. She was naked.

She was perfect.

Her breasts were high and full, her waist narrow, her legs a schoolboy's wet dream.

David pressed a hand to his solar plexus. A silver ring flashed at her navel. She was pierced; there, in that tender fold of flesh, pierced. Why did his blood move faster at the word? Why did his cock suddenly feel twice as large? He wanted to kneel before her and take that ring in his mouth. He wanted to curl his thumbs into her sex and feel her spasm as he sucked the cold, hard metal. David shivered. Evidently, he had interests he'd never suspected.

'Come on in,' she called over the roar of the spray. 'It's not too cold.'

It was hot from where he was standing.

He looked at his polo shirt and trousers, and contemplated stripping down. He'd passed two gardener's assistants on his way here. It was one thing to wander naked through his private rooms, and quite another to wave his willy out here.

'Coward,' she taunted, and dived cleanly into the dark green pool.

He watched the ghost of her bottom flicker beneath

the water. She swam the full length without a breath and emerged directly before the ledge on which he stood. She laughed without sound, her sleepy eyes burning up at him. Her hands snuck out and gripped his ankles, kneading the bone and muscle and dampening his thin cotton socks. Erotic tingles swept up his legs.

Funny. He'd never known his ankles were an erogenous zone.

She blew a drop of water from her nose. 'Come on, Mr Bigshot. Or haven't you skinny-dipped before?'

'I have,' he said.

'In broad daylight?'

He laughed because she'd caught him dead to rights. He'd only risked that pleasure in the dark. She pushed back from the ledge and trod water. 'Take off your clothes,' she said, a delicious, husky growl. 'I want to see that beautiful Bruce Lee physique.'

'I'm not sure Mr Lee has anything to worry about.'

But she pretended to pant when he pulled his shirt over his head, and whistled when he stepped from his trousers. 'Yum,' she said. 'You are one lean, mean fighting machine.'

He was also quite hard, so hard her stare made him self-conscious. His cock throbbed high and thick against his belly, nearly buzzing with excitement. Not even the thought that one of his employees might walk by could dampen its enthusiasm.

Chloe licked her lips. 'Dee-licious. I could stare at you all day.'

But he couldn't stand in the open all day. He cannonballed in, wincing at the cold, at the sting of impact on his scrotum. He was glad Chloe had got her eyeful while she could. He wouldn't be much to look at now.

He tried to catch her, but she was quicker than he was, a lithe little eel. 'Where did you learn to swim?' he demanded.

'At the Y,' she replied and heaved herself on to a sunny rock near the edge of the fall. Her lack of tan lines did not surprise him. She patted the stone beside her. 'Come warm up.'

He hesitated, glancing over his shoulder at the nearest turn of the path. This faux tropical pool was sheltered but not completely screened from the rest of the grounds.

'David,' Chloe scolded. 'It's your house, your pool, your money that pays the staff. If you can't get naked here, where can you?'

'My staff might not care to see their boss in the altogether.'

'I would.'

'You –' he folded his arms on the ledge and kissed her knee '– are a different kettle of fish.'

Refusing to admit defeat, she dragged her hand up the inside of her thigh. Her polished nails flashed in the sun, perfect, coffee-coloured ovals. She curled her fingers over her mons, which she'd shaved except for one black stripe. Beneath the curls, her labia were flushed and plump. She was aroused. Under the water, David's cock defied the laws of physics.

'I don't like to play alone,' she whispered. She pressed her fingers inwards until her lips parted, until her clit peeked pink and shiny between two knuckles.

He was ready to do as she asked. He was ready to bury his face between her legs and lick her until she screamed. Damn the gardeners. Damn everything but driving his prick into that soft, welcoming channel. But that would be giving in and it was far too soon for that, no matter how loudly his body claimed the contrary.

'You'll have to play alone for now,' he said, and swam back to the rock where he'd left his clothes.

She was too cool to argue, too cool to say anything at all. At lunch she pretended nothing had happened; even accepted his invitation for a bike ride into Strathmore.

Once there, she proceeded to enchant everyone in the General Store. She introduced herself as a student on sabbatical from Columbia. David wondered if she'd really attended. She seemed smart enough, but who knew? By the time he'd collected the pastrami sandwiches that were intended to keep Auntie from serving sushi for dinner, Mrs Kleghorn had her photo gallery spread across the counter. He noticed Chloe had memorised the grand-children's names.

'You are a charmer,' he said, as he stuffed his purchases into the pannier baskets on his bike.

Her teeth flashed white in her sun-browned face. 'When I want to be.'

'And when you don't?'

She swung her leg over the seat, her eyes lazy and amused. 'There's not much point pretending to be a saint. I don't think you'd believe me unless you really, really wanted to.'

Her bike rattled off ahead of his. For the space of a few heartbeats, he stood and admired her derrière. Once again, she'd taken him by surprise.

On Sunday evening, Sato obeyed David's summons to the library. They often reviewed the week's plans this way, but Sato sensed his boss had new concerns tonight, concerns with the initial CD. Braced for bad news, he stood at loose attention before David's desk, his hands clasped before him, his feet planted wide. David fiddled with the mouse to his computer, wiggling it back and forth across the pad. No doubt he was dreading Sato's reaction as much as Sato was.

Finally the wiggling stopped. 'I don't want to take Chloe back to New York until I'm sure the threat to her is past.'

A whoosh of happy energy shot up Sato's spine. This was good news.

David lifted his hand. 'I know you won't like this, but – while she's here – I want you to stay at the estate and oversee security. I'll take Lee and Kevin with me.'

Sato opened his mouth, but no words emerged. He did not know how to begin to protest against this foolishness. David leaned forwards and clasped his hands together, just as he did in business meetings. Sato did not like that. David's business self was very hard to argue with.

'I know you consider me your personal responsibility,' David said, 'but, at the moment, I consider this woman mine. She interests me, Sato, and I have reason to believe she needs our protection.'

'Did she tell you that?'

'As a matter of fact, no.' David sat back. His lips were pursed in a way that made Sato's heart turn over. He had never known a man or woman this beautiful, so beautiful it sometimes hurt to look at him. David continued gently, as if he knew how upset Sato was. 'You've trained Lee and Kevin well. They can co-ordinate your staff in New York. The KL agreement is a done deal. We have nothing particularly sensitive in the works. Now is as good a time as any to let them put your lessons into practice.'

'Yes, master,' Sato said.

David laughed. 'I know you're riled when you give me that "yes, master" business. She's just one woman, Sato. It won't kill you to spend a week with her.'

Sato wished he were sure of that. He was sweating and his collar felt tight. He did not want to imagine what trouble Chloe could get up to in a week, but images flashed unbidden through his mind: a rope, a crumpled robe, his mouth hovering above the dimples at the base of her spine.

He shuddered and tugged his lapels. 'A woman like that will be bored all week in the middle of nowhere.'

David's eyes crinkled in amusement. 'She's already

agreed.' He took up the mouse again and drew a lazy circle. 'Don't worry, old friend. I won't make entertaining her your responsibility.'

'I hope you will tell her that,' Sato muttered, though he doubted it would make any difference.

David put off leaving until early Monday morning. He'd thought Chloe might wander into his room, the night before, but she hadn't. Nor did he wander into hers. She did wake early enough to say goodbye, walking him to the helipad in her robe and wooden slippers. Auntie would be annoyed. Those shoes weren't meant to go outside.

The sky was grey with clouds the sun would burn off later. David set his briefcase in the dewy grass and turned to her. He took her hands loosely, so that her palms rested on his fingertips. Her expression was calm, without the chill he'd seen in it before. He took courage from that. 'I'm glad you're staying,' he said. 'This weekend has been interesting. I'm looking forward to getting to know you better.'

She cocked her head sideways, her measuring look. Humour sparked in her light brown eyes. 'It may not be a case of the more you know, the more you love.'

He grinned. 'That's a risk everyone takes.'

'Kiss me,' she said.

The words hit his chest like a gentle fist. He moved closer, toe-to-toe. In one co-ordinated motion, he cradled her head and circled her waist. The beating of his heart seemed louder than the whup-whup-whup of the chopper gearing up behind them. Her hands skimmed his Savile Row suit and twined behind his neck. She went on tiptoe, her weight tugging at him, and then their lips brushed, softly, side to side. A sound broke from one of them, or both, and suddenly, hungrily, their mouths melded together.

Their tongues sucked and held, clinging and sleek. The kiss barely moved, yet grew more intimate by the second. He knew instinctively this was the first honest moment they'd shared. Whatever she'd lied about, it wasn't about wanting him. His hold tightened. He couldn't stop himself, though he feared he might be hurting her. If he was, she didn't seem to mind. She shifted one of her arms and gripped his back with an answering strength. He could feel her bones through his jacket, even the ribs beneath her breasts. Her nipples were points of flame against his chest. Her leg sidled his. She kicked off her sandals and stepped on to his shoes. That much closer to his groin, she rolled her pussy, slow and hard, over his thigh. She wore nothing beneath the robe. He knew because she was wet.

He cursed and shifted the angle of his mouth. His tongue went deeper. She stroked it with her own, giving out mewls of pleasure. He knew the pilot was watching. He'd never kissed a woman in front of someone he knew. He didn't want to embarrass her, or himself, but he couldn't resist sliding one hand beneath her robe to clutch her naked rear. Her bottom was as firm and silky as he'd dreamed.

She rolled against him with even greater force. 'Put your fingers inside me,' she whispered. 'Make me come, David. Make me come before you leave.'

He groaned and slid two fingers past her swollen lips. Her sheath was tight and juicy, slightly rough in its outer reaches, plump and velvety in its depths. He stretched another finger forwards to catch her clitoris. She cried out against his mouth. As eager to feel her pleasure as she was, he worked her in quick, no-nonsense strokes. In seconds, her hips jerked and her sheath tightened on his hand. He didn't let up until her shudders ceased. As if her contractions had held it inside, a sluice of cream dripped down his palm. She arched her spine, her smile a loose, warm curve against his lips.

When she pulled away, he was shaking in reaction, his cock so hard he feared a touch might set it off. He drew a deep, steadying breath and willed his arousal to recede. She buttoned his jacket over the wet spot she'd left, over the bulge she'd inspired. Then, almost as an afterthought, she straightened her robe.

'Have a nice day,' she chirped, like a housewife from the fifties.

He had to laugh. 'I'll be thinking of you,' he said, but he was sure she already knew that.

He held out until Tuesday, at which point his hand jerked to the phone of its own accord. As usual, Auntie picked it up. She was bubbling with gossip: what the chef had said to the pool girl, who had brought their new baby to the General Store. Eventually, she wound down after having told him everything but what he most wanted to know.

He shifted in his chair. 'How's Chloe?'

'Oh, fine, fine,' she said, and lapsed into an uncharacteristic silence.

She was teasing him. She knew he had feelings for Chloe. Auntie had a radar for romance that surpassed the US Military. She'd probably known the minute he brought her home. A hot blush prickled across his chest. 'What has she been doing today?' he asked.

'Who?'

'You know who, Auntie.'

'Oh, you mean that pretty little Chloe. Well, she walked in the garden. She flirted with Angelo and asked why he was tying up tree branches. She drew a smiley face in the gravel of the Zen garden, which upset Master Wu. Ah, and she ate sashimi for lunch and finished every bite.' Her voice grew more emphatic at this. David's eating habits were a constant sore point. 'Then she went to your practice studio, turned the radio up very loud and danced around like – what do they call those spinning men in India?'

'Dervishes?'

'*Hai*, that's it. And now she's taking a bath in the grotto.'

David tangled his finger in the phone cord. This level of detail was unusual even for Auntie. Three of his lines were flashing. He ignored them. 'Auntie, how do you know all this?'

'One of the maids told me. Sato asked them to keep an eye on her.'

So. Now Sato was deputising the maids. Of course, for all David knew, his precautions were warranted. He unwound his finger from the phone cord and knocked a wind-up Laura Fleet doll on its side. Plastic simply didn't do Chloe justice. Although, when you cranked the doll's key, her eyes did shoot sparks. By this time, his chin was on his palm, his heart in his throat. 'Do you think she's bored, Auntie?'

Auntie was silent for a moment. Even if Chloe had charmed her, Auntie was nobody's fool. 'I think you better not spend too much time in the city,' she said. 'This one won't sit around waiting.'

On Wednesday evening, Chloe called him. It was 6.15. David had three designers hunched over the conference table in his office, pouring over reams of code, panicked because Alpha Raiders had developed a bug two weeks prior to release. If they couldn't devise a patch, and fast, they could kiss their delivery date goodbye.

The in-house game team had consulted David about the problem, something they didn't often do since he'd become such a bigwig. He knew they'd called him more to cover their butts than because they thought he could help. They'd been surprised when he followed their explanation. They'd be even more surprised when he offered the solution he was turning over in his mind. It was simple and elegant. He'd spent the last ten minutes searching it for flaws, but so far he couldn't find one. This kind of fix made a programmer grateful for a glitch. It was a pleasure to come up with it. The last thing he needed was an interruption.

But there was no avoiding this one. His face went hot at the sound of her voice. 'Chloe!' he exclaimed.

One of the designers looked up, caught by his tone.

'Are you in the middle of something?' she asked.

'Yes.' He pushed his pen through tense fingers, knowing he should hang up. 'I want to talk to you. Can you hold for two minutes?'

'Sure,' she said. Her shrug was as clear as if she were in the room.

His mind yanked in two directions, he scribbled his solution on to a legal pad and shoved it down the table to Terri Wilcox, the lead designer. A moment ago David had looked forward to announcing the fix himself. Now, he couldn't wait to get away. He jiggled his knee as Terri squinted at his chicken scratch. The designer's eyes widened. He pushed his wire-rimmed glasses up his bony nose. 'Wow. That sure looks like it'll work. But –'

David lifted his hand before Terri could bombard him with questions. 'Give me five minutes. I want to handle this call.'

He stood and moved to his desk, knowing he'd need more privacy than he could find at the conference table. He depressed the blinking line and swivelled his chair to face the picture window. Manhattan's steel and glass flashed under a sunny, cloudless sky. Looking north on Fifth, he could see Trump Tower, the Museum of Modern Art, and the tops of the trees in Central Park. He was far above the world here. The geek from Chicago had climbed to a dizzying height.

'Hey,' he said, all he could manage given the state of his lungs.

'Hey, right back,' she answered. He could hear the smile in her voice. Some of his tension drained away. She'd held the line. She was in a good mood.

He balanced the Laura Fleet doll on the arm of his chair. She was bustier than Chloe, but not nearly as graceful. 'How did you get Shelley to put you through?'

'She's very fond of you, that girl. I told her I'd try to convince you to go home. She says you work too hard. She worries.'

He pulled his heel up on the chair. 'Shelley should worry. I do work too hard. You see, I've never found a really good playmate.'

'Is that what the problem is?'

Her voice had gone throaty. The sound had a predictable effect on his groin. 'It's a huge problem.'

'How huge?'

'At least seven inches.'

'That's funny,' she crooned. 'I could have sworn it was eight.'

'It'll be eight in a minute.'

'Ah,' she said. 'Let me get my stopwatch.'

His laugh burst out of his nose before he could stop it. The designers' excited chatter paused for a moment, then went on. He didn't think they could hear unless they really strained, but the possibility they might guess what was going on was perversely exciting.

'What are you wearing?' she said, a parody of a sex-line operator.

This time he had to cover his mouth to muffle his laugh.

'Never mind,' she said. 'I'll guess. You're wearing a suit. A conservative, charcoal-grey Brooks Brothers suit that makes your shoulders look a mile wide and your hips a foot.'

'Actually, it's a Prada.'

'A Prada. Golly gee, you must have taken your daring pill this morning.'

'Black on black,' he added, smoothing the shirt over his racing heart, 'with a pale gold tie.'

'Sounds natty. Have the trousers got pockets?'

A prickling sensation moved up the front of his thighs. He cleared his throat. 'You know they do.'

'Good,' she said, all hint of teasing gone. 'Put your right hand in your right pocket.'

'Chloe.' His voice sank to a whisper without trying. The skin of his cock felt as if it were stretched to its limit. He knew it was dripping from the way his briefs clung to the tip. 'Chloe. I can't do this right now. I have people in my office.'

'I'm not going to make you come,' she snapped. 'In fact, I forbid you to come until you and I are together again. You're going to save every drop for me. Now put your hand in your pocket and grab your prick.'

He obeyed. He didn't have to. She never would have known. He was David Imakita, CEO of a multinational corporation. He didn't have to answer to anyone.

But it excited him to answer to her.

His hand sweat through the cloth of his pocket, intensifying the intimacy of his hold. His cock was throbbing in time to his heart, as quick and fast as a frightened deer. If he did stroke himself, he knew he wouldn't take long to burst.

'Have you done it?' she demanded. 'Have you got your big, hard dick in your hand?'

'Yes,' he said. His arousal climbed with every word. He couldn't believe he was doing this. He couldn't believe it felt so good.

'Touch the head,' she said.

He touched it.

'Is it wet?'

'Yes,' he said, and shivered, the admission as exciting as the touch.

'Would you like to be inside me right now? Would you like to be stroking deep, deep inside my cunt? My sweat mingling with your sweat? My cream mingling with your juice?'

'Yes,' he said. 'Yes.'

'Give yourself a squeeze, then. A good, hard squeeze. I want to find bruises when I see you again. Every bruise I find I'm going to kiss. One by one, I'm going to kiss them until you beg for mercy. And then, David, my boy, I'm going to give you mercy.'

It didn't occur to him to disobey. He squeezed until the pressure hurt, until he had to breathe through his mouth to quiet his panting. He compressed the swollen flesh with the tips of his fingers, with the edge of his nails. His erection didn't falter. If anything, it grew more rigid.

'Are you still hard?' she asked, eerily in tune with his thoughts.

'Yes,' he whispered. 'Very.'

He heard a sharp intake of breath, but she recovered quickly. 'Good,' she said. 'I think we've learned something here, don't you?'

He closed his eyes. How could she have done this? Turned his world upside down in the space of a five-minute phone call? He'd never guessed he had it in him to enjoy something like this. 'I need to see you,' he said, amazed by how desperate he felt. 'I can't wait until the weekend. I've got a fundraiser to attend tomorrow night, but I'd love for you to go with me.'

'Could I ride the helicopter?'

He laughed, surprised she would admit to wanting to. This evidence of a childish streak delighted him. 'Of course, you can. I'll send the pilot for you tomorrow morning. You can shop for a dress.'

'This fundraiser thing is fancy?'

'Yes,' he said. 'But don't worry. I'll call ahead to Saks and tell them to put you on my account.'

A silence opened on the other end of the line. 'No-o,' she finally said, the word drawn out, hesitant. 'I can afford a nice dress, even at Saks.'

He didn't know what to make of her response. Had he insulted her? Had she wanted to accept the offer, but decided it was bad for her long-term strategy? Whatever that might be.

'Do as you please,' he said. 'But I don't mind paying if you're going to the expense because of me.'

'No,' she said more firmly. 'I'm not a pauper.'

David hung up soon after, his head fogged with confusion. If she wasn't a pauper, why had she been living in a slum?

Chloe arranged to meet him at the hotel where the function was being held. She said she wanted to treat herself to the works: face, nails, bikini wax. Her mention of the last made his chest tight. He arrived on the dot of eight and watched the clock for an hour while he struggled to make conversation with the local glitterati.

A hum of curiosity from the crowd near the door told him she'd arrived. Nothing short of a striking new face could stir that much interest. He turned from the president of the charity to watch Chloe's entrance. Entrance, it was, in true film star style: fashionably late, slinky, seemingly oblivious to the attention she drew. Her hair was swept up and fixed with diamanté pins into whimsical, gleaming sprays. The rhinestones glittered under the chandeliers as her gaze searched the room. When she found his eyes, she smiled.

It was a timeless moment, one that appealed to every

ounce of male ego he possessed. This lovely woman was here for him, was smiling for him. Every other woman paled in comparison. How could they not? Chloe's taste was equal to her looks. She wore a beaded Badgley Mischka gown, a long, drapey, ghost-pink, semi-sheer traffic stopper, the sort of dress that precluded the wearing of undergarments. Revealing as it was, no one could call it cheap; it was too gorgeous and too expensive for that. In truth, the dress was a work of art. The back bared her to the dimples of her derrière. The front swayed enticingly over her breasts. Her nipples stood out like summer berries. Somehow that display, blatant as it was, seemed just as tasteful as the gown, just as inevitable and right. There wasn't an eye in the place, male or female, that didn't turn to watch her pass.

David stood at the opposite side of the ballroom, beside the champagne fountain. Her approach was slow enough that his ogle had time to reach her five-inch silver strap-ons. Her ankles inspired a low, longing sigh. He told himself he was going to kiss them, first chance he got, and that wasn't the only thing he was going to kiss.

She arrived on a faint cloud of lily of the valley. She rose on tiptoe to kiss him, politely, a quick press of lips to jaw. It still made his heart jump. He wanted to drag her into a corner and shove himself straight between those long, toned legs.

'Hello,' she whispered. 'I like your hair slicked back like that. You look dashing.'

He touched her cheek, as lightheaded as if he were in love. 'I can't begin to describe how you look.'

David's companion, forgotten in Chloe's wake, was sharper-eared than he'd expected. 'Quite right,' he said. He stuck out his hand. 'I'm Harvey Simmons and I'm delighted to meet such a lovely young woman.'

Chloe accepted his greeting and turned on the charm,

a demurer version than she'd used to work the crowd at the General Store. Simmons' eyes took on a glaze David had been seeing in the mirror lately. David was impressed. Generally speaking, Simmons wasn't dazzled by anything except a snowy egret or a cheque with a lot of zeroes. She is good, he thought. She is really good.

Chloe assured the round little man that she was happy to be there. His cause was one she felt strongly about. Most people didn't realise how important wetlands were to the maintenance of a healthy water table. David's eyebrows rose. He hadn't told her any details of the fundraiser except where and when it would be held. Then she laid down the kicker. Would Mr Simmons care to accept a small donation?

Flabbergasted, David watched her pull a wallet from her beaded purse. Without blinking, she wrote out a cheque for five thousand dollars. Mr Simmons blinked when he took it. David knew it wasn't the largest donation he hoped to receive tonight. It was, however, far more than he'd expect from a piece of eye-candy like Chloe.

'Thank you for all your good work,' she said, folding his chubby hand over it. 'And now if you'll excuse us, there's something I really must discuss with my date.'

With that, she took David's arm and led him through the crowd. She didn't start giggling until they were out of earshot. 'Gawd,' she drawled, Bronx-style. 'Did you see his face? He's probably wondering if it will bounce.'

David was wondering that himself. Simmons, however, was probably just stunned.

'Are we heading somewhere in particular?' he asked, willing to go along, but hoping she wanted a moment alone as much as he did.

She grinned. 'How about the nearest broom closet? I do have a promise to keep.'

His penis had begun to waver upwards the moment

he saw her, but now a surge of blood shot it out stiff. A broom closet sounded ideal. He pulled her more determinedly towards the door. Kevin, his self-appointed shadow for the night, spotted them before they escaped. David waved the security officer away. At the moment, three was definitely a crowd.

With a skill that both pleased and unnerved him, Chloe found a single-occupant bathroom in a corridor off the marble lobby. The decor was vintage New York, cracked Art Deco tiles and a Tiffany mirror so old their reflections should have been sepia.

David secured the push-button lock and grabbed her for a deep, wet kiss. Their bodies squirmed together through their clothes. She was hot, naked beneath the net of tiny beads. The knowledge that she wanted him was enough to banish his last shred of caution.

She broke free with a gasp. 'Mm, that's good.' She pushed his tuxedo jacket back off his shoulders and reached for his belt. His erection strained his trouser front, having sprung through the vent of his briefs. She rubbed the thick arch, once, from deep between his legs to his waist. 'Let me see,' she said. 'Let me see the marks you made for me.'

Her fingers were surprisingly clumsy, as if she was too eager to take her time. He helped her with the jumble of belt and clasp and zip, not entirely steady himself. He knew what she'd see. He'd traced the bruises this morning, fascinated, alarmed, and horribly aroused. He'd done as she asked, though. He hadn't got himself off. He'd saved all his lust for her.

She cried out softly as he freed his swollen shaft, holding out her hands until he laid himself in them like an offering.

'Oh!' She stroked the bruises with her palm. The marks were faint against his ruddy skin but still visible. The crescent-moon imprints of his nails were the darkest. 'Oh, they're beautiful.'

She knelt to kiss the marks, one by one, just as she'd promised. David's head fell back. Each kiss was as tender as a mother soothing her child's skinned knee. He couldn't believe how sensual it was. The last thing he wanted was to beg for mercy. He couldn't. He was exactly where he wanted to be.

'You've been so good,' she murmured. 'So very, very good.'

'Do I deserve a reward?' He was startled to hear how serious he sounded. The game had turned real.

'Oh, yes,' she said, equally earnest. She kissed the weeping tip of his penis. 'Yes, you do.'

She curled the tip of her tongue across his slit. His face tensed with pleasure. He had to struggle not to close his eyes. He wanted to watch her; wanted to see her take him in her mouth. Her lips were stained with colour but not glossy. She pressed their pout over his glans, then pushed, parting them around his shaft. Her mouth was silky and wet and warm. Her tongue circled the head, then cradled the thick ridge beneath as she took him deeper. She drew him to the verge of her throat, then pulled slowly back. 'You're not to come in my mouth,' she said.

He groaned because, of course, as soon as she said it, he wanted nothing more.

'No,' she reiterated, massaging his balls with her hands. 'Not in my mouth.'

He stroked the soft skin behind her ear. 'You don't like that?'

Her lashes fluttered downwards as she smiled. 'I like it fine. But I have other plans for you tonight.'

'Other plans?' He sounded like a laryngitis victim.

'Shh,' she said. 'I can't talk and work.'

He couldn't argue with that. She sucked him in again, even deeper than before, and he surrendered to her mouth until pleasure beat through him in hot, rhythmic waves; until his knees trembled and sweat broke out behind them. A dangerous pressure built inside his balls. 'I'm going to come,' he said, panting it. 'If you don't stop, I won't be able to help it.'

She let him slip free, gleaming with saliva and ringed by her nearly stay-put lipstick. To his astonishment, her breasts were bare. It was a measure of his distraction that he hadn't seen her slip her gown off her shoulders. Whatever she'd used to stain her mouth darkened her nipples as well, which explained why they'd been visible through the beaded cloth. Enthralled, he circled both areolae with his thumbs. Their centres drew tight. 'My God,' he said. 'I want to suck you like a baby.'

Her breathing quickened. 'Later.'

'Do you always leave things for later? Is that the secret to your allure?'

She laughed, a rush of air without sound. 'A woman should never let a man have everything he wants the minute he wants it.'

'And what about a man? Should he let a woman have everything she wants?'

'That depends on if she's smart enough to get it.'

David was pretty sure Chloe was. He nudged his cock towards her neck, stroking her jawline with the glans, then the hollow where her collarbones met. A sheen of oily moisture followed his caress. His cock was overflowing with excitement. He knew he could come like this, just this, touching her velvety skin with this butterfly stroke. 'Tell me what you want. Tell me what you've got planned for me.'

She didn't answer in words. She rose and perched on the lid of the old-fashioned john. She hiked her glittering dress to her hips and spread her knees, then gestured him to stand between them. Her silence intrigued him, and her stance. He wasn't sure what they could achieve from here. Then she cupped her breasts and pressed them upwards, the rich flesh like cream with a dash of coffee.

'Ah,' he said, understanding. He pushed his cock into the warm, flower- and woman-scented crease.

'Yes,' she said, as he thrust luxuriously up and down. 'Pour yourself over me. I want your seed gleaming on my skin.'

He groaned at the image. She rested her head against his pleated shirt-front. Her breath washed him, warm but shallow. He couldn't restrain himself. He was too far gone and she'd been teasing him since they met. He gripped her shoulders to brace her for his quickened thrusts. Her nipples brushed his hips. His balls slapped her ribs. A sensation like a fist tightening gathered in his groin.

'Now,' she said, and nipped a tiny fold of belly-skin between her teeth.

He came just as the spike of pain snapped through his nerves. His orgasm stuttered for an instant, then swelled so hugely it shocked him. The spasms were deep and strong, squeezing not just his cock but his belly and thighs. He heard himself grunting; felt himself shoot with violent force. His body swayed. He fumbled for a handhold and found the little marble sink.

When he regained his sanity, she was rubbing his semen into her breasts as if it were an expensive, perfumed oil. He could not look away. Tonight her nails were a pale, frosted pink. His cock twitched. Reluctantly, he tucked it back in his trousers. He felt peculiar, satisfied but emptied out. He touched his shirt. Her bite had drawn a tiny spot of blood. He wiggled his finger between the buttons to touch it, to convince himself that it was real, that they'd just done what he thought they'd done.

Chloe did not share his uncertainty. With an air of satisfaction, she stood and shook her dress back to her ankles. Her cheeks were flushed. She glowed with a radiance no amount of make-up could supply.

'What about you?' he said.

She smiled, drowsy-eyed and arch. 'Later,' she said.

He did not have the energy to laugh.

With iron-jawed control, Sato watched them disappear, then re-emerge. He doubted David guessed he was there. He should have. Whatever Sato's opinion of the woman, he would never let her wander through the city by herself. All day he'd remained at her side, watching her primp and pose and do everything she could to torment him. 'What will David think of this?' had been her endless refrain, while her eyes had fed on his irrepressible lust.

She hadn't touched him since that night in the bath.

Now she glowed like she'd been fucked. Jealousy and anger tangled in his belly. If anyone had told him he would ever begrudge David a pleasure, he would have laughed in his face. He studied his master as he wound back through the crowded ballroom. David looked wan and shaken: precisely what one would expect after an encounter with a snake. He hadn't pulled away from her, though. His arm circled her back with a combination of possession and protection. His eyes barely left her face. The pair stopped and David laughed at something Chloe said. As simple as that, the colour returned to his cheeks.

Sato sighed. Whatever the viper had done while they were gone, it hadn't shocked David enough to scare him off.

* * *

The ballroom was even louder than before. A twelve-piece band was playing show tunes – God knew why – and the crowd seemed to have doubled since he and Chloe left. The change was appropriate, David supposed, since he felt as if he'd lived a lifetime in the interim. He spotted Harvey Simmons puffing towards them through the crush. A scruffy young man followed behind.

'There you are,' Simmons said. 'And your lovely lady friend. Perfect.' He squeezed his rotund body next to David's and beckoned the young man closer. Dressed in jeans, a camera hung from a strap around the young man's neck. As Simmons beamed, he lifted it and squeezed off a shot.

Chloe had been looking to the left but the flash brought her head around. 'Excuse me,' she said with icy hauteur. 'I didn't hear anyone ask permission to take a picture.'

'Oh, but you'll dress it up so nice,' Simmons said.

'No,' she enunciated, and took a threatening step towards the photographer.

With the instinct of his kind, he backed up, lifted the camera in front of his face, and snapped another shot. A hand appeared around his shoulder and covered the lens. David started. The hand belonged to Sato. He hadn't seen him come in.

The former sumo wrestler spoke in a slow, measured cadence. 'The lady does not wish to be photographed.'

'Hey.' The man turned innocent. 'I'm just doing my job. Mr Simmons here called me over to take the shot.'

'And you've taken it,' said Sato. 'Now you can leave.'

Wisely, the young man left. Chloe looked as if she wanted to go after him. David felt her hand tremble within his own. Her palm was clammy.

'Are you all right?' he asked.

She blew a spray of hair off her forehead. 'I don't like having my picture taken.'

David was tempted to scratch his head. The woman who'd made an entrance worthy of Scarlett O'Hara didn't like being photographed?

'I could get the film,' Sato offered.

She shook herself like a dog throwing off water. 'No. Don't make a fuss. I'm sure the picture won't come out. I wasn't even looking at the camera that first time.'

Simmons practically wrung his hands. The last thing he would want was to offend a heavy hitter like David. 'I'm so sorry,' he said. 'I had no idea. He said he was from the *Times*.'

Chloe waved him off like a fly, her supply of charm exhausted. Clearly, she didn't care which paper the man was from. She turned to David. 'Could we – would you mind if I left? I'm afraid I've lost my urge to party.'

'We'll both go,' he said, though from a business standpoint there was still plenty of flesh to press. He wanted her to understand that, whether here or in Vermont, he intended for them to be together – at least, so long as she would tolerate it.

Naturally, Sato bridled at the decision.

'She's hiding something,' he muttered as they waited for the valet to collect their car.

David shook his head, but not in denial. Most likely, Chloe was hiding something. He just wasn't sure it made a difference to the tumble he was taking. She'd lured him to the edge already. He could turn back, but he discovered he'd rather see what happened as he fell.

5

Sato could not sleep. The Gramercy Park brownstone had Western beds. They squeaked when he moved. He could not shake the sense that he was going to fall out. Usually, he was able to ignore this, but tonight he could not stop thinking of Chloe, or – more precisely – what Chloe and David might be doing in the bedroom two doors down. He pictured their beautiful bodies twined together, slender and perfect, so hot for each other steam would rise from their glowing skin.

Frustrated, he turned on his bedside lamp. A still life of dead pheasants stared at him from the dark green wall. The brownstone never felt like home to him. David had not put his stamp on the place, not like in Vermont. Most of the furniture had come with the house, awful Victorian stuff: dark colours, heavy lines, a mix of styles that never harmonised. The neighbourhood was the only good thing about the property. Laid out like a London square, Gramercy had the city's one private park. Only residents had keys. Sometimes, when he wasn't on duty, he'd step through the gates and stare at the statue of Hamlet. Hamlet had understood the demands of honour.

The grandfather clock in the hall struck three a.m. Somewhere outside two cars engaged in a honking duel. Truly, this was the city that never slept. Grunting, Sato turned on his side. A floorboard creaked. He tensed. Something touched his arm. He grabbed it and it squeaked. Chloe.

'Are you crazy?' he hissed.

She stood beside his bed in one of the peignoir sets

he'd watched her try on that afternoon. This one was bronze with ivory lace, slit way up her slender thigh. A hint of muscle gave shape to the creamy flesh. Sato swallowed.

'I've brought you a present,' she purred, and climbed on to his bed.

The springs made a noise like mice being slaughtered.

'Stop it,' he said, trying to settle the mattress by spreading his weight. 'I do not want your presents.'

She balanced on her knees before him. Her hands slid over his belly and chest, fingertips exploring his flesh in a way that suggested she liked the feel of him. The unspoken admiration called to more than his pride. He wished he did not sleep in the nude. His organ thickened at her touch, obviously preparing to betray him. It felt extremely heavy.

'You'll want this present,' she said. Her hands slithered behind his neck and locked together. She pulled. He'd been so busy trying to quiet the boxspring, she'd caught him off balance. His face fell into her cleavage. 'Take a good whiff, Sato. This is your master's personal perfume.'

Against his will, he inhaled. A shiver rippled through his body, followed immediately by a flash of heat. He hardened dramatically, painfully. Beneath the scent of flowers, he caught the salt-sharp tang of semen: David's semen. It held the smell of David's body, unique and beloved for the last six years.

A thin keening left Sato's throat. As if she knew what would weaken him most, her touch gentled. She stroked his hair behind his ears, then rubbed his shoulders as he breathed in and out like a bellows. His hands rose, cupping her breasts and pressing them closer to his face. He nuzzled her velvet curves. She was so soft, so warm.

'Yes,' she said. 'Kiss them. Lick them clean.'

He groaned and peeled the lace from her bosom. His

tongue reached for her skin. He licked her; tasted David. His eyes drifted shut on a surplus of pleasure. Her nipples were as smooth as butter. He rolled them on his tongue and trembled when they drew up tight.

'He took me here,' she said. 'He put his cock between my breasts and thrust until he came.'

Sato was lost beyond saving. Her words drew pictures that seared his mind. He saw David's cock, hard and straight, its veins blue in a sea of deeply flushed ivory. He rubbed his face across her flesh. He knew how David's organ must have felt, thrusting through this silken bounty. His own cock pulsed in anguish. 'I want to do it,' he growled. 'Let me do it, too.'

She pushed him back gently, but with more force than he could ignore. When he sat back, she shook her finger like a disappointed schoolmarm. His anger made the blood pump harder through his sex. How dare she mock him?

'No, no, no,' she said with her devil's smile. 'I have something else in mind for you.'

'What else?' he said through gritted teeth.

She brought two items from the pocket of her pei-gnoir, a sealed condom and a small tube of lubricant. She set them in his palm. A quiver raced down his spine, a minnow skittering through an icy stream. His mind wouldn't form the words but his body knew; his body tightened with a dark, ungovernable desire.

'I was wondering,' she drawled, 'if you might be more of a back-door man.'

Her words detonated deep inside his soul. She knew he liked men. She had to. But how could she? If David had not discovered his secret, how could she? No, she was merely perverse, a woman of peculiar tastes. No doubt she thought every man wanted a piece of her arse.

He wished he could deny that he did.

She turned on her knees until she faced the foot of his

bed. Her hands, graceful as birds, gathered up the bronze silk, robe and gown both. Sato sat on his heels, rooted in place. The back of her thighs appeared, her bottom, her incomparable dimples. She stripped the silk over her head and shimmied her arse in invitation. He could not resist. He bent forwards to curl his tongue into the small, satiny hollows. As he did, his hand roved down her cheeks. He found her wetness with his thumb and spread it over the infolded lips.

It seemed natural to open the lubricant then, natural to squeeze it where she'd need it most. Her anal bud was delicate. The thought of breaching it made his heart race with excitement. Or maybe it was terror. He had never taken a woman this way; men, yes, but never women. Senses tuned to her response, he worked the fluid into her tightly furled orifice, teasing the nerves that gathered just inside. His fingers seemed too heavy for the work, but she bit her lower lip as he probed and her hips squirmed towards his hand. When he looked between her legs, moisture gleamed on her inner thigh. The sight brought a smile to his lips. Perhaps this territory wasn't as foreign as he thought.

He donned the rubber. It was thicker than the norm, but he doubted it would dull his pleasure much. The knowledge that she'd planned this, maybe while she'd dragged him from shop to shop, pushed him to the edge of his control. If he did not wish to shame himself, he would need all the dulling he could get.

'Hold tight,' he said, and placed her hands on the footboard.

After one tantalising moment of effort, he slid inside. She had done this before. She knew how to relax; how to surrender resistance until she enveloped every inch of him in warm, pulsing flesh. He cocked his hips and pressed his scrotum to her mons. The angle gained him a precious millimetre more of entry. He closed his eyes, breathing hard to regain his mastery. The task was not easy. There was nothing like this in the world, the tightness, the silky-smooth walls, the curve of a smooth haunch cradling his belly.

In a fog of sensual pleasure, he ran his hands to the nape of her neck. Only from this angle could a woman be taken for a man. Not Chloe, though, not with that violin curve to her back, not with her satiny skin. Moaning softly with enjoyment, he drew back for his first thrust.

The springs chirped like crickets.

She laughed, breathless with her own arousal. 'Guess you'll have to go slower, Sato-san.'

He knew better than to suggest they move from the bed. Instead, he did as she said. He went slower. Even as his body screamed for more, he held himself to a languid pace. She pushed with him, her body undulating in sync with his. It was a dance of mating cranes: hypnotising, elemental. The sight of his cock sinking into her arse made him burn for completion.

'Touch me,' she said. 'I want to feel your hands on me.'

He cupped her breasts; let their weight sway across his palms. Her nipples strafed his skin. Her sphincter tightened on his sex. He could not contain a groan.

'Lower,' she whispered. 'Rub my pussy. Make me come.'

He combed through her tangled fleece, the stripe of hair thick and crisp. The pearl of her pleasure thrust outwards. He pressed it against her and rubbed. She came almost at once, silently, shuddering. Her contractions travelled from one passage to the other, rippling down the molasses-slow pumping of his cock.

He could bear no more. He curled himself around her. He crooked his chin over her shoulder, and folded his hands over hers on the footboard. 'Brace yourself,' he said, because he could not be gentle now. He had to join her or he would die.

'Yes,' she said, gripping him with her secret walls. 'Do it hard.'

He began to pump in earnest, picking up speed as he went, sweat blinding his eyes, the roar of lust deafening his ears. He pressed his face into her neck and tried to muffle his grunts, but he could not contain them. Every collision called a noise from him. *Unh*, deeper, and *unh*, harder. David, he thought, but she was what he saw. She was what he felt. She widened her stance for him. She held firm under his assault. He thrust one finger up her sheath and felt a steady, wet fibrillation. She was coming. She must have been coming for minutes. His eyes burned with sudden fire. His thighs cramped. He thrust.

At last, the agonising tension broke. He flung his head back, jaw stretched wide on a silent scream. The climax pulsed through him, hard and sharp at first. Then, without warning, his pleasure opened like a flower. His head swung forwards in shock. A warm, white-gold light burst in his mind; spread through his chest, his limbs. When it passed, it left a comforting glow behind, as if more than his body had found release.

He did not understand. Somehow, she had drained him of his desperation. He could not imagine she'd intended to do so, but he could not reason away what he had felt. She had good in her: maybe good she did not know was there.

They lay together in the aftermath, their heads towards the foot of the bed.

'Why now?' he asked, because he did not like this pull on his heart. 'We were alone for three days. Why do you decide to seduce me when David is sleeping two doors away?'

She rolled on to her back. 'Don't you like to gamble,

Sato? Everything is more fun when there's something at stake.'

The taunting words revived his anger. 'I think you do not know what is at stake.'

'You mean I might foil my plot to catch your employer in my honey trap.'

'Perhaps a woman like you doesn't make plots. Perhaps you only live to make trouble.'

'So serious.' She mocked him with half-lidded eyes. 'Come on, Sato. It's not as if I'm forcing you to have sex with me. You can say "no" any time you like.'

'Hah!'

'You can.' She lifted one knee and nudged his hip. 'You could even expose me. Oh, David would be hurt, but he'd get over it. His loss of face wouldn't mean as much to him as it would to you.'

Sato sat up and folded his arms. 'It is my duty to protect him. I will not hurt him simply because you wish it. Ach.' He shook his head in disgust. 'I do not understand why you behave this way.'

'Because I can. Because I want to.' She drew a circle on his knee. 'Shall I tell you a secret?'

'You do me too much honour.'

'Ha ha. Sarcasm from the *sumitori*.' She folded her hands across her belly. 'The secret is that, once upon a time, I thought I would never feel desire. I thought I would die without ever making love. Really making love, not just putting the parts together. When I discovered I could feel, could want, I thought God must not hate me after all. Desire isn't something I take for granted, nor is it something I'm inclined to ignore.'

Her explanation confused him; softened the clean, sharp edge of his anger. In spite of himself, he was curious. 'Were you sick?'

'Oh, yes,' she said with a short, bitter laugh. 'Very.'

* * *

David woke when she crawled back into bed. She turned on her side, facing away from him. Her hair was wet.

'You took a shower.' He was surprised. Most women wanted to shower before they made love. He hadn't minded that she didn't; far from it. When they got home from the fundraiser, he hadn't wanted to wait any more than she had. They'd come together with unexpected sweetness, a simple, sighing, eyes-wide-open union. Her body had fit his like a dream.

'You are very good,' she'd said when it was over.

At the time, he'd smiled and kissed her nose, but now he wondered if she hadn't sounded sad. He didn't understand why making love like that would make someone sad. Then again, he didn't understand a lot of things about this woman. He touched her freshly washed shoulder. 'Are you still worried about the photographer?'

'No,' she said. 'But I want to get some sleep.'

The picture from the fundraiser appeared in the society pages. Chloe's face had come out, after all. Her profile had the clarity of a coin. David tried to make a joke of it, but she blistered the air with curses.

'Why are you angry?' he asked.

None of her answers seemed real.

She stopped leaving the brownstone. He caught her peering out the windows when she thought he wasn't watching. She hid behind the curtains and stared at the quiet square as if she expected to see a bogeyman. She made love with a ferocity that broke his heart, striving for every orgasm as if it were her last, as if it were a drug that could erase her fears. He could not make her slow down. The tenderness they'd shared their first night together seemed a figment of his imagination. Finally, he called Sato into his office. 'I want you to find out what's frightening her. Use all your contacts. I don't care if it does violate her privacy. I have to know.'

Sato nodded. He didn't say it was about time, or warn David he might not like what he found. Lately, Sato had been treating Chloe with a care akin to kindness. That frightened David most of all.

Two days later, Sato brought his report to David's office in New York. One look at his face told David he'd better have Shelley hold his calls.

The security chief sat heavily at the conference table. Lines of strain scored his broad, imperial face. He flattened his hands atop a manila folder. David suspected he'd memorised its contents.

'OK,' Sato said. 'Here is what I have found. Chloe Dubois was born Samantha Cohen in an affluent New Jersey suburb. Her father, Gerald, is a district court judge. Her mother, Miriam, is a housewife and an active member of their synagogue. There are two sisters, Beth and Sharon. At age sixteen, Chloe – then Samantha – ran away from home. She ended up in Atlantic City where she worked as a topless dancer.'

He paused, watching for David's reaction. David flipped his pen over in his hand, not terribly surprised, but aware there must be more. 'I presume that's where she became Chloe Dubois?'

'Yes, though she did not legally change her name until she was twenty-one. That's when she left the clubs and was hired as a headliner for one of the casinos. The man who broke into her apartment is probably Ronald Holman, the owner of a strip club called the Golden Buckle. He took exception to her leaving for greener pastures. As of –' Sato looked at his watch '– two hours ago, he is in jail on multiple conspiracy charges. I think we can say he is not a threat for now. Interestingly enough, she was well known, both as a stripper and a showgirl. If you or I were gamblers, we probably would have heard of her.'

'What about her claim that she's a model?'

'She has posed for a few lingerie catalogues, and she really is a student at Columbia. No declared major. She takes a few classes each year: art history, Russian literature. Her global economics teacher –' Sato found the spot in the file '– Professor Birkenstahl, seems to think she's brilliant.'

David got the impression Sato was stalling. He gripped the edge of the table. 'Was she involved in anything criminal?'

'Apart from dancing when she was underage? No. But she seems to have gone from man to man. A string of patrons, you could say. When she is with one, she lives well. When she is not...' His big shoulders lifted on a shrug. 'The odd thing is she's rich.'

'Rich?'

'Yes. She has half a million dollars scattered in different accounts. She must have saved every penny she ever earned.'

Unable to sit a moment longer, David strode to the window and bit the side of his nail. It was an old habit from his childhood, one his mother had worked hard to break him of. 'If she has so much money, why was she living in that hellhole?'

Sato had followed him. He put his hand on David's shoulder. 'Maybe that money is her security blanket. Maybe she is afraid to spend it.' His grip tightened on the muscle between his shoulder and neck. 'There is something else. When she was fifteen, she accused her father of killing their babysitter.'

David turned and stared. Whatever he'd expected, it wasn't this. 'Killing their babysitter?'

'Yes. But it does not seem likely he did it. The police investigated and found nothing to link him to the girl's disappearance. He had no history of violence, then or since. I spoke with the officer in charge of the case. Even he believes Gerald Cohen is innocent.'

'So why does Chloe think he's guilty?'

Sato hesitated. 'She says she saw him do it.'

'Maybe she did.'

'David.' Sato's hand fell from his shoulder. 'Chloe's sisters were with her at the time. They say their father did nothing whatsoever to the girl.'

David recalled Chloe's nightmare. 'Maybe they forgot.'

'Forgot their father strangled someone? In front of them? She was hospitalised, master. She was diagnosed with mild schizophrenia.'

That, at least, David could dismiss. 'I don't know what idiot slapped that label on her, but she's not crazy. Bitchy, yes. Crazy, no.' Of course, maybe *he* was crazy for thinking he could change her, for wanting to so badly. Tears stung his eyes. 'I care about her, Sato. I can't just walk away.'

Sato's sigh came from deep in his wrestler's belly. 'I know, master. I know.'

That night, David found her by the front bow window, the ghost of Gramercy Park, shrouded by the long brocade curtain. She must have heard him approach. She showed no surprise when he wrapped her in his arms. Resting his chin on her head, he followed her gaze to the circle of gold beneath the old-fashioned streetlamp. 'Nothing out there,' he said.

'Couldn't sleep.'

Her voice was heartbreakingly tired. He had to tell her, even if his prying angered her. 'Ronald Holman is in jail, Chloe. Even if he saw your picture in the paper, he couldn't hurt you now.' She didn't ask how he knew Holman's name, merely slid her hand up the curtain's edge. 'I don't get it. You lived in a rough neighbourhood. You were friends with the homeboys. You didn't bat an eye when Holman trashed your apartment. What exactly are you scared of?'

She rubbed one knuckle across her upper lip. In the light from the streetlamp, he saw her beautiful nails were bitten to the quick. 'Chloe.' He held her closer. 'I had Sato look into your background. We know you ran away from home.'

At last she spoke, low and tight. 'You want me to spill my guts, don't you? You want me to lay my intestines on the table and let you poke at them. You think it will bring us closer.'

She almost spat out the last sentence. She didn't push him away, though, so he answered honestly. 'Yes,' he said, as calmly as he could. 'I'd like you to spill your guts, as you put it. I do think it would bring us closer. But I'd never force you into anything, not even if I thought it was good for you.'

She twisted out of his hold. He watched her pace back and forth across the darkened parlour, arms swinging with nervous energy. 'Sit,' he said. 'You're making me dizzy.'

She sat in the nearest chair, then immediately shot up. She pressed her hands together in front of her chest. 'He could always make me do what he wanted. He always found a way.'

He didn't dare step closer. 'He didn't want you to run away, did he? You did that in spite of him.'

She didn't seem to hear. She began pacing again, then stopped in the centre of the faded Oriental rug. 'She was only seventeen.'

'Mary Ryan?'

'Mary *Alice* Ryan. We thought she was so exotic. She had freckles and curly red hair and she always wore a little gold cross around her neck. Me and my sisters used to sneak downstairs to spy on her after she put us to bed. Sometimes her boyfriend would come over and they'd smooch on the loveseat. But one night, someone else was trying to kiss her.'

'Your father.'

A shadow flickered across her jaw. He knew she was clenching it. 'Well, it's a typical male fantasy, isn't it? The nubile young babysitter who'll do anything with anyone. Except Mary Alice wouldn't. Mary Alice was a nice Catholic girl.' She laughed, a sandpaper sound. 'She was so feisty. "I can't believe you did that," she said. "When my father hears about this, he'll kill you."'

'What did your father say to that?'

Chloe's chest sagged with a sigh. 'He was perfectly calm. He told her it was a simple misunderstanding. No harm done. Mary Alice said she thought shoving his tongue down her throat was plenty of harm. She wasn't afraid of him. She laughed in his face. She said she only babysat for him because she liked us. She said she'd known he was a son of a bitch the first time they met.' Chloe grabbed the back of a chair and pushed. Her anger was palpable, a taste on the back of his tongue.

'Then what happened?'

She looked at him, one quick, bitter glance. 'Then he did it. He didn't warn her. He didn't say, "No silly Irish cow is going to ruin my career." He just put his hands around her neck and twisted, as if it were no big deal, as if he'd been waiting all his life for an excuse to do it. I heard a sound like a muffled gunshot and Mary Alice sagged in his arms. He'd broken her neck. I thought she'd fainted, but she must have been dead already.

'The three of us were huddled behind the couch, ready to pee in our pants. Beth made a noise and he saw us. The expression on his face never changed. It was just as cool as it had been when he killed her. "Go back to bed, girls," he said. "Mary Alice isn't feeling well."

'He told the police she'd walked home by herself. He'd offered to drive her, but she said she needed the air; said she had a headache. She only lived four streets away.

The neighbourhood was good. How was my father to know some maniac would grab her halfway there?

'He convinced me,' she said, her voice leaden. 'He convinced me I'd dreamed it.'

'How old were you?'

'Ten. My sisters were five and six.'

David watched her shove the chair again. She seemed to think ten was old enough to do more than she had. 'What changed your mind? What made you think it wasn't a dream?'

She closed her eyes. 'Five years later, I found her cross in the back of his desk drawer. I was looking for a pen and there it was. It had a little pink pearl in the centre. He'd saved it. He'd fucking saved it. One of the arms had blood on it from where it had cut her neck. I stood there, staring at it, and everything came back. I remembered how sweet Mary Alice was. I remembered how she used to decorate our omelets with faces so the vegetables would be more fun. I wanted to steal the necklace, because it was proof, but I heard him on the stairs and I got scared.'

'Scared of what he'd do to you?'

She nodded, the pain she was fighting tightening her face. 'Afterwards, I felt stupid and cowardly. I couldn't go to my mother. I couldn't. But the next day I went to the guidance counsellor at school and made myself tell the truth. I knew she didn't believe me. My father was a judge, a pillar of the community. But she agreed to talk to my sisters. When she did, they said it never happened. They said Dad and I had been fighting and I was just trying to get back at him.'

Her body shook at the memory. David wanted to go to her, but she was wound too tight to risk it. Instead, he dried his palms on his robe. 'What did you do then?'

'Ran away.' She swiped her hand beneath her nose. 'Well, why not? I thought my sisters had betrayed me. It didn't occur to me they honestly didn't remember. They'd forced themselves to forget. He was their father. They didn't want to believe.

'Twice he found me and brought me back. I really went crazy then. They sent me to a private hospital; had to put me in restraints. When I got out, I'd wised up. I realised I needed money if I wanted to keep ahead of him, and lots of it.'

'So you started stripping.'

She nodded. 'Best damn thing I ever did for myself. I was free of his lies. I was safe.' Her body relaxed even as she said it. She sat on the arm of the chair she'd been wrestling. 'I called my mom when I turned eighteen, from a pay phone in the next town over, 'cause – God forbid – the call could be traced. I was pretty paranoid. But I wanted her to know I was OK, not homeless or anything. Maybe I shouldn't have told her I was stripping, but I was proud of it. I was really good, David. I made as much in six months as my dad did in a year, almost as much as the girls with implants did. I was taking care of myself, you know? I was coping.' She rubbed her hands down her thighs. 'Mom said I might as well be a whore. She didn't say it meanly but she said it. Said I'd better come home before I started taking drugs. Shit, I barely took aspirin. Stripping was like worshipping Satan to her. She thought I was totally depraved. She couldn't see it as an honest living. She couldn't imagine what I had to be proud of.

'For a long time after that I didn't even consider calling home. Then, about a year back, I called my sister, Beth. She's the oldest. We used to be close. I thought, by this time, maybe she'd be happy to hear from me.'

'Was she?'

She shrugged. 'She said she was, but I could tell she was uncomfortable. "You aren't still stripping?" she asked, first thing, like that was the biggest evil in the world. I think she wasn't forgetting as good as she used to. Maybe she didn't want the reminder. She's married now. She has kids the same age we were when it happened. It would be hard for her if they knew their grandfather was a killer.'

'Maybe it would be better,' he said. 'And maybe part of you wishes you could forget like she did.'

She pressed her lips together very hard. Her chin was shaking. He knew he was missing something, some puzzle piece that would explain why a fighter like her would choose to run. But he couldn't push her now, not when one more nudge might shatter her control. 'Come here,' he said and held out his arms.

She shook her head at first, then walked into his embrace, still not crying, but trembling like the victim of more recent terrors. She hugged him tightly. 'You're too good for me,' she said.

He did not know how sincerely she meant it.

6

The breakfast parlour glowed a light butter yellow. David loved its faded charm, just as he loved the slightly battered antiques, the threadbare carpets, and the smell of time that hung about the brownstone like an old library. This jumble of forgotten styles was light years away from the department store Americana with which he'd grown up: no plaid couches, no shag carpeting, no clocks shaped like Mickey Mouse. He knew Sato hated the place, but living here gave him the same pleasure as sneaking into a museum at night. This house wasn't trying to be American. It just was.

Chloe seemed fond of it. He'd caught her grinning at the gruesome still lives and the nude marble Mercury on the final of the stairs. Consequently, he was surprised when she set down her cream-cheese-slathered bagel and asked to return to Vermont. 'If it wouldn't be an imposition,' she said. 'I mean, we've never actually discussed how long I'd stay with you. I can make other arrangements.'

He covered her hand where it was pleating the linen tablecloth. 'Do you like staying with me?'

'I like you,' she said.

He fought an urge to press his heart. He wanted to believe her. In fact, he did believe her. A wonderful sense of lightness filled his soul. He tilted her chin on the edge of his hand. 'I like you, too. I hope you'll be with me a long time. Here or in Vermont. Whichever you prefer.'

Her eyes didn't quite meet his. He wasn't used to seeing her unsure of herself.

'I know it's silly,' she said, 'but I feel safer there. There's so much space. It seems so far away from everything.' She smoothed her napkin across her lap. 'I can make the weekends worth your while.'

'Chloe.' His tone was gently scolding.

'I know.' A smile shifted the velvet curve of her cheek. 'I don't have to make it worth your while. You do this out of the goodness of your heart. Let's just say I enjoy paying you back.'

'In that case –' he said, and pulled her in for a soft, bagel-flavoured kiss.

Weekends weren't enough. Damning the expense – which he could, after all, afford – he had the helicopter take him home at least two nights a week. Sometimes she'd be there at the landing pad. One moonless night, she waited just beyond the reach of the lights and knocked him to the ground with a flying tackle. The grass was thick and cool under his back. She had his trousers open before he could catch his breath.

'Hard already,' she said, drawing him up in admiring hands.

The sight of the house from the air, knowing she was close, had brought him to this state. Rather than tell her so, he slid his hands under her thin silk robe. He found her slippery folds. 'Wet already,' he teased.

She threw her head back as he played, rocking her pelvis into his caress. His heart pounded just watching her, his arousal a hot, delicious ache between his legs. He'd never known a woman with such an animal enjoyment of sex. From a distance, he heard the chopper blades begin to spin. As if this was a sign, she pushed his hands aside and impaled herself on his erection. The shock of entry was sharp and very sweet.

He cried out, jerking instinctively deeper. Her sheath was hot. Its walls squirmed in the way that signalled she was nearing orgasm. He wrapped his hands around her hips. 'You were ready for this, weren't you?'

She nipped his earlobe between her teeth. 'I was masturbating when you landed. I had my fingers up my cunt.'

When he stiffened at her words, she laughed, a full-throated sound he didn't often hear from her. 'You're crazy,' he said, breaking into a chuckle himself.

She stole his breath with a quick, swivelling thrust. 'I'm crazy all right. Crazy enough to bet I can make you come before that bird lifts off again.'

He wasn't brash enough to bet against her. She rode him with swift sure strokes, as if her hips were oiled. Under such relentless stimulation, he was helpless to resist the climb. Forget holding back. Forget worrying about her pleasure. The only thing that kept him from coming in seconds was the fact that his body literally couldn't react fast enough. For one long minute, she held him at an incredible pitch of sensation, one he hadn't known himself capable of sustaining. He hung at the edge of release, gritting his teeth, groaning for relief, then lost his breath in a harsh, involuntary cough as the first burst of lightning kicked up his spine.

The chopper's lights swept over them as he came. A picture froze in the hot white glare: Chloe's powder-blue robe fluttering in the backwash, its lapels fallen to her elbows. Her breasts shook from her ride and flesh gleamed where their bodies met. His cock was half buried, her pussy half filled. Both were wet, both dark with engorging blood. She whipped her hips again, deepening the pain-pleasure of his peak.

Perhaps the pilot watched. Perhaps he didn't. David couldn't bring himself to care. All he saw was the halo around her head, the sweat dripping in streams of diamond-glitter down her neck. She cried out, high and wild, beginning to crest. The hoop at her navel quivered in time to her inner pulses, which fluttered deliciously down his shaft. He dug his heels into the turf for purchase. His buttocks clenched. He surged into her with all his might. He would pierce her soul if he could; would break her open with his lust. He growled with effort as one last burst of seed squeezed through his prick.

'Yes!' she answered, coming hard, the tendons of her neck corded tight.

Then the light was gone. The chopper swooped away. Her contractions slowed. She sank on to his chest, breathing hard. 'Aw,' she said. 'You won.'

But he thought they both had.

Chloe wheeled her bicycle out of the garage. One of Sato's men, bored with the quiet, had reconditioned the ten-speed for her. He'd done a good job. Now it whirred instead of rattled. Chloe seemed as fond of it as she was of David's bottle-green Ferrari. She drove too fast, of course, but her reflexes were good. He had no qualms about handing her the keys.

'I'm riding into Strathmore,' she said. 'Do you want anything from the shop?'

He smiled at her. She wore a bright tie-dyed T-shirt with a pair of khaki walking shorts, both bought in town because she didn't own casual clothes. Her hair was caught back in her nice-girl's braid. Her cheeks were pink from being outdoors. She looked happy, even content. The expression might have been another of her masks, but it didn't feel like it.

'Hold up five minutes,' he said. 'I'll change into shorts and join you.'

She looked him up and down, a grinning, lascivious once-over. 'Yeah,' she said. 'I can tell you need the exercise.'

He laughed to the house and back. The day was perfect: warm in the sun, crisp in the shade. The first leaves were beginning to turn along the narrow country road. They pedalled and laughed, joking about nothing, teasing each other. A pair of blue jays darted in front of them, their trajectory low and straight. 'Newlyweds,' she said. 'Taking the short route home.'

The words stirred a daydream. He thought of the future, of being able to take her presence for granted. The image wasn't as hard to form as he'd expected. He could picture her with grey in her hair and one large diamond on her hand, maybe not rocking on the porch, but there at his side.

They left their bikes in front of the barber's, locking them to the rack out of city dweller's habit. Strathmore was virtually crime-free until the tourists came through, and even then it wasn't bad. Arm-in-arm, they strolled towards the General Store. The town was quiet. Painted signs creaked in a gentle breeze. Six cars filled the slots on Main, all slanted into the street. Strathmore didn't believe in parallel parking. Strathmore was an old-fashioned town.

A car door opened ahead of them. A tall man emerged from inside, slim, distinguished, silver-haired. David wouldn't have noticed him if Chloe hadn't stopped in her tracks the moment he appeared. Her face had gone chalk white. In the time it took him to ask what was wrong, the man had reached them. 'Thank God,' he said. 'I thought I'd never find you.'

Chloe did not answer. Her lips had formed a thin white line. David's first thought was that this was an old lover. He didn't really want the reminder that he was one of many, but Chloe should have known he wasn't going to act the idiot. He squeezed her elbow in reassurance.

'Get the fuck away from me,' she said, spitting each word like a stone.

David stiffened, thinking she meant him, but the man flinched even more. His face took on a wounded cast.

'Samantha,' he said. 'I only want to make sure you're all right. We've all been worried sick.'

That's when David knew. That's when he saw the likeness in their faces: the elegant bones, the full, sensual mouths, the sleepy, dark-amber eyes. This man had killed in front of his daughters. He'd made a ten-year-old his accomplice. Anger began to rise but it was quiet, like a wave gathering out to sea. Rage might come later, but for now David was calm. He pushed Chloe behind him. 'I think you'd better leave.'

Something flickered across the man's face, something calculating and cold and not unlike excitement. The last scrap of David's doubt disappeared. Chloe's father was looking forward to a confrontation. Chloe's father enjoyed fooling the world. Was that the real reason he'd strangled Mary Alice? To revel in a secret the people around him would never suspect? Did what he'd done change his perception of every woman he met? Did he think: if she pisses me off, I'll kill her, too?

David wasn't terribly religious, but he knew, one day, a higher judge would exact a price for what this man had done.

Unfortunately, one day wasn't good enough for Chloe. Chloe needed protection now.

'Leave,' he said, leaning forwards, his knees soft, his centre rooted deep in the earth. Sato had taught him this. Sato had given him the confidence to know no ordinary man could overpower him.

The man sensed David's strength even if he didn't understand it. His expression turned; took on a parent's concern. He would not retreat, but he would change direction. 'You don't understand,' he said. 'She's my daughter. Her mother's been so worried.' He reached past David's shoulder, beseeching with his hand. 'Samantha, please.'

Chloe didn't move. Perhaps she couldn't. She screwed her eyes shut and began to scream: a child's scream, shrill and endless. The man faltered back towards his car. Her public display cowed him as David's well-mannered threats could not. People began to emerge from the stores, shopkeepers, customers. Chloe gulped a breath and went on, her body taut with strain. Her father got into his car and started the engine. 'Please,' he said again.

Her eyes flew open. She rushed him. She pounded on the window he quickly rolled shut, pounded on the hood as he pulled away, so hard she left dents in the shiny metal. 'Bastard,' she screamed. 'Murderer!' His tyres squealed on the asphalt.

As soon as the car was gone, she began to sob.

David pulled her into his arms. 'Hush,' he said, kissing her, holding her. 'Hush.'

'You heard him,' she said. 'He looks like a father. He talks like a father. Like he cares. Like he loves me. But I'm not crazy. I'm not.'

'I know,' he said. 'I know.'

'Is she all right?' asked Mrs Kleghorn, plump and kind and steady. A handful of townspeople surrounded them, worried, but not pushing close. This was New England, after all. People cared, but they didn't crowd. David smiled at them and rubbed Chloe's hitching back.

'We've got some new Ben & Jerry's,' Mr Kleghorn offered. 'Maybe that would settle her.'

Chloe actually laughed against his shoulder, but he knew she wasn't up for questions, or for ice cream. 'If I could borrow your truck,' he said. 'I'd like to drive her home.'

'Of course,' said Mr Kleghorn, and handed him the keys.

David kept her hand on his leg as he drove the old pick-up, squeezing her icy fingers whenever he didn't have to shift. He watched her from the corner of his eye.

'He can't stay away from me,' she said. 'He likes that I know. It gives him a thrill. What good is getting away with murder if no one knows?'

David thought she was right, but it didn't seem wise to say so, or to wonder why she'd never pulled a stunt like this where people who counted could see. The courthouse steps struck him as a fine option. But maybe she thought no one would believe her. Maybe the judge was really good at convincing people she was nuts. 'You faced him down,' he said. 'You didn't let him hurt you. You did just what you should have.'

She nodded, a little jerk of motion. Her eyes were glassy, her breathing rough. Was she in shock? He could hear her teeth chattering over the grumbling engine. He wondered if she'd even heard him. 'We'll put you in a bath,' he said. 'We'll get you warmed up again. We'll have Auntie brew some tea.'

She made a funny sound, then covered her mouth with her fist. He thought she might be afraid she was going to scream again. He lifted her hand from his leg and pressed a kiss to its back. Her gaze darted to him and away. 'You'll stay with me, won't you? At least until I'm calm?'

'Absolutely,' he said. 'Until you're calm and then some.'

She nodded again. He had a feeling she didn't trust her voice.

Auntie brought tea to the bath. Chloe drank one tiny cup and started crying again. The older woman tugged her up from the tub. 'Come sit on the little stool. I'll wash your back.' She shooed David out with sharp little flutters of her hands. 'Go,' she said. 'Crying is for women.'

David didn't agree, but Chloe could probably use some mothering. She was crying more easily now, not fighting it. Auntie would call him if Chloe asked. He left them with a last backwards glance and went to find Sato.

He suspected they hadn't seen the last of Gerald Cohen.

7

The dream woke him. There were spiders in it and a long, dark hall. Though he tried to shake it off, his skin crawled with a sense of dread. He couldn't imagine why. Sato's men were on patrol. The grounds were secure. He rolled his head towards Chloe's side of the bed, and his pulse jumped in his throat. She wasn't there.

He forced himself to breathe. Her absence wasn't necessarily cause for alarm. She often woke in the middle of the night. She liked to sit in the Zen garden and draw silly pictures for Master Wu to shake his head over in the morning. Once she drew a giant phallus like they kept at Taga-jinja shrine; covered the whole stretch of gravel with it. The gardener had leaned on his rake and laughed until tears ran down his weathered face. In the end, she'd charmed even him.

David had to make sure she was safe.

He descended the outside stairs to the roof of the second floor. The garden was empty – as it had been designed to be. No plants grew here, no statues or fountains. The garden's entire contents consisted of two masses of granite that rose from a bed of pale beige river gravel. Every morning, Master Wu raked the pebbles into the same straight lines and contoured loops, a silent encouragement to meditate on the eternal. At the moment, David merely meditated on Chloe.

A thread of music floated out from the house. He turned towards it.

Someone was using his practice room. It was a large, bare space with plain white walls and hardwood floors.

Sato had a *dojo* behind the garage where he drilled David in self-defence. This room was David's alone. He used it when the weather kept him from exercising outside. Sometimes he sat drinking tea and staring at the garden. On a cool, rainy day, nothing could be more peaceful.

Tonight, a different energy had entered the room, a dangerous energy. An array of votive candles lit the far end, their cut-glass holders creating a ruby-and-pearl glow. The window, which rolled upwards into the wall, was halfway open. David ducked under the gap and slipped into a shadow. He wasn't the fighter Sato was, but he had good balance and he was quiet. When he didn't want to be heard, he usually wasn't.

As he'd expected, Chloe had taken possession of the room. She faced away from him, towards the bank of stereo equipment. Modern Flamenco music issued from the speakers. David picked out a lone guitar and a clarinet that moaned like a man in carnal agony.

This was not one of his CDs. Jazz made him nervous. This particular jazz crept into his blood: heavy, warm, pooling in his groin like sunbaked sand. Or maybe the music was sugar because, as he padded further into the room, the sight of Chloe made it melt.

She wore a bra and panties he'd never seen before: black with spider-fine lace. A thong formed the back of the panties. A pair of shiny stiletto heels encased her feet. Any normal woman would have been teetering, but the shoes seemed not to hamper Chloe. She was dancing gently, barely moving. His eyes followed a roll and dip of shoulders, a shuffle of feet. Her hips inscribed a lazy figure of eight in the beeswax-scented air. He wanted to press his own hips into that rotation, to let her rub that firm, rounded flesh across his rising cock.

He could not have been more aware of his nakedness, of the air currents moving like water over his sex. They'd made love twice tonight; thorough, strenuous encounters, Chloe's chosen remedy for her scare. Now he felt as if he'd been celibate for weeks. His veins throbbed with longing. His hair prickled with energy. He pressed his hand over his belly as if that would hold his desire in check. It did not, but he stayed as he was. She didn't seem to know he was there. Right or wrong, he wanted to remain undiscovered. He wanted to watch who she was when she thought no one saw. The thrill was guilty but irresistible.

She reached out to increase the volume. The music pulsed over him in spicy, sinuous streams. She turned. Her nipples were sharp silhouettes beneath the black flowery lace of her bra. Her breasts swayed. She moved more purposefully, not just her hips, but her arms, her belly and her neck curved and counter-curved. Her hair swung loose to her waist. She smoothed it back with both hands, then snapped three turns to the centre of the room, as neatly as a ballerina.

Now she danced a body length away. She reached behind her back. Her hands met between her shoulder blades to undo the clasp of her bra. Sweat broke out across his belly. It didn't matter that he'd seen everything she had. This was different. This was private. She peeled the lace away and threw it to the opposite wall. Her palms skimmed up her waist. She touched her breasts. For a moment, the pain of his erection was so intense he had to close his eyes.

He'd seen strippers before. They were popular in Japan. For a businessman, a trip to a sex show was a common cap to an evening of drinking. He'd also seen strippers in America, less frequently, but he had. They were nothing like this. They were bored, most of them, scornful or fake, going through the motions. Chloe was more like belly dancers he'd seen in Egypt; not the dancers who shook their booty for the tourists, but the dancers who performed for the locals after the tourists went to bed.

There wasn't a man alive who wouldn't understand the message in her rolling hips, who wouldn't want to obey the beckoning curl of her fingers. No law, no custom, no habit of repression could dull this. This wasn't just the power of sex; it was the power of sex offered freely, with a hint of mischief, a promise of lust met and welcomed. Her dance was not a parody; it was a celebration of all the earthly delights a woman had to offer.

She touched her nipples, her waist, the soft slope of her inner thighs. She was showing off, but she was enjoying the touches, too. She turned in a slow circle. She undulated down to the floor, leaned back on her heels and humped the shadowed air. This was a copulatory dance. Her arms rippled out from her sides like snakes. She was Kali the destroyer, a goddess, a force of nature. Sweat bathed her shaking breasts; dripped down her ribs. He heard one of her joints pop as she arched her back. So, she was just a woman. But that was all she had to be to bring him to his knees. He could fuck a woman, after all; could hold a woman in his arms.

He wanted to grab her, to turn those undulations into the act they mimicked. At the same time, he wanted to watch her all night. His lust felt good. It was a shot of adrenalin, a megadose of life. He touched his cock for the first time, squeezing it between thumb and forefinger and pulling upwards, just once, to feel how strong it had grown.

The music ended as he reached the slippery, lust-drenched head. Chloe sat up, breathing hard but evenly. Her hair clung to her sweaty back. She rose. Clack, clack, clack went her heels as she crossed the room to collect her bra; clack, clack, clack, as she strode past him towards the garden. She swung the scrap of lace as it dangled from one finger: insouciance incarnate. Her walk was a dance in itself. Her hips swung with it. Her spine swayed.

She stopped before ducking under the half-raised window. 'Thanks for coming,' she said, looking straight at his shadow. 'It's always better with an audience.'

He knew if he let her get away, he wouldn't find her in his bed. He recognised her teasing mood, one he most definitely did not share. He caught her before she reached the outside stairs, spun her around and forced her back against the garden's tallest rock. Its peak reached her shoulders. She didn't resist. 'I'm going to fuck you,' he said, his voice slurred like he'd been drinking. 'Harder than you've ever been fucked in your life.'

She smiled with heavy-lidded eyes. 'That will take some doing.'

He growled at the implication, then gave it his best shot. His rage helped. He took all of a second to rip off her thong and jam his prick inside her. He stood to do it, putting his full weight behind the penetration, pushing her hard into the stone. God, she was wet. She laughed and wrapped her legs around his waist. Her hands fisted in his hair and they were off. Sweat flew with every thrust. Their hips slammed together. He knew they'd both be bruised tomorrow, but they held nothing back, giving the coupling all their strength, all their passion. He hoped no one would wake to hear their cries because he damn well couldn't hold them back.

'More,' she said, nails gouging his shoulders, heels digging into his butt. 'I'm almost –' Then she came, snarling with it, hair lashing from side to side. A second later, he followed. Gouts of feeling pulsed up his legs, through his cock, like honey set on fire. He could barely stand when it was over. His knees didn't want to hold him. Her calves slid down his sides. She bent to pick up her shoes. 'Thanks,' she said, while he panted and shook.

'That might not have been the hardest I've been fucked, but it was pretty damn close.'

He went to bed angry. Worst of all, he went to bed alone.

He woke angry as well, but he couldn't remain so long. A dark blue Lincoln Town Car appeared outside the gates: her father's car. The not-so Honourable Judge Cohen parked on the verge of the public road and sat there. He left at sunset, then reappeared at dawn, a vampire in reverse.

The distance to the gate was considerable, but the car could be seen from the fourth floor windows. Chloe stood behind the curtains and watched, just as she had in Gramercy Park, the only difference being this time the bogeyman was there. For the present, David did nothing. He wasn't sure what she wanted him to do. Their relationship had reached too delicate a stage to risk making the wrong move. Moreover, he wasn't sure what he could do. It was a public road, and the charges against her father had never been proved.

'He must be peeing in a cup,' Auntie said. 'None of the staff have seen him get out.'

'I don't care if he's pissing down his leg,' Sato growled. 'He doesn't belong there.'

He and Auntie had joined David, seemingly by chance, in the library. David sensed their impatience with his inaction. They didn't care as much as he did about staying within the law. They only saw how deeply the judge's presence troubled Chloe and, by association, him. David came around his desk to press Sato's shoulder. 'Don't do anything until I talk to her,' he said. 'She may have a preference as to how we handle this.'

Sato grunted and rattled the newspaper he was pretending to read. David knew this was as close to a promise as he was likely to get.

Stomach tense, he climbed the stairs to talk to his sequestered lover. He found her in the southernmost end of the front hall, the room Auntie optimistically dubbed the nursery. A rocker of unknown origin sat in the corner on a round braided rug. The windows were dormers. Chloe stood within one, its lacy ruffled curtain gathered in her hand. He came up behind her. She didn't turn. The roof of her father's car glinted in the distance.

'We can call the police,' he said. 'Try to get a restraining order.'

She shook her head. 'He can't stay there for ever. He'll have to go back to work.'

'I don't mean to be negative, but this may be his idea of a vacation.'

'Raking everything up again would only upset my family. They don't want to face what happened. I have to respect that.'

He didn't know if she believed what she was saying. She sounded calm, restless maybe, but calm. He would have preferred anger. This lack of emotion seemed a step backwards. He didn't know how to combat it. She'd left her edges too smooth.

The next day, Chloe requested the keys to his Ferrari.

'I'm not letting you leave here alone,' he said. 'Not while he's out there.'

She exhaled forcefully through her nose. 'Your car is faster than his, and I'm a better driver. I'll leave him in the dust.'

'Not on a public road, you won't. Not when one of you might hit a passing tourist.'

'Have Sato's men box him in until I'm gone.'

This was not good enough for David. The man had murdered once to save his reputation. He might not have done it since, but no one could guarantee that would remain the case. 'I want you to take Sato with you.'

She planted her hands on her hips. 'I won't be spied on.'

'I'm not trying to spy on you; I'm trying to protect you.'

Her expression remained mutinous. He sighed. 'Take Kevin, then. I'll give him strict instructions to respect your privacy unless you seem to be endangering yourself. I'll order him *not* to report back to me.'

She rolled her lower lip between her teeth. He could see she wanted to refuse even this precaution. He suspected he didn't want to know why.

'All right,' she said. 'And thank you.' She dug the toe of her sandal into the polished floor. In her flowered yellow sundress, she looked a bashful angel. 'I know you don't have to do anything for me. It's your car and your house, and my father is my problem, not yours.'

He stroked her shining hair behind her ears, then bent to gaze at her lowered face. 'I care about you, Chloe. I don't want anything to threaten what we have a chance to build together. That makes your father my problem, too.'

Her cheeks grew pink. 'We do kind of have something, don't we?'

Lord, she could be precious. He kissed her forehead. 'Yes, honey, we do.'

He made up his mind. He would protect her whether she wanted him to or not. As soon as she was safely off, he dialled Sato's cell phone. 'Talk to that bastard,' he said. 'I want him gone before Chloe returns.'

Sato was a man of principle. He believed in duty and honour, in paying his debts, and in defending women and children. He would have welcomed this assignment even if he hadn't harboured a reluctant admiration for the viper. He still wished she weren't part of David's life, but since she was, he would not allow her to be harassed.

He marched down the drive, opened the gates and rapped sharply on the Town Car's driver-side window. His favourite automatic was shoved in the back of his belt. He didn't expect violence, but he also didn't believe in giving scum like this man the benefit of the doubt.

Machinery hummed as the judge rolled the window down. He was freshly shaved, crisp. He looked like a driver who'd been pulled over by a policeman and could not imagine for what. 'Yes?' he said in a cool, condescending tone.

Sato leaned into the window, forcing the judge to lean back. 'I am the head of security,' he said. 'I am here to tell you you're not welcome in Vermont.'

The judge smiled faintly. 'I wasn't aware Vermont had a head of security.'

'It does for you.'

The judge tried another approach. 'Look,' he said, one man to another. 'I just want to make sure she's safe. My daughter is a troubled young woman.'

'Yes, and we both know how she got that way, don't we?'

Skin creased around the judge's mouth. He turned in his seat so he could face Sato, so he could deceive Sato as he had deceived the rest of the world. He was a stupid man if he thought Sato would fall for this. But maybe he was used to people trusting him.

'You may not know this,' said the judge, 'but when Samantha was a teenager, she spent time in a private mental hospital. She released herself over the objections of her doctor. No doubt we should have insisted she stay, but we didn't have the heart. She's always been delusional.'

Sato had had enough. Chloe might be a lot of things,

but delusional was not among them. He reached through the window and put his hand on the judge's shoulder, hard enough to let him feel its weight. The judge stiffened. Perhaps he disliked being touched. Too bad. Sato had no intention of letting go.

'Mr Cohen,' he said, purposefully leaving off his title. 'I don't care if Chloe thinks she's Genghis Khan. You are not welcome here. If you do not leave her alone, I will make sure the whole ugly story is splashed across the newspapers.'

The judge's eyes narrowed. 'Sammy would never do that. Her mother –'

Sato cut him off. 'I did not say she would. I said I would. So what will it be, Mr Cohen? Do you leave or do I call my contacts at the Associated Press?'

The judge began to splutter about libel and lawsuits.

Sato laughed in his face. 'Mr Cohen, you are just a little fish compared to David Imakita. Suing will cause you far more inconvenience than him. You know how public opinion works. The average American does not need proof; he merely needs suspicion. The more outlandish the suspicion, the more entertaining he finds it. I assure you, many people will be wondering what really happened to Mary Alice Ryan. As for me, if you hurt David or Chloe, I will be more than happy to tear you to little pieces and grind you under my heel. If there is enough of you left to take me to court, you will be welcome to do so.'

'That's a threat,' said the judge.

'Now you are catching on.' He gave the judge's cheek a smack and pulled back. A second car rolled up the drive, a tank-tough Mercedes with Lee Wurtzmueller behind the wheel. 'Ah, just in time. Mr Cohen, your escort has arrived. Mr Wurtzmueller here will see you safely across state lines. We would not want any harm to befall you along the way.'

Pure anger shone from the judge's eyes. He knew he was beaten, but he did not like it. He started the ignition and leaned out of the window. 'If your employer harms my daughter, he'll answer to me.'

Bile rose in Sato's throat. Even now, the man clung to his lie. 'We both know who has harmed her,' he said, 'and we both know who will not do so again.'

The judge pulled on to the road. 'Remember my warning,' he said.

Sato spat at his tail-lights, then waved Lee after him. Lee would have no trouble trailing the man, not with the tiny tracking device Sato had planted inside the door. He smiled to himself. He hoped the judge did try something. Sato would enjoy enacting a nice, clean, untraceable revenge.

He pulled out his cell phone and called David. 'It is done,' he said.

'Good,' said David. 'Have you got someone to watch his movements?'

'A hair will not fall from his head without us knowing it. If he is stupid enough to do anything to give himself away, my investigator will see the Ryan case reopened.'

'Good,' David said and broke the connection without saying goodbye.

Sato did not mind. He knew his master was pleased.

David snapped the cell phone shut and sagged back in his chair. Sato had sounded very sure of himself. He hoped the worst was over, but he suspected saving Chloe from her father would be easier than saving Chloe from herself.

8

His fears came to pass two weeks later.

'I have a surprise for you,' she said with her old coy glitter. She led him to the Ferrari. Since her father had left, she'd been taking it out every afternoon, without Kevin's protection. When she returned from wherever she went, she'd be lost in her thoughts for hours. Maybe now he'd find out where she'd been going.

She followed Route 9 into the Green Mountains, glowing now in all the shades of fall. Rather than talk, she flipped on the radio. Her flimsy sundress, white with red poppies today, was topped by a bright red cardigan. She pushed the sleeves to her elbows and tapped the wheel to the rhythm of The Doors. The lyrics made David grimace. No one had to ask Chloe to light their fire. She did that by breathing.

Left without conversation, he settled back in the bucket seat. He'd driven this way when he first moved to the area and wanted to find his way around. The woods touched him with melancholy. Gold and scarlet, lemon and rust, they seemed primeval, removed from the modern world. The forest knew only the changing breath of seasons, the rustle of squirrels, the plop of falling berries.

He hoped he meant more than that to Chloe.

He snapped from his reverie when she turned off the highway and on to a gravel road. It was the approach to the Old Mill Inn. Since the restaurant had folded the previous year, he knew they hadn't come to share a meal.

A minute's ride completed their journey. Set against a backdrop of flaming foliage, the inn gleamed with nine-teenth-century charm. The clapboard shone white, the shutters black. The porch swings spoke of lazy afternoons drinking lemonade in long, high-necked gowns. The building was a good deal sprucer than he remembered, a change accounted for by a number of board-toting, bucket-hefting workmen.

Chloe stepped on to the newly poured asphalt turna-bout. She spread her arms. 'Welcome to The Seven Veils, Vermont's newest dinner theatre.' Catching his hand, she pulled him through the front door, past a graceful entry and into the dining room. High windows lined the walls, spilling sunbeams that swirled with clouds of sawdust. A stage was taking shape at one end. It sloped gently towards an audience of sawhorses and orange electrical cords.

David's nose tightened with an urge to sneeze. 'You bought a dinner theatre?'

'I bought an *erotic* dinner theatre.' She bounced on her toes. 'Isn't it great?'

'Great' wasn't the word he would have used. He tried to imagine the locals watching Chloe strut bare-breasted across the stage. He bit the side of his thumb. 'Who are you, uh, expecting to come?'

'Whoever I ask.' She skipped blithely around a ladder and executed a light-footed twirl. Her sundress floated out from her thighs. One of the workmen grinned. 'You'd be surprised how many people I know.'

He wouldn't, but he kept that to himself.

'I'm planning two shows a month,' she bubbled on. 'Attendance by invitation only. Men and women, but strictly high rollers. I'll hire a caterer for the weekend and make everyone pay through the nose.' She chuckled at his expression. 'Don't worry. It's not going to be a strip show. No bump and grind. No grubby bills shoved down sweaty G-strings. No touching period. What I'm planning is more of an erotic shadow play.' She laughed, an exultant burst of sound. 'Or a fucking ballet.'

'Hear, hear,' said the workman who'd grinned. She punched his shoulder in a manner that suggested too much familiarity for comfort. Unfortunately, David's frown went right over her head.

'These are going to be top-drawer acts,' she said, 'acts a man can take his wife or girlfriend to and they'll both go home hot. Here –' She grabbed him by the arm and pulled him into a back hall. 'These are the dressing rooms. Nice, huh? I always hated sharing. I'm hiring a regular troupe just like a repertoire company. I've already started tryouts.'

Tryouts? Exactly how did one try out for an erotic dinner theatre? No. He didn't want to know. 'You're not going to perform yourself?'

She twinkled at him through her lashes. 'I might. If I'm in the mood.'

He felt dizzy. He pressed his fingers to his temples and squeezed.

'What?' she said. 'Aren't you happy for me?'

He sighed. He knew this would get him into trouble, but he couldn't keep his feelings to himself. 'You're a smart woman,' he said. 'You've attended Columbia. You could start any business you wanted.'

'Sure I could, but I'd be stupid to ignore my vocation.'

'Stripping is your vocation?'

She crossed her arms. She hadn't buttoned the cardigan and her breasts swelled into the neckline of her dress. Petite though she was, she still managed to look down her nose. 'Not stripping *per se*, but the mechanics of exhibitionism and voyeurism; the power that comes from tapping into someone else's fantasies. Those things I understand. Those things I know how to use, as you yourself can attest.'

'Chloe.' He coaxed one hand from her arms and pressed it over his heart. Though she didn't resist, she watched him like a cat watches a rival over the supper dish, coolly suspicious. He forced himself to go on. 'You're still not over the shock of seeing your father. Are you sure you're not retreating to an activity that made you feel safe, only this time you'll control the how and when?'

She snatched her hand away. 'You think I'm totally neurotic, don't you? You think I'm a charity case you have to take care of until I get better. Well, you know what? I don't care what you think. I'm doing this and I'm going to make a success of it, with or without your precious approval.'

She stormed through an outer door, into the woods behind the inn.

'Wait,' he said, hurrying after her. 'Damn it. That's not what I think. I just –' He tripped over a rock and fell flat on his face. 'Shit.' Feeling like an idiot but too angry to care, he smacked ground litter from the front of his pullover. Chloe was halfway down a long, wooded hill. The trunks rose like masts from a sea of crimson leaves. He touched his nose to make sure it wasn't bleeding, then picked up his pace. 'Chloe! Do you even have enough money to do this?'

'Fuck you,' she said.

'But maybe I could help.'

She spun around, red with fury. 'You are not horning in on my business.'

She couldn't have enough money. Half a million was a lot, but not enough for all this. And what bank in their right mind would give an ex-stripper a loan? He skidded to a halt in front of her. 'Better me than a loan shark.'

'I have the fucking money. And you know what?' She jabbed his chest with her finger. 'I am really proud of myself for spending it. I've been hoarding every penny for years, afraid to spend a cent for fear I'll need to run again. But I'm done with running. I know I can face my father down now. I may not have banished all my demons. Maybe I never will. But I've taken the first step. I'm sorry you can't be proud of me, but that's really too damn bad.'

Her eyes shimmered with angry tears, maybe hurt tears, too. He rubbed the spot she'd been trying to gouge out of his breastbone. 'OK, I apologise. But it's not a good idea to sink all your money into a speculative enterprise. A silent partner wouldn't hurt.'

She scuffed the toe of her shoe through the leaves. She wore heels. How had she been able to outrun him in heels? She sniffled once, loudly, as if impatient with her own vulnerability. 'How silent?'

He wanted to laugh, but he didn't. 'Virtually incapable of speech.'

Something like a smile tugged the corner of her mouth. 'You'd do that for me?'

'Yes.'

'Even though you disapprove?'

'Even though I disapprove.'

She dashed a tear off with the back of one knuckle. 'I'm such a bitch. I know I don't deserve you.'

'Maybe I don't deserve you.' He cupped the side of her face. 'Maybe you're about to make me a ton of money I haven't earned.'

He didn't believe it, but – as it happened – it was true.

Sato stuck his head around the door to David's office. Beyond the picture window, fuchsia clouds streaked the sky, setting Manhattan's stone and glass ablaze. When David looked up, his reading glasses shimmered pink. He must have had a difficult day if he had broken out his horn-rims.

'The pilot will be ready in twenty minutes,' Sato said.

David groaned and dropped his head on to a scattered pile of papers.

Sato closed the door behind him. 'Is something wrong? You know Chloe's club holds its first performance tonight.'

'I know. I know.' He lifted his head and wagged it. 'I've got an emergency meeting with the lawyers. I'm not going to make it.'

To Sato's surprise, disapproval curled through his belly. His master knew how important this was to Chloe. Even if he thought her enterprise unwise, as Sato himself did, he had said he would be there. He should keep his word no matter what. In Sato's experience, a lawyer's idea of an emergency was not worth breaking a promise over. 'I will go,' he heard himself say. David's eyes widened behind the scholarly frames. Sato tugged his jacket straighter. 'A friend should be present for the début of a new enterprise.'

A smile fought for control of his master's face. 'That would be kind of you.'

Sato understood his amusement. If Sato could be considered Chloe's friend, her life was in a sad state. Then again, maybe Sato's was, too.

Sato's progress to The Seven Veils was blocked by a line of cars, big, expensive cars in subdued metallic colours: platinum, bronze, gunmetal green – or maybe it was money green. Sato handed his keys to the valet with a feeling of unreality. He was a guest tonight, not a chauffeur, not a bodyguard.

Standing sentry at the door was a man with the build of a football player. His tuxedo did nothing to hide his blocky frame. He stopped Sato before he could follow the people ahead of him inside. 'Got a token?' he said, his hand planted firmly in the centre of Sato's chest.

With great self-control, Sato ignored the discourtesy.

He removed a gold-plated disc from his inside jacket pocket. David's name was inscribed on the back. Its face held The Seven Veils' logo, a veiled Venus on the half-shell. Everyone here had received one of these chips in return for their membership fee. As Sato understood it, after tonight, they would pay an additional sum to attend a performance. The bouncer stared at the chip, then at Sato, a slow, steely intelligence moving behind his pale blue eyes. 'You smell like cop,' he said.

Sato smiled, suddenly understanding the problem. 'I am head of security for Imakita International.'

The bouncer's face cleared. 'Forgive me, Mr Takemori. The boss told us to expect you. A table has been reserved. Please make yourself known to one of the waitresses.'

Sato was impressed. David must have called ahead, and Chloe must have briefed her people well. He stepped into the spacious entry, then turned. 'Are policemen not welcome here?'

The bouncer grinned over his shoulder. 'They are if Miss Chloe invites them.'

He said 'Miss Chloe' as if he were fond of her, and maybe familiar with her, too. Perhaps he knew her from her showgirl days? Whatever the case, Sato approved his appointment. The man was not just intimidating, but intelligent: an effective combination.

The attractive young woman who escorted him inside seemed equally competent. She did not fawn, but led him with dignity to a round, white-draped table near the stage. Purple chrysanthemums spilled from the vase in its centre, the arrangement far simpler than David's *ikebana*, but cheerful. A bottle of Tattinger's chilled in a bucket of ice. At his nod, the waitress popped the cork and poured him a glass that smoked with cold. The champagne was delicious, crisp and dry, but not bitter. Better than warm sake, truth be told. The last of Sato's trepidations burst with the tiny bubbles. Whatever else might be said of Chloe, she had not embarrassed herself here – or David.

He discovered he was looking forward to the show.

Curious, he gazed around the room. He had already marked the points of entry, of course, but now he took in the decor. The walls were a soft, dark gold, broken by white pilasters and balconies. A chandelier hung from a copper medallion in the ceiling. He was searching for lighting booths when he spotted Chloe moving among the tables.

Her hair was twisted off her neck and a 1920s flapper dress draped her body. The thin black silk was weighted by jet embroidery and fluttered with beaded fringe. She did not wear a stitch beneath it. Her breasts swayed as she moved. Her mound moulded the cloth. The dress was not lined. Only the beading saved it from indecency. No doubt, his master could have named the designer, but Sato did not need to. The surge of interest in his groin told him more than he wanted to know.

He watched her as she squeezed a hand here, kissed a cheek there. Out of reflex, his gaze surveyed the crowd. They were an interesting mix, a little rough, but well heeled, and well mannered enough. He spotted two pro wrestlers, a junior congressman, and a young rap artist whose Eurasian companion was so stunning she put even Chloe in the shade.

Evidently, Chloe knew her. The woman rose and hugged her, pressing the lines of their bodies together. Sato could not suppress a shiver of speculation. Had they been strippers together? Friends? Close friends?

His fancies kept him company as he enjoyed the meal. Chloe's caterer served roast squab with baby vegetables. The skin was crispy, the meat fell from the bone, and the vegetables were steamed to perfection. More wine oiled the progress of the food. Laughter bubbled through the crowd, but the tone was hushed, as if everyone was anticipating the show. Dessert was a rich chocolate mousse Sato did not even try to resist, though these days he had no need to put on weight. It did not matter. Tonight was his to enjoy. By the time the lights dimmed, his mood was very mellow.

Full dark had fallen outside, a deep woods blackness. As it filled the room, murmurs swept the audience, a sound that soon diminished to the rustle of expensive clothes. For the first time, Sato heard music, soft and sleepy and haunting, the accompaniment to whatever lay ahead. His body tightened. The footlights came up, glowing against the creamy, swagged hem of the stage curtain. The cloth rose.

A second veil remained behind the curtain, this one black. Sheer enough to see through, it lent the scene behind it the air of a dream. A man and woman were playing pool in a smoky bar, or miming playing pool. There were no balls on the green felt, nothing to make a sound except the rising swell of the music. The woman was very pretty, small and blonde, with barely any breasts. Her tight gold dress left little to the imagination. It was cut low both front and back, and clung to her succulent bottom. Her partner was older, edgier, lean and tall with a slashing black moustache above a thin sardonic mouth. He wore a fitted leather jacket and a black fedora. Completing his outfit were black jeans, black boots, and a black silk shirt with a silver clasp at the collar. His long dark hair was tied behind his neck.

The woman was flirting, teasing the tiger. She pretended to need his help with a shot. He smiled and strolled to her, all lazy masculine confidence. He cupped his body over hers, his intent so blatant a flush crept over her cheek. He stroked her hips where they bent forwards, then her hand where it had forgotten to aim the cue. She squirmed away, half-coy, half-frightened. The man stepped back and grinned at her, the hands he'd propped on his hips pushing his jacket back. He was hard and well hung and proud of it. The arch of his organ was apparent from the audience. The woman shook a scolding finger, but seemed pleased with this evidence of her power. Her cheeks were pink with it. Her little bosom rose and fell.

The dance that was not a dance continued, following the music but not precisely. The man sank his last ball, then pulled the woman into his arms for a teasing rumba. He was as smooth on his feet as a professional. The woman twined her hands behind his neck, thumbs stroking his angular jaw. Their eyes shot slow fire at each other. The man's hands drifted over her rounded buttocks. With a bottom like that, the caress could only stir envy. Sato shifted in his chair, grateful for the darkness that hid his reaction. Lust throbbed between his legs. He longed to touch himself, but the restraint imposed by being in public had its own excitement. He wondered if everyone were controlling themselves, or if some of the heavy breathing he heard came from watchers more indulgent than he.

The actors on the stage were breathing heavily, too. Their chemistry seemed genuine. The woman's flush crept all the way down her shallow cleavage. The man's expression was fierce. Sato didn't think he was angry, simply caught in the grip of a strong desire. Still dancing, he curled his fingers under the hem of her tight gold dress. The woman stiffened. The man was touching her, stroking her sex with long brown fingers.

The moment her neck sagged in reaction, he scooped her up and laid her across the billiard table. He kissed her deeply, until her struggles melted away. She lay limp with surrender, seemingly ready for whatever he might propose. He broke the kiss and looked down at her. His dark brows arched in question. She nodded, shakily, but without hesitation. The man grinned and kissed her again, softly this time. He reached into his jacket and drew out a condom.

A concerted gasp rippled through the audience, astonishment colliding with titillation. Apparently, this was not going to be a simulated sex show; it was going to be the real thing. That was the question the man had asked his partner. And she had given permission. Sweat broke out on Sato's face. Like everyone else, he was afraid to make a sound. He sensed the performers needed to pretend they were alone, even if knowing they weren't heightened their arousal. No wolf whistles broke the breathy silence, no crude instructions. A single voice whimpered in the darkness. The sound was immediately cut off.

The man removed the woman's shoes, then pulled her stockings down pale, shapely legs. From the angle at which she lay, the folds of her sex could not be seen. The man required no such concessions to modesty. Eyes locked on the woman's face, he opened his jeans and spread the flaps. The pressure of his erection limned it against his briefs. The woman licked her lips. The man shivered and speared both hands into the stark white cotton. For a moment, he massaged himself, his expression glazing with pleasure. Then, in one determined motion, he lifted out his weighty package, phallus and scrotum both. Sato swallowed. The woman was lovely, but this man's organ deserved to be carved in stone. He was big, uncut, so hard and thick the shining eye of his cock glared at the ceiling. A net of veins wound up the darkened skin. Slowly, as if he enjoyed his own touch, he rolled the condom down his shaft.

His erection remained on display while he shrugged out of his leather jacket and unbuttoned his flowing black shirt. He tossed his fedora and it lit neatly on a coat rack. The audience chuckled, but not for long. There was too much else to admire. The man's body was wiry, his nipples small and erect. A thin cloud of hair swirled over his chest, binding point to point. Muscle ridged his belly.

The woman reached out, touching his stomach but not the towering shaft that shadowed it. The man smiled, closed his eyes and covered her hand. Gently, he coaxed her caresses over the planes of his torso: his pectorals, his shoulders, the long, strong cords of his neck. Touch me, said the gesture. Touch me all over. When her hands began to move on their own, he leaned over her, his thighs spreading hers. He ran his fingers over her hem, again asking a silent question: would she let him raise her dress?

She shook her head, too shy for this. He kissed her, the gesture saying it was all right; he understood. His mouth drifted down her throat, over her breasts and on to their small, beaded peaks. He sucked them through the tight gold cloth, then tugged them with his teeth. Her back lifted like a wave billowing at sea. His face twisted. Then, in a move too swift to follow, he entered her. Her body jerked with the force of his penetration, but clearly she was not hurt. At once, they began to rock together, strenuously, hands roving, heads tossing. Their silence amazed Sato. He doubted he could have matched it. He could see the reason for it, though. Their expressions were all the more intense for having no verbal outlet.

The man in particular looked as if every thrust were a turn on the rack. His torso was sheened with sweat. His mouth gaped for air. If he came too soon, not only would the show end prematurely, but his lover would not be satisfied. The woman had no such discipline, nor pity for his dilemma. Her motions grew faster, more erratic. She must have been killing him, but he merely cupped her thrashing head and stilled her with his hands. He stared into her eyes, watching, willing her to come. Sato's nails scored his palms. The woman bit her lip, arched, and then her hips danced against the man's. Spellbound, the room watched her spasm with pleasure. It was too much for the man. He shuddered and came hard, his face stony with it. Sato was so close to the stage he heard the man's climactic expulsion of breath, like a cough that cannot be suppressed.

The sound echoed in his ear as their motions slowed, as the theatre plunged into darkness, as the audience audibly caught its breath. The darkness lasted at least a minute and when it ended, the chandelier was turned up very dimly, to perhaps a quarter of its previous illumination. The golden glow washed flushed faces and starry eyes. Hands reached for champagne glasses. Throats tightened on cooling swallows.

The curtain had fallen around the stage. Chloe appeared from behind it and spoke quietly, soothingly. She said she hoped everyone had enjoyed the maiden voyage of The Seven Veils and that they would return many times. For anyone who wished to stay, she was pleased to offer champagne and dancing in the ballroom next door. For anyone who wished to leave, she sincerely hoped the rest of their night would be made more pleasurable by what they had experienced here.

She earned a laugh for that, then a swell of applause that ended in a standing ovation. She laughed herself as she bowed, but tears stood in her eyes. Sato was happy for her, happier than he expected to be. She was making a success of this. She was finding a path of her own.

Despite his upbringing, he was not such a chauvinist that he believed a woman did not need her own place in the world. Also, it would be better all around if Chloe grew less reliant on his master. Pleased with the fruits of the evening, he watched the dancing, then went in search of his hostess.

Sato strode down a hall of dressing rooms. Muffled thumps and moans issued from behind one door. Either some of the guests couldn't wait to get home, or tonight's performers were continuing where they'd left off. His cock thickened at the possibility. The freedom to make noise must be welcome after such restraint.

Chloe's office took up the end of the hall. The door was open. Windows lined two of its walls, tall windows, filled with neat, square panes like a French country home. Uncurtained, they looked out on the woods. The light from the club caught the edge of the trees, their thinning leaves like flames floating on a pool of darkness. A fitful wind whispered through the unseen branches: the ghosts of foreign ancestors. What Sato's ancestors would make of this night he could not say.

Chloe stood behind a polished wooden desk, flipping through a pile of papers. A huge bouquet of roses brushed her shoulder. Despite her sexy black dress, she looked surprisingly businesslike. She smiled when Sato knocked on the open door. 'Well, hello. I'm glad you made it. I hope you enjoyed the show.'

'Very much. It was quite a production.' He tried to keep his voice bland, but his reaction must have seeped through. Her eyes crinkled with amusement. She came around to the front of the desk and propped her bottom on its edge. Sato tried not to stare at her legs, but there was quite a length of them to avoid.

The beads of her dress rustled as she crossed her ankles. 'You had a good view, I trust?'

'Fine,' he said, his throat a little thick. He hoped she wasn't going to try to seduce him. He wasn't sure he could resist her tonight.

She crossed her arms beneath her unfettered breasts. 'Bonnie is very pretty, isn't she?'

'Bonnie?'

'Tonight's female performer.'

'Ah, yes. Very pretty.' A vision of the man's abdomen swam before his eyes: the thin arrow of black hair, the rippling muscle, the huge, wavering shadow of his organ. He could not meet Chloe's eyes.

'I forbade them to sleep together before the performance,' she said, as if abstinence had been a uniform she'd asked them to wear. 'I knew they wanted to screw each other silly as soon as they met, but I made them promise to hold off. I think it added to the intensity, don't you?'

He gave in to the urge to clear his throat. 'Very much so.'

'It's not surprising, really.' She crossed her ankles the other way. 'The things we can't have are usually what we want most.'

He looked up then. Was she alluding to his feelings for David? Was she aware of them? Her sleepy, smiling eyes told him nothing. 'I do not imagine there are many men you could not have.'

She gazed at her nails, her lashes dipping in a slow, lazy glide. 'There are different kinds of having, though, aren't there? There's the kind that lasts a night, and the kind that lasts a lifetime; the kind that offers everything, and the kind that's no better than a single sip of water to a man dying of thirst.' She folded her hands at the crux of her thighs. 'You know I'm not a woman who believes in taking a single sip.'

'If you have something to say, say it,' he warned. 'Do not play with me.'

Her lips drew back from straight white teeth. 'I'm not playing with you, Sato. But perhaps you wish I was?'

'No,' he said gruffly, quickly. It was not entirely true.

Chloe knew this, of course. She came to her feet and smoothed his lapels around his neck. As always, she smelled wonderful, spring flowers and a dash of spice, a hint of feminine essence. He began to harden under her touch, helplessly, primed by all that had gone before.

'I'm turning over a new leaf,' she said in a voice as seductive as any he'd heard her use. 'Dedicating myself to your lord and master. From now on I'm a one-woman man.'

'I will believe that when I see it.'

She chuckled, low in her throat, and he could not help smiling. She was so bad, so unredeemably bad he almost had to admire her for it. 'David wanted to come,' he said. 'He was very disappointed when the meeting came up.'

'Of course, he was.' Irony dripped from the words. She swept her arm towards the bouquet. 'And, look, he sent roses to apologise.'

Sato did not respond. He could not take her side against David, even if he thought she might be right. 'May I drive you home?' he said instead.

She shook her head, throwing off her annoyance with a sigh. 'No, thank you. I have the Ferrari, and a few cheques to write before I go home.'

'It is late. One of your male employees should lock up.'

She patted his shoulder. 'I'll let them, Sato. But I'd like a little time alone to savour my success.'

'I would be happier if you would do your savouring in the daylight.'

'Don't worry. I'll be careful. I have the cell phone. I'll call you if I need you.'

'Call me when you leave,' he said. 'Then I will know when to expect you.'

She nodded, her eyes sparkling with laughter. Then, unexpectedly, she pulled him into a hug. 'Thank you for coming,' she said, the words warm against his neck. 'Thank you for being so good to me.'

Flustered, he pulled back as soon as she would let him. He bowed before he could stop himself. It was a low bow, a bow one gave a teacher. He straightened and tugged the hem of his jacket. 'Call,' he said, almost barking it out.

She promised she would.

9

To Sato's surprise, when he returned from the club he found David in the library. A stack of CDs sat by his computer on the curving glass desk. As he manipulated the joystick, the noise of simulated explosions came and went. Bursts of reflected yellow washed his handsome face. His sleeves were rolled up, his tie yanked past the third button of his shirt. Usually, he played with boyish abandon, but tonight his expression was grim. Sato did not know what to make of this mood, but he suspected it had nothing to do with lawyers. He tossed his jacket on to the back of a sleekly modern leather chair.

'Your meeting ended early,' he said, carefully neutral.

David glanced at him. 'Unfortunately, not early enough to make the show. I brought some demos home to test drive. This one looks promising. We may buy it.'

Sato said nothing. David paused the game and shoved the joystick aside. 'How was it? Not too painful, I hope.'

'It was good. Impressive.'

'I'm sure it was very professional.'

Sato's spine stiffened at the scorn in his voice. David said 'professional' as if Chloe had been whoring for the audience. 'It was impressive,' he repeated. 'I am sure you will get a good return on your investment.'

David waved his words away and rose; he paced across the room until his way was blocked by a globe the size of a beach ball. He spun the sedately coloured sphere, then stopped it by clapping both hands on the sides. 'This won't last. The club is just a toy for her. She'll tire of it soon enough.'

'I do not think so, master. She seemed very –'

'She's never stuck with anything else, has she?'

She had stuck with stripping, but it did not seem wise to say so. In any case, David was probably referring to her sexual history, not her career.

His master rolled down one sleeve and buttoned it. 'It's just a phase. Her father's appearance threw her off balance. She feels more comfortable following an old pattern. Ever since she saw her father try to rape that babysitter, then kill her, she's been screwed up about sex.'

Was that all her business was: a symptom of an old trauma? Sato stroked his jacket over the back of the chair. He remembered how she'd called her desire a triumph over coldness. To a certain extent he believed her, though such promiscuity could not be healthy. Or could it? He scratched his chin. Back in his wrestling days, Sato had as many partners as Chloe, perhaps more. He was a man, of course, but –

He shook his head, unable to see the right of it. He was sure, however, that The Seven Veils was not a phase. Chloe had put too much of her heart into it, and had done too good a job. But there seemed little point in telling David so. He would have to see her dedication for himself. 'She missed you,' he said instead, which was probably the most important information he had to convey.

David looked at him, then away. The young-boy hope in his eyes made Sato's chest ache. His master spun the globe again. 'Did she say that?'

'She did not have to say it. She missed you. She cares for you. I am sure she would be very pleased to see you at the next performance.'

David grimaced. 'I'll go. Next month.'

But when next month came, David had a conference in LA. He broke the news at the dinner table. Chloe did not seem surprised, or even angry; at least, not on the surface.

She sipped her steaming cup of sake. 'A man's gotta do what a man's gotta do.'

'If I could get out of it, I would,' he said, chopsticks poised over a morsel of gingered fish.

'I know you would,' she said.

If Sato had not grown familiar with her expressions, he would have believed her. He opened his mouth to say he would attend, then shut it. Chloe was pretending David's absence did not matter to her. If Sato volunteered, it would suggest that she needed support, that she deserved pity. He would not undermine her pride that way. Instead, he topped up her sake cup, bowed, and excused himself from the table.

David loved to lie on his bed and watch her after a shower. She would emerge, rosy, glowing, her hair clipped atop her head, her body wrapped in one of the dark blue *yukatas* that, in a way, marked all in the house as his. Her moisturising ritual began with the robe still on. She liked to sit in his leather director's chair, the one fronting the secretaire that held his phone. She'd treat him to flashes of thigh as she smoothed in the cream. Then she'd undo the belt and massage her belly and breasts. Her nipples always tightened beneath her hands. Her eyes always closed. He didn't think this was a put on. She enjoyed her own caresses. They took her far away.

Tonight they took her farther than he liked. Tonight she looked untouchable. He'd broken the news before her shower: business obliged him to leave town. Once again he would miss her monthly show. That made three in a row. She hadn't complained, but she couldn't be happy. He rolled on to his belly, his cock a thick warmth beneath him, not yet stiff, but getting there. At the moment, he doubted she was interested in its condition. 'Are you angry?' he asked.

She rubbed a dollop of cream into her neck. 'Of course not. Your deal with the Koreans made your Japanese partners nervous. You have to reassure them that you still value the association.'

'I could postpone this trip.'

She shrugged the cotton robe off her shoulders, baring the clean, satiny lines of her back. Her body hovered on the edge of thinness, seeming more vulnerable from this perspective than it did from the front, where the fullness of her breasts hid her ribs. 'It doesn't matter to me when you go, but I'm sure it matters to them. They've made plans for your visit. If you put them off, they'll be insulted and inconvenienced.'

She was right and she was being reasonable. Why this stirred such guilt he couldn't say. He only knew he had to touch her; had to smooth his hands up that fragile queue of vertebrae. He rose and took the moisturiser from her hands.

'Ow,' she said when he kneaded her shoulders too firmly.

He gentled his touch, sliding his fingers to the curve of her buttocks, then up, then down her arms and around her waist. She was still beneath his caresses, accepting, but not reacting. This had been happening more often, ever since she'd started working at the club. She did not fight for her orgasm the way she had before. He fought for it, and sometimes he didn't win. It was hard for him to hold back. His body responded to hers, no matter what she did. Sometimes her mildest sigh of pleasure could push him over the edge. Even her withholding had the power to arouse him. But that did not mean he liked it. That did not mean he wanted it to continue.

An increasingly familiar panic squeezed his chest. She was slipping through his fingers and he didn't know how to stop it. She was embracing her past; rejecting her future. He pictured her as she'd been that night in his practice room: stripping, strutting, flaunting her beautiful body for a few soiled bills. He couldn't let her return to that life. Somehow, he had to draw her back.

He crossed his arms around her chest and kissed her hair. A mirror hung above the secretaire, its edges bevelled, its frame a plain dark square of wood. He aligned their faces in the glass. How alien he seemed next to her. Everything about him was different: the planes in which his features sat, the tint of his skin, the texture of his hair. The basic structure of his body was not that of an American. When she looked at him, did she see a foreigner? He wondered why she wanted him at all. Had it all been a lie? Was she growing tired of the pretence? The reflection of their eyes met and held. Hers were so sad it shocked him.

'Come with me,' he said, tightening his hold until her breasts swelled cool and soft over his forearms. 'We'll visit Japan together.'

'The club isn't going away,' she said softly, almost pityingly.

'I never said I wanted it to.'

She patted his cheek as if she knew better.

The gesture frightened him. He knelt before her and clasped the wooden arms of the chair. 'Surely you can put someone else in charge for one performance. Come on, Chloe. We need some time away. Just the two of us.'

She sighed. Her finger traced the curve of his scar. He kissed her palm and willed his feelings to reach her heart. 'All right,' she said. 'I'll go to Japan with you.'

He hugged her. 'You won't be sorry.'

In answer, she only stroked his hair.

They took a commercial flight, first class, of course. Chloe sat in the aisle seat, thumbing through her guidebook while the business passengers shuffled by. Most turned their heads for a closer look. Chloe certainly deserved it. She wore a suit of rich indigo wool, a fifties-style Dior. Beside the vibrant blue, her skin glowed like a peach. A thick gold slave chain circled her neck, its gleam no brighter than her straight, dark hair. She looked a prosperous woman of business, self-contained and elegantly fuckable. The women blushed when David caught them staring. He and Chloe had been in Strathmore so long he'd forgotten the effect she had on strangers.

For once, she honestly seemed oblivious to the attention. She pointed to one of the traveller's phrases in the back of the guidebook. 'How do you pronounce this?'

He told her and she repeated it precisely, down to the intonation.

'You have a good ear,' he said.

She grinned at him, pleased with the compliment, pleased with herself. He cupped his hand around her smile, stroking her cheek with his thumb, finally certain he was in love because the warmth in her eyes brought a sting to his own. God help him, he didn't want to lose her, not to The Seven Veils, not to anything. 'I'm glad you're here,' he said. 'We really do need this.'

Her eyes sparkled. 'Teach me another phrase.'

He whispered something dirty in her ear, then had to clap his hand over her mouth before she parroted it back. Chloe giggled into his palm. A mother with two children in tow smiled at them the way women have been smiling at lovers since the beginning of time. David released Chloe's mouth. She wagged her brows at him. 'Later you'll have to tell me what you said.'

'Later I'll demonstrate.'

She stroked his hand where it lay on the armrest between them. Her nails, frosty bronze today, slipped between his knuckles and fingers. The motion was blatantly coital: four slender cocks sliding into four waiting channels. The hair on his nape lifted and the beginning of an erection uncoiled between his legs. She continued to caress him, up and down, down and up. His cock stiffened until it hurt. Her gaze slipped sideways beneath her lashes, towards his crotch. A tiny smile curved her cheek. She knew what she was doing to him. She always knew.

'Will I be able to sightsee while you're having meetings?' she asked, her expression a teasing imitation of innocence. Her hand slipped over the armrest to touch his outer thigh. At the contact, his cock jumped with embarrassing force. He moved her hand back to his arm and patted it. His throat felt thick.

'Mr Narita's wife will take you around.'

'She doesn't have to work?'

'Most Japanese wives stay at home.'

Her eyes went round. 'Most? Even today?'

'Even today. They only work until they marry.'

She appeared to think this over. Some indefinable emotion flickered across her features. He knew better than to ignore it. 'It's their culture,' he said. 'It's accepted.'

She withdrew her hand and smoothed her narrow skirt over her knees.

'I didn't say I approved,' he said.

She shook her head. He didn't know what she was denying: that she'd never imagined he approved, or that she didn't believe him. And if that was the case, was she right? Could he honestly say he didn't wish she were more demure? Or that she spent her days more respectably? His lips twisted. He couldn't deny it unless he lied.

She flipped a sheaf of hair behind her shoulder, her expression misleadingly serene. 'I suppose I shouldn't mention The Seven Veils.'

He wanted to say she could mention anything she liked, but the thought of Mr Narita's shock stopped the words in his mouth. Ironically, if he'd had an American face, his hosts would have accepted Chloe's background, and David's relationship with her, much more readily. Americans were supposed to be outrageous. Fairly or not, his associates expected David's genes to make him wiser. He looked out the window, away from Chloe's knowing eyes. Doing business in Japan was a matter of respect, showing it and earning it. A man might have a mistress who owned an erotic club, but he would not treat her with the care David intended to show Chloe. A mistress was not an equal. No female was an equal. Half the time, foreign businesswomen were treated as if they'd sleep with anyone who asked. A woman who stripped for a living might as well be a whore. He watched the tyre-streaked runway as the plane taxied towards it, searching for the right words to explain. Unfortunately, he wasn't sure they existed.

'The Japanese are more reserved than you're used to,' he said. 'They won't expect you to share your life story. If they knew what you did for a living, they might not treat you with the respect you deserve.'

'The respect I deserve.' Her tone was bitter, but she didn't accuse of him of trying to protect his own reputation. That, more than anything, heightened his shame.

He gathered her hand and pressed it to his shirtfront. 'It would be easier if you said nothing, but I want you to do what you think is right.'

'You'd prefer I said nothing, though, wouldn't you?'

She was forcing him to admit it. He kissed the back of her hand. 'I would prefer you said nothing.'

She nodded as if she'd been expecting this. Her eyes closed. When they opened, her face gave nothing away. Her stillest mask was in place.

'There's one more thing I should warn you about,' he said.

Her mask broke long enough for her to roll her eyes. 'Yes?'

He squirmed in the contoured seat. He'd have given a great deal not to explain this right now, but it would be far more awkward if he waited. He drew a fortifying breath. 'They think you're my fiancée.'

'What?'

His face grew hot at the volume of her amazement. 'I had to call Mr Narita's secretary to explain I was bringing a guest. She doesn't speak much English and I'm afraid my Japanese isn't subtle enough to explain what sort of female companion I meant. The best I could come up with was "special girlfriend". She started congratulating me on my engagement and, well, it just seemed easier to let her believe it was true.'

Chloe was laughing, little snorts of air escaping through her nose. It was not, however, happy laughter. 'I'm sorry,' he said, squeezing her fingers. 'I can explain when we get there. It simply isn't customary for a man to bring a woman on a business trip.'

That threw a bucket of ice on her amusement. 'Well, of course not. We little ladies might get in the way.'

Fuck, he thought. He wasn't even Japanese and he was getting blamed for their chauvinism. Yes, he wanted to avoid making waves, but this was business. That didn't make him a monster. He turned back to the window. He still held her hand but it didn't matter. Her shoulder was rigid, the moment of amity gone. What a way to start the journey that was supposed to heal their wounds!

As far as Sato was concerned, the trip went downhill fast. First, they were given adjoining suites at the hotel, a gleaming, futuristic tower in downtown Tokyo. Sato would have preferred Eastern-style rooms, but the real problem was that the two bedrooms shared a wall. Sato could hear his companions squabbling as he unpacked. Chloe had wanted to complain to the airline about a dent in her suitcase. David insisted she not make a fuss. Neither of them could let the matter drop.

Sato was sure he would hear anything else they did in that bedroom as well.

His master's meetings proceeded as all Japanese business did: slowly, with everything discussed in detail and nothing decided until consensus was reached. Then and only then would new projects move forwards. David knew this. David accepted this. But, for some reason, he could not contain his impatience today. He paced; he jiggled; he snapped a pencil in the middle of one manager's presentation. Finally, their host, Mr Narita, asked David if there was somewhere else he needed to be. More time was wasted smoothing the waters with excruciatingly polite apologies. By the time the meeting broke for the night, a tiny muscle fluttered beside David's scar.

They rode back to the hotel in silence, except for David grumbling under his breath at the typical bumper-to-bumper traffic. The cabbie offered to drive them to a bar. He winked at Sato. 'Your boss need plenty sake. Maybe pretty lady, too?'

Sato declined. Any more pretty ladies and David might implode.

Chloe met them in the lobby. A famous Japanese sculptor had erected a stainless steel bamboo grove in the centre of the atrium. The light beneath the arching stalks was eerily alive. Like disembodied spirits, silver flashes danced along faces and clothes. Chloe's hair was disarrayed from her shopping tour with Mrs Narita, and the brisk November air had put roses in her cheeks. She looked good enough to toss into bed, but her appearance did not cheer David, especially when she confessed she'd made the mistake of going into ecstasies over a kimono at the Ginza's fanciest *depato* store. Naturally, Mrs Narita had felt obliged to make her a gift of it.

'I tried to refuse,' she said. 'Honestly, I did. But she

kept pressing me to take it until it just got ridiculous. She made it sound as if I'd be, I don't know, spitting on her ancestors if I refused.'

David pressed his fingers to his temples. 'Tell me it wasn't a brand new kimono.'

Chloe cocked her head. Apparently, she had no idea antique kimonos could be obtained for a fraction of the cost of new. 'I don't know. It looked new. She certainly pulled out a big stack of yen to pay for it. It had to have been a thousand dollars. For me. A perfect stranger. I felt so bad.'

'Well, it can't be the first time it's happened,' David muttered.

Sato's stomach dropped. Chloe blinked. 'I'm going to pretend I didn't hear that.'

David rubbed his face and sighed. 'I'm sorry. I shouldn't have said it.'

'No, you shouldn't.' She folded her arms, pressing her smart navy coat beneath her breasts. Sato imagined this was to restrain herself from hitting David in public. Embarrassed for both of them, he stared off through the silvery fronds and pretended to be deaf and blind.

'Damn you,' she said after a moment of silent fuming. 'I wasn't trying to get her to give me a present.'

David shuffled his feet. 'I know you weren't.'

'Do you? Do you really? I've never asked you for anything, you know. You always volunteered. I can pay back every penny you put into the club, any time you say.'

'I'm not asking you to do that.' David's vocal cords were so tight Sato could barely hear him. He surrendered to temptation and looked at the angry pair. Both their eyes shimmered in the dancing light; both their faces were taut.

Do not do this to each other, he thought, helpless not to. For the first time since Chloe and David met, he did not look forward to their parting. They loved each other. Any fool could see it, just as any fool could see they would not last much longer.

'We should dress for dinner,' Sato said. 'Our hosts will send the limo in an hour.'

Chloe was the first to shake free of the eye-lock. She brushed a nonexistent speck of lint from the arm of her velvet coat. 'I'll be up in a bit. There's a nice store in the lobby. I want to see if I can find a gift for Mrs Narita.'

David reached into the inside pocket of his coat, where he kept his wallet.

Chloe stopped him with one trembling finger. 'Don't you dare,' she said. 'Don't you fucking dare.'

Dressed for dinner, Sato reached the pavement outside the hotel before either of his friends. The awning, two gull-wing arcs of concrete, overlooked a busy intersection. Thick streams of Tokyoites spilled over the crosswalks: housewives with shopping bags, salarymen with briefcases and cell phones, office ladies in the latest designer clothes who still managed to look more conservative than half the businesswomen in New York. Sato knew many were hurrying to dinners they hadn't the space to cook in their closet-sized flats.

The sea of Asian faces eased his tension, a tension that crept over him whenever he left Japan. Though he had not been happy here, here he was home. Here he did not stand out. Here the rules of behaviour came as easily as breathing.

He did not think David experienced this phenomenon in quite the same way. David's face might belong, but his heart beat to different rhythms. He knew the rules, but he had not been steeped in them as Sato had. Despite having Japanese parents, David's nature had been brewed in an American pot.

Chloe, at least, was spared that confusion. When she

pushed through the revolving door, she simply looked lost, one bright violet in an ocean of daisies. He sensed that her ignorance of how to charm anyone here frightened her. She knew a few things about the Japanese, but not enough to shine as she had at home.

He noticed she carried a little white bag with a Gucci logo. With a hesitance he had never seen in her before, she showed him the beautiful silk scarf it contained. He assured her it was not too small a gift and that Mrs Narita would appreciate the famous international brand. 'But you must not be insulted if she does not open the gift in front of you. To us, the proper behaviour is to wait until one is alone. Also –' He touched the sleeve of her coat and searched for the right words. 'You must make clear that the gift is a thank you for acting as your guide today, not a payback for the kimono.'

Chloe looked like a schoolgirl with her first apple for teacher. 'When do I give it to her?'

'When you meet. Thank her for showing you around, but do not fuss. Speak of your gift as a very small thing.'

Chloe nodded as if everything he said were vitally important. He wondered at that. In fact, he wondered at her reaction to the whole incident. He knew from his investigation into her past that she had accepted many gifts from men. She may not have been a 'kept' woman, but she had come close. Was this show of independence part of her plan to catch his master? He knew her affection for David might not exclude an interest in his money. She had behaved without honour before.

From the corner of his eye, he studied her earnest face. Had David changed her? Or had she, perhaps, been trying to change even before they met? Though she'd been dating the musician from Boston, her residence had been modest. If she'd truly wanted to live off other men's money, she could have done it then as well.

No wiser than before, he returned his attention to the

passersby. A young office lady smiled shyly at him as she waited for the light. Perhaps her boss had encouraged her to husband-hunt. Perhaps she was tired of living with her parents and was testing her powers among the wider world of men. Sato was well dressed, solid, dignified in demeanour: a good catch. If she could attract his attention, she would feel better about her prospects. He smiled back for the pleasure of watching her giggle behind her hand. How easy his countrywomen were to read, and how impossible was Chloe! More than her foreignness accounted for the trouble. He suspected she did not understand herself.

David couldn't seem to shake his anger. It bubbled inside him, dark and bitter, feeding on itself.

Chloe had dressed while he showered, choosing a snug Dolce and Gabbana sheath with a scoop neck that bared half her cleavage. Naturally, the dress was red. If he'd seen it before she'd removed her coat at the restaurant, he would have sent her back to change. None of Mr Narita's men could look away from her breasts. Every inhalation fascinated them to the point where all three were tugging at their ties, so overstimulated they were choking. Contrary to custom, two wives had been invited to make Chloe feel more comfortable. They couldn't look at her at all.

She might as well have worn her G-string.

At the end of the strained meal, Mr Narita announced that he had arranged for them to visit a private geisha bar. As expected, the wives excused themselves, pleading responsibilities at home. 'But, of course, your delightful lady must come,' Mr Narita said when Chloe failed to follow their example. 'She has no important household matters to oversee.'

Chloe was oblivious to the implied rebuke, or the fact that Mr Narita was only being polite. She tucked her arm through David's with an intimacy that made everyone stare, then said: 'I'd be thrilled. I've always wanted to meet a real live geisha.'

Once she'd said 'yes' so enthusiastically, David could only grind his teeth.

'What is your problem?' she hissed as they slid into the hired limousine. 'You've been a mute all evening. I thought these after-work get-togethers were supposed to loosen everyone up.'

'They are,' he said. 'But as you may have noticed, you're the only woman left.'

She pressed her lips together until the skin around them whitened. 'I see,' she said.

But she didn't see, or she would have begged off with a headache as soon as Mr Narita and the others piled into the two facing seats. Instead, she turned on the charm, flirting with their hosts and exclaiming at the neon blaze of nighttime Tokyo. Colourful glowing signs climbed the narrow shopfronts, stacks of them sometimes, shouting for attention in both *kanji* and English.

Chloe leaned towards the window. She'd unbuttoned her coat in the heated car and her breasts spilled against her neckline, creamy mounds of smooth pale flesh. Mr Narita's VP, who sat between her and the window, practically drooled down her dress.

'Why do all those signs say "soapland"?' she asked.

'Soapland is for sex,' said the VP, his eyes glued to her tits, his cheeks pink from the beer he'd consumed at dinner. He was more than a little drunk.

'Why?' Chloe asked, wide-eyed and innocent. 'Do prostitutes make their customers wash before they visit?'

All the men except Sato and David giggled like eight-year-olds. Recovering first, Mr Narita explained that for a basic fee, the masseurs who worked in these districts soaped their clients down. For an extra payment, they used their bare hands and body. 'Any part of their body,' added the VP, the direction of his leer making clear which part he meant.

'Hm,' said Chloe. She laid her hand across the curves of her bosom. The motion seemed casual, but it forced the VP's eyes back to her face. When she smiled, there was neither fear nor flirtation in it. She was, with a small sardonic curl of her lips, putting the VP in his place. David had a feeling he was witnessing the man-handling skills she'd perfected as a stripper.

The VP blushed and squirmed under her gaze, but he also looked delighted. No doubt her clients had been delighted, too.

'I assume,' she said coolly, 'that some masseurs would not condescend to use their bare hands, no matter what the price.'

'Ah, er, perhaps,' said the blushing VP.

Mr Narita peered at Chloe with greater interest. She had not shown her claws before this. Many Japanese liked the idea of a kitten with a whip, possibly because they didn't meet very many. Obviously, the senior businessman was one of them.

Perfect, David thought. Just perfect. Chloe might not be embarrassed, but he foresaw having to sidestep more than one proposition before the last cup of sake was drunk.

To David's relief, the geisha bar was elegant, despite the raucous *pachinko* parlours on either side. A sumptuously dressed *maiko*, or geisha in training, ushered them down a mulberry-coloured hall. The silk of her pink and white kimono swished with each swaying step. Ornate hairpins, cherry blossoms and willow fronds trembled in her lacquered hair. The men hushed as if they'd walked into a museum, though their grins were broad.

They entered a large room with pale gold tatami mats and erotic *shunga* unscrolled across the walls. The softly lit space was empty except for a low table in its centre. Unlike the restaurant, the geisha bar did not offer Western-style seating. Childishly, David hoped Chloe's calves would fall asleep. Of course, his probably would, too, even if he did have the option of crossing his legs.

Once they were settled on the flat floor cushions, three more geisha entered, all in full regalia. The first wore bronze with a yellow sash around her waist. The second wore purple and green, and the third wore cream silk with a beautiful bamboo pattern embroidered in gold and silver thread. Here was a thousand-dollar kimono, maybe more. David wondered if she were the proprietress. The *obi* that wrapped her waist matched the mulberry walls.

The last to enter, she knelt, set down her lacquered tray, and slid the rice-paper door shut behind her. As she rose again, a pool of light crossed her face. A frisson of pleasure shivered down David's spine. Beauty was not required in a geisha, but she was truly lovely. The stylised white make-up she wore only made her more so. Her tiny red mouth turned up at the corners when she caught his stare. The smile made his heart beat faster. He knew she found him attractive.

She was the first woman he'd felt any interest in since meeting Chloe. As if it were fated, she knelt between him and her and filled their cups with warm, clear sake. Each motion was precise. For thousands of years, women had been pouring wine just so, had been brushing back their flowing sleeves and exposing the willowy bend of their necks. 'I am Kiku,' she said in clear but accented English. 'Welcome to the House of the Seven Blossoms.'

Chloe made a sound of surprise, half laugh, half cough. The geisha turned to her, wide-eyed and smiling. Chloe smiled back. 'I own a club called The Seven Veils,' she explained, then pressed one finger to her lips to show it was a secret.

'Ah.' Kiku's eyes sparkled at being the recipient of a confidence. 'It is most rewarding to own one's own establishment.'

Chloe's smile widened to a grin. The two women exchanged a look of complicity, each satisfied she'd found a kindred spirit. David suffered a twinge of annoyance, followed by shame. He'd wanted Chloe to feel uncomfortable. He could have prevented her *faux pas*. Instead, he'd been a bastard since they'd arrived.

If Kiku hadn't been sitting between them, he'd have taken Chloe's hand and squeezed it, maybe even whispered an apology. He knew better than to believe she'd forgive him without one.

Resigned to waiting, he turned to the rest of their party. Mr Narita, the VP, and Mr Lee – who oversaw their operations in Hong Kong – were engaged in a drinking game with the other two geisha, something silly involving Trivial Pursuit-like questions which everyone tried to answer with as much double-entendre as possible. This flirtation, this wit, was one of the geishas' arts, as prized as dancing or singing or playing the *shamisen*. For many, it required as much training. Japanese women were not raised to behave this way, nor did Japanese men want such boldness in their wives.

Since he'd grown up here, Sato knew how to appreciate their skill better than he did. David watched him smile at the better sallies, though he refused to join in. His sake cup was planted firmly upside down. Even here, he considered himself on duty.

'Your associate is very sober,' Kiku commented.

'He is my ... fiancé's bodyguard,' Chloe said.

Kiku's painted face turned grave. 'He is right to be serious, then. It is quite a body to guard.'

The sake that had been halfway down David's throat spurted out his nose.

'Thar she blows,' bellowed Mr Narita.

The VP put his elbows the table. 'Tell us, David-san: are all your emissions so forceful?'

'Let us hope they are not so precipitous,' teased Mr Lee.

Kiku thumped David's back as he continued to choke. 'Surely not,' she said. 'Or how could he keep such a beautiful *gir furendo* happy.'

'No, not girlfriend,' said the VP. '*Koibito.*' He made a graphic gesture with a circled finger and thumb to demonstrate that *koibito* meant lover.

'I'd watch where you stick that finger,' Chloe drawled. 'Someone might mistake it for a little shrimp and bite it off.'

The VP collapsed with laughter, sake-soaked tears rolling down his face. His glasses fell into a bowl of white rice the geisha had brought to snack on.

Lord, David thought. How much lower could the evening sink? Much lower, he feared. In this country of conformity, of stringent rules and near-universal politeness, being under the influence of alcohol was an accepted – perhaps necessary – excuse to act like an idiot. Always the least favourite part of his visits, having Chloe pour oil on the blaze made it more galling than ever.

He glanced at Kiku. She had folded her hands in her lap and was laughing softly, as lovely as a flower. In that moment, she seemed perfect to him: utterly feminine, demure, but also erotic; naughty in a sweet way as opposed to a brash one. Her body was girlish, its curves obscured by the swaddling silk of her kimono and *obi*. Nonetheless, he knew if he unwrapped the cloth he'd find a woman inside.

He filled her sake cup, striving for some of her grace. Their shoulders brushed as he poured. Perhaps he imagined it, but he thought her cheeks grew pink beneath their paint.

'*Domo arigato*,' she said, almost a whisper, as if emotion had made her breathless.

He bent closer, his heart pounding with a thrill both terrible and delicious. 'I think *you* need a bodyguard,' he whispered in Japanese.

Kiku dipped her head and caught her lower lip between her teeth. Just beyond her, Chloe watched, her mouth smiling, her eyes cool. She looked like she could guess what he'd said without a translator. David didn't want to admit it, but knowing her gaze was on him intensified his excitement.

'Kiku,' Chloe said in her kindest, gentlest voice. 'Why don't you show me that scroll over there? I'd like to see what those folks in the picture are doing.'

'Of course,' said Kiku, still breathless as she rose from her kneeling pose. 'I would be interested to hear what you think of the artist.'

But as they stood by the *shunga*, whispering behind the screen of Kiku's hand, they didn't appear to be discussing the long-dead pornographer's skills.

They appeared to be discussing him.

10

David gazed around the empty suite. He called Chloe's name, but no one answered. She'd sent him to the hotel pharmacy for aspirin; said all that sake gave her a headache. But she wasn't lying across the cream-coloured couch any more.

Perhaps she'd gone to bed?

The hair at the back of his neck prickled. He had an odd feeling, as if a stranger had been in their rooms. He could almost smell a faint, alien scent. He shrugged off his jacket and padded across the thick ash-grey carpet. Everything seemed just as he'd left it. Chloe's coat was still draped over the back of the desk chair, and his laptop still blinked on the cherrywood dining table.

He tried to shake off his jitters. Most likely, the evening had left him on edge: fighting with Chloe, the quips he couldn't keep up with, being attracted to someone and knowing she knew it. He'd never been in a relationship like this, all storm and thunder. He wasn't sure how much longer he could stand it, and yet he didn't know if he could bear to let her go. The core of her, the real Chloe, called to him more strongly than any woman he knew.

He loosened his tie, hoping she'd want to make up the way he did, in bed, naked and sweaty. Already half aroused, he pushed the bedroom door open. A single light was on, a wall light with a frosted, semi-circular shade. The bed was empty, but someone was kneeling at its foot with her hands crossed in her lap. The someone wasn't Chloe.

Kiku, the beautiful geisha from the House of the Seven Blossoms, looked up at him and smiled. She had removed her make-up and wig and wore a much simpler kimono, little more than a robe with a sash. If anything, her looks improved without adornment. Her natural hair hung like thick black silk to her waist. Her mouth was almost as small as the one she'd painted on. Her dark, almond-shaped eyes were liquid pools of sweetness.

His skin heated at the sight of her, as if he'd stepped into the sun. Warmth pooled in his groin, moving him, stretching him. 'What are you doing here?' he asked, unable to make the question anything but husky.

She gazed down at her hands, still wearing that Mona Lisa smile. 'Your fiancée thought you would like a present.'

'Chloe?'

She nodded. '*Hai*.'

He raked his hair back with his hands, the warning about Greeks bearing gifts flashing through his mind. 'She paid you to sleep with me?'

Kiku's little mouth turning down like a cartoon. 'I am not *korobi*, not roll-over geisha. Your girlfriend said you were fascinated by our culture, that you would welcome the chance to experience bedplay with a traditional Japanese woman.'

David laughed under his breath, anger close to the surface of his skin. Whatever Chloe's motives, they weren't simple generosity. This was a test, probably one he couldn't pass no matter what he did.

He touched Kiku's hair where it curtained her cheek. 'What do you get out of this?'

When she lifted her face, it shone like a girl at communion, her cheeks rosy, her eyes starred. 'You are the most beautiful man I've ever met, and I have never slept with an American. I hear they are good lovers.' She touched the back of his thigh, just above his knee.

Feeling shot up his leg, through his sex, cold and electric. She kissed his hipbone through his trousers, her hair whispering over the wool. 'It will be good, David-san. I will be Japanese for you, and you will be American for me.'

His hands found their way to her delicate skull, stroking it, cupping it, helplessly pressing her closer. 'I'm not sure I know how.'

'There is nothing to know,' she said. She rubbed her cheek across the growing ridge of his erection. 'You should do what you wish and you will be what you are.'

Her words unravelled his last knot of resistance. To hell with it. If Chloe was going to play games, he'd do what he pleased and she could live with the consequences. After all, why should he assume she'd been faithful to him? All those days at the club, training her 'troupe'. Who knew what she'd been up to? She'd made no promises. She'd never even said 'I love you.'

He shut his eyes on a sting of hurt and let Kiku undress him. She did not rush. Her hands were gentle, soothing. Each item of apparel was removed with the care afforded a ritual in a tea ceremony. She spent as much time stroking his clothes as she spent stroking him, as if all the textures – skin, wool, linen – were worthy of appreciation. When she pulled his shirt over his head, she brought it to her face and inhaled. 'You smell of America,' she said, shining with happiness.

He slipped his fingers into her hair and drew them outwards. 'Now you.'

Her breath came faster as he unwound her sash, folding it neatly before parting the open halves of her kimono. Her breasts were small, almost flat, their nipples the size and hue of pennies. He sat on the bed and drew her between his open legs. As he suckled her, she cried out, soft but sharp. 'Oh, yes,' she said in Japanese. 'That is very good.'

Her tiny hands slipped down his torso, fingertips testing the hardness of his muscles. He kissed a path across the spoon of her chest and drew at her other nipple. Her fingers tensed at his belly, then clasped the vibrating column of his shaft. The novelty of her touch aroused all by itself: a new hand, a new caress. Her thumb massaged his weeping glans while her fingers probed the softer flesh of his abdomen. He jerked as she found an unfamiliar sweet spot.

She licked the shell of his ear. 'Do you have a condom, David-san?'

He shivered at the flick of her tongue. 'Yes.'

'Good.' She pushed his shoulders gently and he fell, his spine as limp as soba noodles, his cock as hard as jade. Her hands trailed up his thighs, nails rasping softly in his hair. 'We will finish this with *hon-ban* then, the real thing. But first –' She kissed his quivering knee. 'First, I will show you how a true geisha serves her *danna* . . .'

When Sato opened the door to his room, the light from the hall struck Chloe's legs. Oddly enough, he recognised the shape of her calves. They were crossed. One foot wagged slowly, like a hypnotist's pendulum. The shoe that dangled from its toes moved as if her foot were fucking it.

Immediately, he wished he were drunk, anything to numb his body's reaction to her.

She bared her teeth in more than a smile, her glee dark and tightly wound. He knew she was planning something bad, something destructive. He flipped on the light, tossed his cardkey on to a chair and crossed his arms. The door clicked shut behind him. 'What happened to the one-man woman?'

She smirked and moistened her upper lip. 'Rules change.'

A wave of mingled fatigue and melancholy rolled

through his body. 'Chloe, don't do this. Don't make it harder for you and David to work things out. You care about each other.'

'Oh, please.' She swiped her thigh-hugging skirt. 'David cares about the woman he wishes I were.'

'The woman you could be.'

Her chin dipped at his rejoinder. '*Et tu*, Sato? But no –' She waved her perfectly manicured hands. 'It doesn't matter. Tonight, I'm giving him what he wants, perhaps what you want, too.'

'Chloe, whatever you are planning, do not do it. No matter how angry you are, it isn't worth the risk.'

She laughed, sharp and brittle as glass. 'Too late. The deed is being done.' She pushed her body from the chair and stalked towards him, one incomparable leg at a time. When she reached him, she brought her forefinger to her mouth. 'I thought you might want to watch.'

Watch? No, he did not want to watch. Except ... he could not repair damage whose cause he did not know. He repeated this like a mantra as she wrapped one hot hand around his wrist and pulled him through the adjoining door to the living room. A single lamp was lit, the one in the entryway. The bedroom door was ajar. That room was dim as well. Sato heard nothing, but the light shifted as shadows moved inside.

'Come,' Chloe breathed, and tugged him forwards.

Despite himself, excitement tingled up his nerves. His fingertips were almost numb with adrenalin and arousal. The stiffness of his sex changed the pattern of his walk. He knew David was in that room. He knew he was about to see something intimate.

They crouched beside the crack in the door, below the normal line of sight. Chloe's fingers dug into his bicep, vice-tight, either to balance or to hold him captive. He could not hear her breathing, but he could feel it.

He looked inside and had to bite his cheek. The

woman from the geisha bar was removing David's clothes. She began with his shoes, then his belt, then his trousers. Each inch of skin she revealed was both gift and torment. Sato had shared baths with his master; had wrestled him shirtless in the *dojo*, but he had never caught more than glimpses of him naked. Certainly, he'd never watched David's cock arch up beneath his briefs, nor seen the flush of lust on his chest and throat.

'Now you,' said David, and tugged the woman's sash. His touch roved her slender body, first over the deep red robe, then under. Awe for her beauty, for her delicacy, invested every gesture. He kissed her tiny breasts as if she might break, as if she were precious. Sato had done the same himself with unfamiliar partners. One did not want to offend, or to hurt.

But he wished Chloe were not watching. Chloe would not see David's behaviour as he did. David's gentle care towards this woman would likely wound her beyond forgetting, perhaps beyond forgiving.

Or was that what she intended, to prove to herself that David did not love her?

Sato knew this infidelity did not prove it; knew – too well – that a man could feel tenderness towards another without lessening the intensity of his heart's true choice. This stranger was only a dream to his master. Come morning, her memory would fade away like mist.

But Chloe's hurt would not.

'We should leave,' he whispered close to her ear.

She resisted with an angry jerk, her jaw set so hard the tendons in her neck stood out.

A sound drew his attention. The geisha had pushed David on to the bed and was pouring a river of kisses up his legs. Sato could hear them now: the soft percussion of her lips, the catch of David's sighs. His arms were flung wide and his head rolled back and forth across the covers. He was so hard the blood pounding through his organ barely moved it. Sato found himself memorising its shape, its colour, the distinctive pointed flare of its tip. He licked his own lips as the geisha took the shaft in her mouth. David's neck arched with pleasure.

Chloe's nails broke the skin of Sato's arm. He rubbed her hand until her grip eased, then stroked the velvety hollow of her cheek. 'Come away,' he said. 'Do not torture yourself.'

When she shook her head, a tear spilled free of her lower lashes.

A sound called his attention back to the bed. The geisha was mounting David, her body swaying like a reed. She settled gingerly, as if his organ were too large for her. 'Now,' she said in breathy Japanese. 'You ride me, Mr American.'

David rolled her beneath him and began to stroke, his hips pushing and drawing in slow, liquid rolls. He had such lovely, muscular buttocks. Sato knew his master was not thrusting as deeply as he might. Even now, he was careful of his partner. Once he'd established a rhythm, he braced on his elbows and looked into the woman's eyes. His hands bracketed her skull. With both thumbs, he stroked her hair from her perspiring forehead.

Chloe stiffened, startling Sato's gaze to her. She'd bitten her lip until it bled, but she did not cry out. David's gesture must have been one he had used on her. Sato drew Chloe's head to his shoulder, his strength too great to resist. For a moment, she rested there, letting him shield her eyes. Then she pushed away.

David and Kiku neared their finish.

The geisha was uttering tiny kitten cries, murmuring endearments in Japanese. Her hands fluttered over David's back. His thrusts quickened, deeper now, and harder. David's shaft disappeared completely inside the geisha's body. Sato could barely breathe. His master was going to come. David's stomach tensed. His eyes screwed shut. His head fell back. Kiku clutched his shoulders and slid her knees to his armpits. David shoved in deep and groaned.

'Your lover is watching,' Kiku gasped.

In an instant, his groan changed from pleasure to dismay. 'No,' he said, his head turning towards the door, his hips fighting to undo his thrust even as he shuddered in release. Still twitching, he pulled free and swung to the floor.

Chloe did not wait for him to find her. She fled, one fist pressed to her mouth, the other to her breasts. Sato stood and moved back from the door. He heard David cursing as he stumbled into his trousers. He was zipping them as he ran.

He never saw Sato in the shadows. He never knew Sato had seen.

David and Chloe returned within the hour. They must have reached some accord because Sato heard them making very gentle love. The headboard did not thump. The mattress did not squeal. Only David's low murmurs seeped through the wall. They sounded pleading, loving, sad. They brought an ache to Sato's chest he could not rub away. Chloe moaned when she came but, as far as Sato could tell, that was the only noise she made.

Her silence lasted through the long plane ride home, then filled the house in Vermont. When she wasn't at The Seven Veils, she walked the gardens. Even at night, she walked. She only spoke when spoken to and barely that. Sato did not understand why she had not left, why she had not found her own home, away from David. Her spirit was gone already.

The answer would come later, with a bitter, tragic logic.

She had not left because she had not destroyed her chance for happiness, not yet, not utterly. But she would.

11

The house in Vermont went into mourning. Chloe had turned ghost again: not sad, not frightened, just wound up like a watch spring that wouldn't tick.

David shoved his hands in the pockets of his fleece-lined bomber jacket. His back rested on a boulder by the first of the garden's ponds. Fallen leaves hid the tattered remains of the lily pads and a koi slid through the murky water, a flash of orange in the green. November was drawing to a close. Whether Chloe would stick around for Christmas was anyone's guess. They hardly talked. She'd moved back to the Green Room. They hadn't made love since their return from Japan. She'd stopped flirting with the staff and the staff had stopped sucking in their guts. Always curt, Master Wu had grown surly, muttering about early frosts and spider mites in the greenhouse.

David knew the old gardener missed a different sort of pest.

He wondered if she'd come walking today or if the sight of him would stop her. Admittedly, he was lying in wait. He'd do anything to break this impasse, even – he closed his eyes – even let her go if he believed she really wanted him to.

He couldn't forget her tears. They'd stood in the hotel corridor, he whispering furiously, she refusing to respond. Guilt warred with anger in his breast. 'You pushed her on me,' he said. 'You did everything but spread her legs. What did you think would happen? Why did you watch if you didn't want to see?'

Her hands shoved weakly at his chest, bare because

he hadn't taken time to grab a shirt. Her head wagged from side to side, a silent 'no, no, no,' while tears rolled down her cheeks. He pulled her closer, forcing her to cry against him. Her arms folded between them. Her tears fell hot to his skin. A maid trundled by with a cart of towels, her eyes widening at the picture they made. David felt himself flush, but he ignored it. 'You can't think I love her,' he whispered against her hair. 'You can't think it was anything but anger and curiosity that made me do it. I love you, Chloe. I love *you*.'

She gasped for air against his breastbone. 'I'm scared,' she said, her whole body burrowing close.

'Of what, honey? Tell me and I'll try to help.'

But she wouldn't tell him; wouldn't speak of the matter at all after that. When he finally coaxed her back to the suite and they made love, his heart broke with every thrust. There wasn't enough tenderness in the world to erase what he'd done. The right and wrong of it didn't matter. The knowledge was there, dark and heavy in her eyes. She was comparing every touch to the touches she'd seen him give the geisha.

Now he sighed at the lowering sky. They might get their first snow tonight. The clouds were thick and grey. They even smelled grey.

A hand touched his shoulder. He spun. 'Chloe!'

She held something out to him, but he couldn't look away from her eyes. They were cognac shot with splinters of coffee, more mysterious than an Arabian night. 'You forgot your gloves,' she said.

He took them, but didn't put them on. 'Chloe.'

'Yes, David-san?' The echo of Kiku stung them both. She lowered her gaze.

David slapped the gloves against his palm. 'I'm coming to your next show.'

The promise seemed to inspire more weariness than joy. 'I thought you might,' she said.

Her eyes swam with tears. He dropped the gloves and cupped her face. 'Chloe, I love you. Can't we find a way through this?'

She swallowed hard but did not spill over. 'I can't change who I am.'

He didn't know what to say. That he thought she could? That she needed to? That he believed only fear kept her from it? None of those answers were likely to bear good fruit. 'Would loving me be such a terrible risk?' he asked, his voice as light as he could make it with a lump the size of Newark in his throat.

She bit her lower lip, teeth sinking into full, red flesh. God, he missed her mouth. His involuntary sigh had too much sound to be hidden. She smiled, a small curling at the corners of her mouth. 'Poor David. Too good for his own good.'

She tilted forwards and kissed him playfully, but he'd been too hungry too long to leave it at that. He wrapped her in his arms and sank as deep as he dared, reaching into her mouth, loving her tongue with his, her teeth, the sleek-soft cushion of her cheeks. She began to melt against him. He hardened the kiss. He would not let her go this time. He would take her here on the bare cold ground if he had to.

But he didn't have to. She unzipped his jacket and reached inside. She smoothed the button-down cotton over his pounding heart. He moaned, his throat aching with need even as he slanted his lips for a better fit. 'Touch me,' he said, close to her mouth. 'Put your hands on me.'

She unbuttoned the waist of his jeans and cupped the painful pressure at his crotch. She lifted him up against himself, almost forcing him to his toes. Then she rubbed his bulk with the heels of her palms. The heat of her hands bled through the denim in slow, firm circles. It was good, almost heaven. He nuzzled her ear. 'Inside,' he said. 'Put your hand inside my jeans. Touch my cock.'

She pushed back to arm's length, lips parted for breaths that misted in the wintry air. Her beautiful mouth was swollen from his kisses. She knelt. Her skirt fanned across the browning grass, gold with tiny printed violets. She held his knees for balance, thumbs in front, fingers in back. She kissed the pulsing ridge of his erection.

'I'm dying,' he said, the words gusting out. 'I could come in two seconds.'

She nuzzled the wet spot that overlay his glans. She drew down his zip. The sound made him shiver. Her fingers searched, gentle and warm. He wanted her to hurry. He could barely stand still. He waited, though, his blood pounding, his cock a solid ache. She lifted him free of his briefs, the cold a shock until she ran her parted lips up his raphe. The soft tip of her tongue left a trail of fire and ice. She breathed on him, blew on him, then swallowed the head and bore down.

He cursed, overwhelmed with pleasure. Sweat broke out on his face and chest and back. Her lips sank towards his belly. Her fingers kneaded the bunched muscles at the back of his thighs.

It didn't take two seconds, maybe thirty. He ground his buttocks into the boulder, afraid if he didn't he'd shove himself down her throat. Her tongue cradled him as she pulled and teased him when she paused. He gripped her shoulders hard enough to bruise. She chuckled around his cock, low and throaty. 'Chloe,' he groaned. 'Please.'

She took all of him to the root and hugged him with her cheeks. She sucked him as if he were a sweet that could melt and she was starving for the taste. Her mouth contracted around him, rhythmic, intense. The base of his spine ached, pulsed, the feeling tightening in his balls and cock. She squeezed his thighs and drew hard. Gold-white spots danced before his eyes. His hips convulsed. He came, one deep, bright, spear of heat, and another, and another. He sighed with the relief of it. After all that waiting, after all that wanting, she'd finally taken him back.

As she stood, she clasped his shaft between her hands. The gesture moved him. She was protecting him from the cold. Gently, she tucked his penis back inside his clothes. He smiled, feeling cherished and wanting to return the gift. 'Come here, you,' he said.

She shook her head. Her smile was crooked, her eyes sleepy and shuttered. 'I'll save you and Sato a seat,' she said, and left him to his shock.

Chloe didn't merely save them a seat, she saved them a private box overlooking the stage. The balcony projected from the wall between two doors, its front curved, its curtains dull gold tapestry. The view couldn't have been better. In honour of the season, fresh greenery – gathered up with red satin bows – decorated the white balustrade. The box had just enough room for two chairs and a café table.

Since it was obviously a trysting place for lovers, sharing the space with Sato struck David as odd. It was, however, preferable to sitting among the crowd downstairs, where he'd be forced to witness reactions he'd just as soon not see. A shudder of unease coursed down his spine. Chloe's mood had been strange these past few days: too bright, too tight. He rubbed his knuckle across his upper lip as the waitress cleared their plates. They'd been served turkey with cranberries. A rich bread pudding with rum. Ho ho ho.

'Enjoy the show,' said the waitress, and closed the door behind her.

Sato tugged at the knees of his loose grey trousers and resettled in his upholstered, high-backed chair. Apparently, he wasn't comfortable, either.

'Do you think she plans to perform?' David asked. He wouldn't put it past her to make him watch what she could do to other men, what she'd done to other men for years.

Sato shrugged. 'I saw her working the room a few minutes ago, in a business suit.'

David wished that reassured him. Chloe had something up her sleeve. The dread that clenched his belly was too strong to dismiss. Before he could even try, the chandelier dimmed, rainbow sparks spinning off the crystal as the rest of the lights followed suit. The crowd below them murmured in anticipation, then hushed. A hiss marked the rising of a stage curtain. David set his forearms on the pine-prickled railing and peered into the darkness. Squinting didn't help. Apart from two tiny red bulbs above the exits, the room was black.

A new sound joined the rustle of the audience: music, a caper of strings as light and clear as sunshine. He recognised it at once as the 'Dance of the Sugarplums' from *The Nutcracker*. Lights rose behind the smoke-thin scrim that veiled the stage. He made out the shadow of a Christmas tree, then couples in modern evening dress waltzing in circles around its base. A line of windows stretched behind the ornamented pine. Snow fell, catching the light like fairy dust. It was a fine illusion. The audience hummed with pleasure.

Gradually, the illumination increased to day-like brightness. David's breath hitched in his throat.

A woman with straight dark hair twirled across the floor with a light-footed partner. She was slim and vibrant and familiar. She turned, and David pressed a hand to his pounding heart. It wasn't Chloe, just a woman who looked like her. Her partner was very elegant. Dressed in white tie and tails, he held her with a care that conveyed not just lust but affection. The woman's dress, a sheer, sparkly concoction in pale, pale pink, bared most of her slender back. The man's long, dark hands – he was Spanish, David thought – edged past the cloth, his fingers claiming more of her than the audience could see.

It was hard to look away from them to watch the other couples. These two had an unmistakable chemistry. They moved together well, fluidly, their legs brushing with the steps, their eyes seeing only each other. A separate spot followed them around the tree, bathing their heads and shoulders in a rose-gold glow.

David smiled and bobbed his head to the well-loved music. He'd been a fool. If this was Chloe's show, he'd been worrying over nothing. He would apologise for misjudging her, with pleasure. He'd go down on his knees if he had to. He'd –

Sato choked out a sound, yanking David's thoughts from the pleasantly erotic place they'd been drifting to. He looked at his chief of security. Sato's face was pale in the light shining up from the stage. The whites of his eyes showed around his pupils. Clearly, something had alarmed him. He followed Sato's line of sight. For the first time, he noticed a solitary figure in the far upstage corner by the windows. A portly Hawaiian stood beside a potted palm, feet braced wide, hands clasped loosely before him: a casual, at-the-ready pose Sato could have trademarked.

The Hawaiian's gaze never left the golden couple. His face was impassive, stern even, but something in his demeanor suggested yearning. David looked back at the Spaniard and the woman in the beaded dress. Now he saw. The gown was like the one Chloe had worn to that fundraiser in New York. In fact, it might have been the very same. If the woman was meant to be Chloe, he supposed, in a pinch, her partner could be a stand-in for himself.

Was Chloe suggesting Sato was in love with her? Was that why Sato was upset? If so, she was trying to sell the wrong bridge. Sato's attitude towards her had mellowed since the early days, but David wasn't gullible enough to mistake kindness for infatuation.

He turned to his old friend, a reassuring smile on his lips. Sato never saw it. The action on stage held him in a spell, and not a pleasant one. His hands were fisted on the table like a man braced for disaster. Beads of sweat trickled down the edges of his hair, plastering it to his face.

Perplexed, David gazed back over the balcony. The gilded couple had danced into a portion of the stage that had been dark before. Now the lights revealed a small art deco bathroom, black and cream, complete with a mirrored sink and toilet. The couple grappled into a kiss as if they'd been waiting an eternity to touch each other.

So, David thought, Chloe was re-enacting what they'd done at the fundraiser. He pinched his lower lip. What was she trying to prove? That she held nothing sacred? Why did she think he'd care after all the other stunts she'd pulled? Her disrespect for their privacy was annoying, yes; embarrassing, certainly, but hardly the end of the world. Who would guess but he and Chloe? That Spaniard didn't even look like him. He had a ponytail, for God's sake.

Torn between snorting and rolling his eyes, David watched the man ride the woman's breasts until he came. He had to admit the man did a good job. He made what David knew to be an awkward business look grace-ful, even erotic. He could not deny his groin was heavy by the time the man spat what appeared to be genuine semen from his formidable nine-inch cock.

David wondered if he ought to be flattered by Chloe's choice of stand-in.

The woman rubbed the semen over her skin as if that, in itself, were an orgasmic experience. The man moved towards her and the lights fell, plunging the room into darkness.

David thought this a strange conclusion to the piece until the lights came up again, low this time, on the other part of the stage. The Christmas tree and ballroom and been removed. In their place stood a near-perfect replica of Sato's room in the Gramercy Park brownstone. It had the same heavy still lifes, the same dark green walls and off-white trim. The Hawaiian was sleeping fitfully in the double bed. He appeared to be naked except for the sheet. When he rolled on to his back, an erection almost as prodigious as the Spaniard's tented the cloth. A female shadow appeared at the door.

David knew what was coming as surely as he knew his own name. Memories returned, heavy with new meaning. He and Chloe had made love for the first time that night. She'd been so impatient she hadn't showered until after, while he slept. Because he'd slept, he had no way of knowing how long she'd been gone, or if she'd been showering off someone else's smell besides his own: Sato's, for instance.

Anger pounded between his temples like a migraine. The thought of Sato's hands on her, Sato's mouth – his oldest friend . . .

He ground his molars and fought for control. He knew what Chloe was. He knew what she could do to a man's better judgement, even a man as honourable as Sato. Sato must be miserable, mortified, having his breach of faith unveiled this way. He reached out to cover his friend's white-knuckled fist. 'It doesn't matter,' he said, squeezing to make the words go deep. 'I swear, Sato, it doesn't matter if you slept with her. I know what she's like.'

Sato had closed his eyes. He shook his head from side to side, reminding David eerily of Chloe's response in the Tokyo hotel. Whatever was wrong, Sato obviously didn't think David understood. 'What?' he said, even as Sato lurched to his feet. 'What is it?'

Sato wouldn't meet his eye. 'I'm sorry, master.' He spoke to the tips of his shoes, his chin trembling like a young boy's. 'I'm sorry.'

He left, tearing his sleeve from David's grip and blundering through the door.

David gaped after him. Then, not knowing where else to look for answers, he returned his attention to the stage. The fake Chloe kneeled on the fake Sato's bed, acting out by gesture what David had done between her breasts. The fake Sato looked horrified, then enthralled, and then he fell on her, sniffing her, kissing her, licking the dried semen from the cleavage of her bronze and cream lace gown.

David's stomach sank like a lift cut free of its cable. Everything inside him slowed. His blood ticked in his ears. The man was nuzzling her skin like a starving dog. And now he was pleading for something. He pressed the woman's breasts together. He mimed a thrusting motion with his hips. He was begging to do what David had done, to get himself off between her breasts.

David covered his eyes. His breath came in ragged gasps, drawing in the scent of pine, the taste of sorrow. It wasn't Chloe Sato loved.

It was him.

All his care, all his loyalty, all those years, he'd been in love with David and David had never known. How hard Sato must have worked to keep him from discovering his secret! They'd bathed together, wrestled together, pissed side by side in the executive washroom. David hadn't seen a look, a touch, so much as a word out of place. But there must have been. There must have. Because Chloe had seen the truth in – what – a matter of weeks?

Good God, he was blind. He hit his forehead with his palms. Chloe had used the strength of Sato's love to seduce him into betraying it. How many times? How many nights had she crawled into Sato's bed, stinking of David's sweat, and offered herself as a proxy for Sato's unrequited lust? A dozen? A hundred? Last night?

He gripped the balustrade, pine needles prickling, bleeding sap. No. He stared unseeing into the fog-like blur above the stage. Not last night. Not even recently. Because Sato had forgiven her. Sato had, in his own quiet way, begun to take her side. David had seen the disapproval in his eyes whenever he thought David had let her down. Sato wanted David and Chloe to have a future together.

Sato wanted Chloe to be happy.

And this was how she repaid him.

David pushed to his feet. From the crowd below a long intake of breath sounded, a gasp like waves breaking into foam. He didn't know what was happening on the stage and he didn't care. He yanked open the balcony door and strode down the narrow hall. He took the stairs two at a time, the heels of his dress shoes ringing on the cold concrete. His jaw ached but he wouldn't relax it. He and Chloe were going to have this out. Now. Tonight.

And he wasn't going to pull a single punch.

No snow fell behind the tall windows in Chloe's office. In the distance, the blare of light struck the bare grey skeletons of trees. All evidence of holiday cheer was absent: no ho-ho-ho, no ribbons, no music, no denial of the cold, hard truths of the world.

She was waiting for him. Like an old film goddess, she lounged in the sleek leather chair, her ankles crossed on the blotter, her cobalt velvet suit as fresh as the moment she'd put it on. Her face held the same icy serenity he'd seen after her fight with Ian Quist.

David wouldn't give her the satisfaction of slapping her around, but he had to admit he was tempted. Were all her boyfriends the same? Did they all think they loved her, only to end up nearly insane with rage?

He came to a halt on the Persian carpet, panting with anger, his thoughts too tangled to know where to start. She blinked once, slowly, and then her lips curled in a smug, cat-in-the-creamery smile. She stroked one red-tipped finger up and down the neckline of her jacket, a jacket beneath which she wore nothing but skin. David's eyes followed the teasing trail. His blood heated. Even now she could arouse him. Surely this, more than anything, ground his nose into the completeness of her victory.

Her finger circled the hollow between her collarbones. 'Enjoy the show?'

'Damn you.' His body trembled with fury while his voice quavered on the edge of tears. 'You just wouldn't quit until you'd convinced me you were a bitch. Well, congratulations. You sure as hell have done it.' He slammed his hands on her desk, to either side of her shapely calves. A bill fluttered to the floor. Her eyes narrowed, but her smile didn't falter. 'Why, Chloe? Why Sato? Maybe I disappointed you, but he never did. He protected you. He defended you. Obviously, at some cost to himself. Why in God's name would you do this to him?'

Her smile grew beatific. 'He loved you, and he was so loyal.' She spread her hands, palm up. 'The challenge was reason enough.'

'The challenge.' His laugh was as bitter as any he'd

heard from her. Her eyes laughed back, daring him to hit her, to be like the rest. He turned away and clenched his hands. The muscle beneath his scar was ticking, annoyingly out of sync with his pulse. He drew a deep, tight breath that ached as it filled his lungs. 'Don't come home tonight.'

'And tomorrow?' she purred, velvet and ash.

He stared at the closed door, his eyes hot and dry. She wouldn't stop until he slashed the ties between them. Maybe she couldn't help herself. Maybe nothing but fire and destruction would satisfy her wounded soul. Maybe she literally didn't know how to accept the love he'd offered. The thought broke his heart but, at the moment, he hated her too much to care.

He shoved both hands in his pockets. 'Don't come home tomorrow, either.'

She said nothing to that. He couldn't even hear her breathe. He bit his lips to still their trembling. His feet felt as if they'd been cemented to the floor. Even now, he wanted to turn, to hold her close and kiss her shining hair.

He took one step towards the door, then two. He reached for the knob. He had to clasp it tight to keep it from slipping on his sweat. He turned it and pulled. 'Goodbye,' he said, without looking back. 'Keep the money I gave you for the club. I don't want it any more.'

He closed the door behind him. Only then did tears spill down his rigid cheeks.

The knowledge of what she'd done chased her from the club, chased her like the memory of Mary Alice Ryan's soft white throat. Her heels clattered across the car park. One slid on the gravel and her ankle turned, a stab of pain shooting up one tendon. She ignored it. She could see the car.

You're not to speak of this, her father would say. *It was just a bad dream.*

She battled against the driver-side lock, a sob tangling with her curses. Fucking thing.

The key turned and she flung herself inside the poison-green Ferrari, alarm bleating until she did the fucking seat belt. She gunned the engine; pulled on to the road with a squeal of rubber.

But she couldn't outrun the memories any more than she could outrun her fear of forgetting. *This never happened. Never happened.* Except it had. She'd meant to do it and it was done. She'd hurt David beyond forgiveness. She'd shown him what she was, what she'd always been, what he'd been too Sir Galahad-ish to see. She was who she was and now he could live with it, too.

She didn't think where she was going: just drove down the dark, winding road, past the Cumberland Farms shop and on to the highway.

She could go back to Atlantic City; perform again. She still had it. Everyone said she had it. She could feel the slick, cool pole between her hands, pressed against her barely covered sex. She could feel the eyes in the darkness; the hard-breathing, faceless men; the power she'd gather like a palmful of smoke. She shuddered at the memory of their sweaty fingers slipping bills under her G-string: fives and tens, twenties and hundreds. But she had money now, plenty of it. David didn't know the half of what she had. If she wanted, she could spend the rest of her life in bed. Alone.

She punched on the radio and let it blare through all six speakers. Mick wailed at her. He couldn't get no satisfaction. My man, she thought, her grin a snarl. She'd give David what he wanted. She'd give them all what they wanted. She'd be the whore everyone thought she was. The lights of the highway swept past her, sulphur-yellow brightness whooshing like the cars, like the short white dashes between the lanes. The tyres hummed on the surface of the road. *This never happened. Never happened.*

She clenched her jaw until her molars ached.

'It happened,' she said out loud, barely able to hear above the radio. 'Deal with it, bitch.'

The headlights came out of nowhere. For a millisecond they glinted on the old rain spots that bordered the windshield: diamonds and pearls. Then the glare blinded her. It was too bright, too close. She shifted down and jammed on the brake but she knew this was it. Her number had just been called.

'Fuck,' she said, surprisingly angry. Something big hit the car dead on, something huge. The shadow behind the headlights had an intolerable weight. Brakes squealed like tortured souls. As the world crumpled towards her in slow motion, shale-black shards of pain burst inside her skull.

'David,' she whimpered, but all that came out was *Day–*. The rest was swallowed by a cotton-wool fog. Her body disappeared.

I'm dead, she thought.

This never happened, said a familiar, acid voice.

But it wasn't her father's voice.

It was her own.

Surrender

12

Pressure. That was her first thought: walls closing in, a knife arcing ... Her hand tightened on the hilt, her whole body aching with the effort of holding tight. She felt nothing as she slashed, but wounds opened in her flesh. Her heart bled.

She opened her eyes. The ceiling was white with small grey holes. The light made her head hurt. She had a sense of mental vertigo, of something missing.

A man was crying.

Carefully, gingerly, she turned her head towards the sound. She was lying in a railed bed, a hospital bed. The knowledge fell into place with a satisfying snick. She was in a hospital. She must be sick.

She looked at the man. He was slim with long legs and broad shoulders. Hunched in a blue vinyl chair, he'd propped his elbows on his knees. His face was hidden in his palms. He wore a business suit, black, with the tie yanked to the centre of a crisp white shirt. A matching jacket draped the back of the chair. Forearms corded with slender muscle emerged from his rolled-up sleeves. His hair gleamed blue-black under the thin fluorescent light. Cut short against his neck, a thick shock fell across his forehead. A tiny spray, a – she fumbled for the word – a cowlick stood up at the crown. She smiled, her fingers twitching weakly with an urge to reach out and smooth it. How endearing. A cowlick. Just like a boy.

But the man didn't look as if he'd appreciate her humour. As she watched, he sat back and pressed his fisted hands against his mouth.

She could see his face then. He was Asian, his features graceful and cleanly carved. A small crescent moon scar bracketed his right eye, one imperfection amidst a sea of ivory beauty. Tears trembled in his lashes. He lowered his hands and squeezed his knees. The sight of his mouth brought an odd tightness to her chest. It was a lovely mouth, a blend of masculine firmness and feminine allure. Both his lips were equally full. She found herself wondering how he would taste – which was probably not the most appropriate reaction to have towards a weeping man.

'Are you all right?' she asked, the words rasping her throat like burrs.

He leapt to his feet. 'Chloe!'

Who was Chloe? she wondered.

He kissed her hands as tears rolled down his face. 'Thank God. Oh, thank God, you're all right.'

This was getting embarrassing.

'I'm sorry,' she said as he pressed his lips to her palm. 'Do I know you?'

He stared at her, his beautiful face pinched with confusion and hurt. That was embarrassing, too. Obviously, she was supposed to know who he was.

Then it struck her. She didn't know who *she* was, either. An icy wave washed over her. 'Oh, God,' she said. 'I don't remember anything.'

She fought to sit up, to escape the terrible realisation. She had to remember. She had to. Something caught on the bend of her arm, an IV tube. Pain strobed in her head, red, white, red. The man pressed her back into the pillows. 'Lie still,' he said. 'You've had a bump on the head.'

His eyes were bitter chocolate, steady and reassuring. Her lungs stopped trying to hyperventilate. 'A bump on the head,' she repeated, clinging to his gaze.

He smiled and cupped the curve of her cheek. His

touch was so tender her eyes stung. 'You were in a car accident. You've been unconscious for nine hours.'

She reached up and found a bandage on her brow. 'Am I –' She swallowed. 'Am I hurt badly?'

He stroked the line of her nose. 'You had a bad cut in your forehead, but other than that and the concussion, you're fine. Nothing broken. The airbag deployed just right and you were wearing your seat belt.' He shook his head in wonderment. 'The Ferrari looks like Godzilla stepped on it.'

'The Ferrari.' The words triggered nothing. She knew they ought to. 'Did I –' She took a breath to get the question out. 'Is anyone else hurt?'

'No, no. Don't worry. The accident wasn't your fault. A trucker ploughed through the crash barrier. He'd been driving too long and started to nod off. His eighteen-wheeler barely had a dent. He's fine, apart from being terrified he killed somebody.' His eyes crinkled in a smile. 'I imagine he'll be as glad as I am to hear you're awake.'

'But who am I? And who are you?'

He hesitated just long enough to make her wonder why. 'I'm David Imakita,' he said. 'And you're Chloe. You're my wife.'

Her head pounded at the words. What he'd said seemed so wrong. Chloe. What kind of name was Chloe? She felt no connection to it, no connection to him except ... His beauty, that tugged at her, and his tears. They made her feel bad inside, a dark, uneasy coiling in her stomach. She saw a flash of something gold, then hands around a soft, white neck. She closed her eyes.

'I don't remember,' she whispered. She rolled her head against the pillow. It hurt, but she couldn't stop herself until he laid his hand across her cheek.

'Hush,' he said. His voice soothed her. Maybe she did know it. Maybe he was her husband. He spoke again. 'I'll call the nurse. They'll want to know you're conscious.'

She nodded. She felt very small, a child afraid of monsters. She clutched his hand. 'Don't leave me.'

He smiled and kissed her cheek. His lips were soft. 'Just try to get rid of me.'

A feather of darkness brushed her mind. She shivered, but it was easier to give in to his comfort than to worry.

The doctors would not release her until she spoke to the hospital psychiatrist. They'd been poking her for two days now. Apparently, they could find no organic cause for her memory loss.

At least they'd let her wear clothes. David, her husband – how odd that sounded! – had brought a brand new pair of jeans and a slouchy lambswool sweater that had to be his from the way it fit. Didn't she own anything casual? She would have asked, but the doctors had warned David she needed to find her memories on her own. Telling her wouldn't help. In any case, she didn't mind wearing his big grey sweater. It smelled good. Actually, it smelled terrific: a hint of aftershave and man and soft, expensive wool.

She stroked one sleeve as she waited in the doctor's claustrophobic office, fighting a panic that threatened to close her throat. This trumped-up broom closet had no receptionist, no carpeting, no view, no soothing music – not even a couch. It barely had room for a bookshelf, a cluttered metal desk, and two of the hospital's omnipresent vinyl chairs. A yellowed cartoon curled from the bland green door. It showed a patient lying on a couch in an office much posher than this one. 'Say, Doc,' said the patient. 'How many shrinks does it take to screw in a light bulb?' The doctor responded. 'Hm. What exactly do you mean by "light bulb"?'

Har-de-har. She was ready to bust a gut over that one. Evelyn Perkins must be a good ol' gal to have such a whip-cracking sense of humour about her profession.

Chloe felt warm and glowy just reading it. But at least she'd discovered something new.

She had a knack for sarcasm.

And she didn't like shrinks.

She twisted her hands in the hem of David's sweater. She hoped this instinctive aversion didn't mean she'd been a mental patient.

A noise at the door pulled her hands from their telling pose. Dr Perkins had arrived. She was tall and lanky and dressed like a librarian. Her navy cardigan drained every speck of colour from her sallow cheeks and did nothing to minimise her hips. Chloe's gaze travelled downwards. Good Lord, she was wearing orthopaedic shoes.

Self-knowledge point number three, she thought. I am a fashion snob. She forced a smile. Being disliked made one vulnerable. People could tell lies about you and be believed. Where that bit of wisdom came from, she didn't know, but it resonated so strongly she didn't dare ignore it. She would do her best to be liked.

'Sorry, sorry, sorry,' said the doctor as she clunked a pile of folders on to her overburdened desk. 'Got stuck in a consult.' She turned in a circle as if she'd forgotten something. 'I apologise for the humble digs. This is a teaching hospital and – Ah-hah! There's your file. Now.' She sat and clasped her hands atop the manila folder. Her smile revealed large, coffee-stained teeth. 'I usually do chit-chat at this point, but I'm running late. Would you mind terribly if I cut to the chase?'

Chloe hoped her answering smile didn't look as stiff as it felt. 'Please do.'

'Good. Good.' The doctor pushed too-large glasses up a long, sloping nose. 'First of all, you should know that total episodic memory loss, the type you're suffering from, is very rare. It hardly ever lasts more than a day or so. Given the relative mildness of your head injury – you weren't unconscious long – I'd expect to see a loss of, oh, maybe the hour immediately preceding the accident. The reason for that is those events wouldn't have had time to be transferred to long-term memory.' She paused. 'You understand these terms, don't you? I can explain.'

Chloe shook her head. So far she understood everything. She even knew that episodic memory was the memory of life events, as opposed to skills memory, which was the tasks one had learned to do: reading, driving, tying one's shoes. 'I think I must have gone to college,' she said.

Dr Perkins nodded in approval. 'Columbia, according to your husband. Anyway, the good news is you'll probably get everything back except, as I said, a short period of time previous to the accident.'

'And the bad news?'

The doctor beamed and wagged her finger as if Chloe had told a good joke. 'The bad news is you've been here three days and you ought to have started remembering already. Your husband tells me everything is still a blank?'

Chloe didn't want to mention the flashes she'd got, the dark, bony hands, the creeping sense of unease. Those weren't memories, after all. They were just fragments, feelings. She shrugged. 'I'm afraid so.'

The doctor couldn't quite reach Chloe, but she patted the stack of phone messages on the far side of her desk. 'Don't worry. It'll come back when you're ready. The point is, there's a chance your amnesia is, well, self-induced. There may have been some trauma associated with the accident that led your subconscious to engage in a wholesale repression, a clean sweep, if you will. Your husband admits it's a possibility.'

'He does?'

The doctor folded her hands beneath her chin. The pose seemed casual but, behind the thick corrective lenses, her eyes were keen. Chloe's nails pressed the wood veneer on the arms of her chair. Did the doctor think she was lying? Did she think she'd made this up?

'I'm afraid your husband wasn't particularly forthcoming about the details. Which is his right, of course.'

Dr Perkins sounded as if she disapproved. For some reason, this angered Chloe. 'The doctors warned him not to tell me things. They said I have to remember on my own.'

'Quite true, but if your husband is the cause of your trauma...'

'No!' Chloe jumped from her seat. Unfortunately, there was nowhere to go in the office. She knew it looked bad, but she couldn't help twisting her hands in David's sweater. 'I'm sure he didn't hurt me, or beat me, or whatever you're thinking. I'm sure I'd remember that.'

Dr Perkins rose and squeezed around her paper-strewn desk. She took Chloe's shoulders in raw, gentle hands. 'You might forget if you loved him enough, or if you thought you'd be helpless without his support. People often do. And David Imakita is a powerful man.'

Her words had the strangest effect, like being plunged under cold, murky water. She saw a young girl, scrubbed, her hair in braids and ribbons, sitting in a too-big chair. Her yellow plimsolls swung above the floor. *Daddy would never hurt anyone*, she said in a righteous little voice. Chloe wanted to strangle her.

She came back with a gasp.

'What is it? Did you remember something?'

Chloe massaged her chest. It was hard to talk. 'Just a flash. I don't know of what. But nothing to do with David. Oh, God!' She grabbed Dr Perkins' arm, her fingers digging into the unfortunate navy cardigan. 'I don't have kids, do I?'

'No-o,' said Dr Perkins. 'You haven't been married very long. Why do you ask?'

Chloe fumbled behind her for the chair, her knees too

rubbery to hold her. She sat on the creaky arm. Of course, she didn't have kids. That little girl wasn't David's. She couldn't be. David wouldn't hurt a child. 'I just thought how hard it would be if I had kids and I didn't remember them.'

'Yes,' said Dr Perkins, though she sounded suspicious. 'That would be awkward.' She peered closely at Chloe and Chloe willed herself not to blush. Finally, the doctor patted her shoulder. 'It does seem promising that you're getting flashes, however unnerving they might seem without a context to put them in. It will probably happen more often when you're among familiar surroundings. When you're ready, you might want to return to the scene of the accident. That can be a powerful trigger. Just remember not to force it. A relaxed, open mind is the most receptive to memory retrieval. Of course, if all else fails, you can always try knitting.'

Chloe smiled. 'Knitting?'

To her relief, the doctor twinkled back. 'Induces alpha waves in the brain. And now I'm afraid I really must be going.' She reached behind her to pull a business card from a small ceramic dish. She laid it in Chloe's palm and folded her fingers over it. 'This has both my office numbers, and my home phone. If I don't answer, my service will. They know how to handle emergencies, or minor snit-fits, if it comes to that. You can call any time, day or night. Remember, Chloe, you don't have to be alone. You don't have to feel helpless.'

Chloe nodded, her throat tight. The urge to lean on this nice, homely woman was almost as strong as her fear of doing so. 'I'm sure I'm not in any danger. My husband seems like a good man.' She remembered his tears. 'A compassionate man.'

'Oh, dear heart. I've met child molesters who presented like Mother Teresa. I hope you're right, though. I truly do. In any case, the biggest dangers usually come from here.' She touched Chloe's heart. 'Or from here.' Playfully, she rapped Chloe's forehead.

Chloe struggled to smile naturally. 'You mean we like to trip ourselves up.'

'Don't think of it that way. If your amnesia is self-induced, it's a protective mechanism. You have to trust that your subconscious meant well, even if it seems inconvenient right now.'

'So don't beat myself up for forgetting.'

'Precisely.' Dr Perkins rubbed her upper arm. 'One more thing. Don't be surprised if the oldest memories come back first, things that happened when you were a child, skills you learned young. Those memories are the most deeply engraved.'

Chloe saw the knife again, the arc of silver, the welling blood. Was it real or metaphor? Fighting a shudder, she shook the doctor's hand goodbye.

The oldest memories. She wondered just how painful getting them back would be.

Sato sat in his office behind the *dojo*. The furnishings were bare, the room unheated. Streams of December air trickled through the chinks in the plaster walls. He had neither computer nor phone, but this place was his, more than any other on the grounds. No one would bother him here. Here he could sit and think, though his brain did not seem up to the task at the moment.

He stared at his resignation. He had begun writing it as soon as he returned from The Seven Veils. The letter included a restructuring plan, as well as suggestions for who might be hired to replace him. It was logical and well thought-out. Resigning would save David the awkwardness of asking him to leave. It would save Sato the pain of watching David's friendship turn to wariness, to wondering what repellent desires lay behind Sato's words, Sato's glances, Sato's loyalty – such as it was.

Most of all, resigning would give Sato a chance to get over his infatuation. He needed that. He craved that like an insomniac craves sleep.

In spite of this, he opened the drawer to his battered wooden desk and dropped the resignation inside. He could not leave David now. David needed him. Humiliating as it was to admit, Chloe's brush with death had pushed anything to do with Sato from his master's mind. Sato had rocked David in his arms while Chloe lay in the hospital, offering a comfort David was too anguished to think twice about accepting.

'My last words to her were words of hate,' he said. 'If she dies . . .'

But she hadn't, and now David thought they had another chance to make it work. Wonder and hope had hushed his voice. 'All her emotional baggage is gone, Sato – the murder, her stripping, our fight – all of it swept clean, nothing left but who she always was inside. This is our chance to be close with none of that between us.'

'And when she remembers?'

David's hands had clenched. He turned away. 'When she remembers, if she remembers, we'll have new memories between us, memories that could help us heal. Don't you see? I have to try.'

Sato saw. Sato saw that the prospect of losing Chloe for ever had deepened David's love. David believed what his heart told him to believe. Sato knew better. A leopard was a leopard even if she lost her spots.

He would not leave his master alone with the beast.

13

The estate took her by surprise. The silent chauffeur, another Asian, as blocky and solid as a boulder, drove them through the wrought-iron gates and down a long avenue of boxwoods. The hedges were so tall they must have been growing for generations. From the front, David's residence resembled an overgrown Civil War farmhouse. The rough stone façade – real stones, not blocks or facing – rose four storeys. A queue of narrow, arched windows marched across each level. The top floor, where the roof sloped, had dormers.

Chloe half expected the ghost of Mrs Danvers to be hiding behind the curtains.

David took her elbow and helped her from the car. The house stood on a rise surrounded by rolling farm-land, only hinting at green this time of the year. Between the farms, isolated stands of trees followed the curves of the earth. Their winter-grey trunks did not obscure her view of a road ribboning off into the distance, a road entirely devoid of traffic.

A person could enjoy a lot of solitude out here.

Chloe's thumb nudged the diamond solitaire she wore on the third finger of her left hand. David had retrieved her valuables from the hospital before they left. They'd included a slim gold watch and this, a large diamond in a marquis cut. The stone was water-clear with lots of flash, not huge, but expensive. The band was loose. She supposed the cold explained the imperfect fit. David's wedding ring looked freshly polished.

'Shall we?' He gestured towards the imposing front

door. The knocker was a snarling Chinese dragon, the wood heavy, iron-bound planks. Chloe glanced back at the car. The chauffeur – Sato, David called him – already had her overnight bag.

Now there was a dangerous character, the perfect villain. All he lacked was a bowler hat with a razor-sharp blade in the rim. His eyes were cold, almost black, and his movements had a strange, slow grace. She bet none of his bulk was fat. She also bet he didn't like her: not good enough for his precious master. Most likely, no flesh and blood woman would be.

With an inward sigh, she followed the men inside. She barely noticed when David knelt, Prince Charming-style, to replace her shoes with wooden sandals. The spacious interior caught all her attention. Here were David's roots, a clean, modern taste of Japan. Two floors had been knocked together to form one large space at the front of the building. Cool white light flooded in from a plate-glass window that spanned the entire length of one wall. Through it, she saw both the crumbling shell of the old construction and the dips and swells of the landscape beyond.

Inside, dark wooden beams supported the walls. Plants dotted the room, ferns and ficuses and other greenery for which she had no name. The effect was lush but not overwhelming, a mannerly display. The area was split into levels. Gleaming oak floors stepped down to conversation pits, which stepped up to airy perches that probably had no purpose beyond providing a platform to admire the changing views. This was a sculpture one could live in.

With a feeling of reverence, Chloe entered the space, her felt-bottomed sandals shushing as she went. 'It's beautiful,' she said. 'Like something out of *Architectural Digest*.'

She stepped into an octagonal depression where a

Bokhara rug in muted gold and green warmed the floor. A sand-white sectional couch followed the curve of the steps. As she moved, a square of glass caught the light, a single photograph propped on an end table. She lifted the frame in both hands. The sepia print showed Asians in American uniform: World War II vintage, she thought. The man who knelt in the centre of the front row held a plaque that said '442nd Regimental Combat Team'.

Knowledge clicked as she touched the young, serious face. 'This is the all-Nisei regiment, from the internment camps, the most decorated unit in World War II.'

'Yes.' David was close enough behind her that she smelled the sweet spice of his bay rum soap. 'My mother was a girl at Manzanar. Her father enlisted when the call for volunteers went out. He thought it was the only way to stop his countrymen from thinking of Japanese-Americans as traitors. He survived, though he lost an arm in the fighting.'

He gazed at the picture and laid his finger precisely where hers had been, over the young soldier holding the plaque. 'This was my great-uncle, Auntie's brother. She lived in Japan then. It was hard on the family, having young men fighting on both sides. My other great-uncle was a kamikaze pilot.' He slanted a glance at her as if expecting her to disapprove.

'He fought for his country,' Chloe said. 'Just like your grandfather.'

'Yes.' His shoulder brushed hers. His muscles were hard beneath his soft brown pullover. Their warmth slid straight to her groin, as if a length of mink were being rubbed between her legs.

Uncomfortable with her reaction, she shifted her weight. 'You told me about your grandfather, didn't you? I must have remembered.'

'As far as I know, you've never asked about this picture before.' His eyes lifted to hers, bringing yet more heat to her vulnerable flesh. Such beautiful eyes he had. They were long under their narrow lids, lined as if with kohl by his curly lashes. She could not read what he was thinking, though he seemed to be thinking hard.

She laughed nervously. 'Well. I wonder how I knew.'

As soon as she said the words, a memory came. She was a young girl walking beside her mother with an armload of books so heavy her arms were dragging out of their sockets. Leaves scuffed underfoot and the smell of fall mingled with the must of ageing paper.

'Oh!' She cradled the photo to her chest. 'The library. We had a rule when I was a kid. We weren't allowed to check out more books than we could carry. I can still feel them in my arms. I had so many I was staggering.' She laughed. 'My mother used to tease me. "Sammy," she'd say. "You'll never read all those in two weeks." Then we'd bet. We'd bet for Baskin Robbins ice cream. Oh, David, I remembered something real.'

'Yes, you did.' His expression was warm and quiet. He didn't press her for more, which she appreciated. That bit was all she had. That bit, however, told her something else.

'I said "we", "we had a rule". I must have siblings.'

'You have two sisters, both younger than you.'

'Sisters.' She set down the photo for fear of dropping it in her excitement. 'Do you think I should call them? Will they be worried about me?'

He hesitated. 'You're ... estranged. I don't know much about your relationship.'

'Estranged.' An ache spread outwards from her heart. She might not remember them, but she remembered missing them. He'd said they were younger sisters. How could she, as the oldest, have let them grow apart? Wasn't it her responsibility to stay close to them, to protect them? What sort of big sister was she? She touched her throat with her hand. 'I suppose it wouldn't be a good idea to call them, since I don't remember why we're estranged.'

'It might be awkward,' David agreed. 'Perhaps we should see what you remember on your own before we try that.'

She bit her lower lip. 'That does sound sensible.'

'Hey.' He bent closer. 'No one says you have to be a prisoner of the past. If you want to mend that rift, you will.'

'But what if it was my fault? What if I did something bad?'

He stroked her hair behind her ear, his thumb following a gentle arc across her cheek. 'There's such a thing as forgiveness. For everyone.'

The caress stirred something. 'You've touched me this way before,' she said. 'I remember this.'

Smile lines bracketed his eyes. 'Good. I want you to remember happy things.'

'Are there unhappy ones?'

His expression sobered. He didn't answer. Because the doctors had warned him not to? Or because they hadn't been wallowing in marital bliss?

'I suppose every marriage has its rough spots.'

'Yes.' He wrapped his arm around her shoulders and gave her a bracing squeeze. 'Come on. I'll show you your room. You must be tired.'

Her room was on the third floor. Chloe's breath caught at the sight of it. It was lovely, with sliding doors that opened on to a covered veranda. The walls were a deep, earth green, a Japanese green, like tea that had been steeped a long time. Tightly woven tatami mats covered the floor. The bed, which lay on a low platform, was a comfortable-looking futon. A painted screen cordoned off one corner and a spectacular kimono hung opposite the bed as decoration. It, too, was green, with water lilies and carp swimming up its silken sides.

A small table stood to one side of the kimono's alcove. On it sat a small but stunning flower-arrangement. A mass of white gardenias spilled from a clever horizontal vase whose exterior was a rich, deep red. Three branches of greenery – azalea, she thought – curved in different directions around the flowers. The space they enclosed had a pleasing asymmetrical balance, as if the emptiness were part of the arrangement. She knew the effect wasn't accidental. Someone had posed every leaf. 'These are gorgeous,' she said.

David blushed. How delightful. He must be the *artiste*. How sweet of him to leave them for her homecoming. 'We, uh, moved your things in here,' he said. 'I thought you'd feel more comfortable, since you don't actually remember being my wife.'

Until he'd explained, she hadn't considered she ought to share his room. To her surprise, amusement bubbled inside her and, with it, an urge to tease. 'What?' she said, hand to breast. 'You want to deprive me of the thrill of sleeping with a stranger?' David looked startled. She covered her mouth. 'I'm sorry. I shouldn't make a joke of it. This must be hard on you, your own wife not remembering you. Honestly, you've shown the patience of a saint.'

He gazed down at his stocking feet as if embarrassed, then grinned. 'It's no hardship. I think I'll enjoy getting to know you again.'

Who could resist that boyish twinkle? Not she. Still, she let him leave without protest. Too many questions remained unanswered. There would be plenty of time to get close once she felt surer of herself and him. In the meantime, she had a room to explore. Who knew what might trigger another discovery? Not that she was in a hurry. Mostly, she wanted to prove Dr Perkins wrong. She wasn't traumatised. She wasn't repressing. She was just slow.

She opened the top drawer to a brown lacquerware bureau.

Underwear met her gaze, lace and silk, like Technicolor spiderwebs. She pawed through the heap, lifting items one by one. The neatly folded scraps hadn't been designed to cover much. There wasn't a plain white panty in sight, or a bra that didn't rely on advanced engineering. She had to admit they were pretty. Like a child counting treasures, she spread the lingerie in a rainbow across the bed. They posed a question: what sort of woman wore such racy undergarments? Answer: a woman who was sure of her looks.

That wasn't a bad thing, was it? To be sure of herself?

Come to think of it, though, what did she look like?

She wandered into the adjoining room. Strange. It had a sink and toilet, but no bath. A full-length mirror hung on the door. She faced herself. Her eyes caught her attention first, light-brown, sherry-coloured eyes. Her lashes were black and thick, her gaze haunted. She didn't see how a person could forget her own eyes, much less what had put those shadows beneath them.

You need a good night's sleep, she told her reflection. Then she took in the rest. Wow. She lifted her baggy sweater. Double wow. Her face broke into a grin. She was gorgeous, top to bottom gorgeous, not to mention one of very few women on the planet to appreciate her beauty as a stranger would. She was centrefold material. She compressed one creamy, uptilted breast and encountered nothing but softness. So. Her parts were original. What luck. She could use this.

The thought stopped her glee in its tracks. She dropped the woollen hem. Why did she have to 'use' her looks, as if they were a weapon? Why couldn't she just enjoy them; be glad she had them to share?

Frowning, she returned to the bedroom and peered

behind the folding screen. There she found an old-fashioned desk, with a curved top and cubbyholes. She swung into the rolling chair. A leather-bound book lay on the blotter. Gold embossed lettering declared it 'THE SEVEN VEILS ACCOUNTS.' Inside was a neat listing of expenses for a business. A restaurant, she thought, though she wondered what sort of workers 'Performance Staff' might be. Whoever they were, they earned much more than 'Wait Staff'. The business seemed to be making money, though it had not paid off its debts. Curious, she scribbled a few words on an envelope. Yes, these accounts were written in her handwriting. The Seven Veils must be her business ... unless she was a bookkeeper, which – given her taste in underwear – she sincerely doubted.

She stroked the smooth, ruled pages. Imagine, she'd written all this out by hand. Surely she knew how to use a computer. Yes. If she closed her eyes, she could feel the keys beneath her fingers. This account book was kept for pleasure, then. Something she could carry home with her. She snorted. Maybe she slept with it under her pillow.

But a business. That was a good thing. She was gainfully employed. She didn't spend her days mooching off her powerful husband. Although – she tapped the edge of the leather portfolio – if she had a business, she'd need to get back to it soon. If her memory didn't return, she could only hope she had enough ingrained skills to get by.

With a quiet sigh, she pressed onward. The cubbyholes at the top of the desk revealed account statements from several brokerage houses, all in the name of Chloe Dubois. Dubois. Her brow furrowed. She supposed she'd kept her maiden name. Well, no crime in being a modern woman. She pulled out the folded pages. The balances widened her eyes. The withdrawals had been significant as she poured capital into her business. Nonetheless, this was a good deal of money. Was she some sort of heiress, or had she earned it? A now familiar tension tightened her belly. Memory shimmered. She saw a metal pole between her hands; felt muscles strain as she swung her weight off the ground. The air curled with smoke as dark as her sense of triumph.

Later, she thought, and shuddered the image away. She'd deal with that memory later, when she had a context for it. She opened the bottom right-hand drawer. She found a closed laptop and, under that, a ream of blank white paper. She closed the drawer, then opened it again, nagged by something out of place. There was no printer here, so why was there paper? It wasn't stationery. Her pulse picked up a notch. She lifted out the laptop and the paper. Neatly arranged beneath were more account statements, slit open, but still in their mailing envelopes. They bore the return address of a large Swiss bank.

With a sense of dread, she slipped out their contents. Good Lord. Her elbow clunked on to the desk as she pored over them. Her mind converted the amounts to American dollars with a facility she didn't have the presence of mind to wonder at. *Oy*. One point two mill. One of the envelopes contained a personal letter from her account executive, in German. She translated that just as easily as she had the money. He called her *Fraulein* D and congratulated her on taking advantage of the falling yen; said next time he'd 'take a flyer' with her. He sounded young, which made sense. A million was nothing to a Swiss bank. She probably had a junior, junior trader overseeing her account. But she was buying and selling currency? Where did she get the balls? Most of all, what had happened to her money while she was in the hospital?

She reached for the sleek black phone, halfway towards dialling a long international number she didn't even know she knew. With an effort, she stopped herself. She was breathing hard, almost panting. She looked at the records again. It was all right. Most of her money was in high-grade bonds. She'd only risked a portion on speculative ventures, a portion she could afford to lose until she remembered what the hell she was doing.

Good Lord. She pressed her shaking hand over her pounding heart. A person would have thought that money was her firstborn child. She slid the statements back into their envelopes and returned them to the bottom of the drawer. She hesitated, then replaced both the ream of paper and the laptop. She didn't know why she wanted to hide these assets but, until she did, she wouldn't feel comfortable leaving them in the open.

A sound from behind the screen snapped her away from the desk. She let her breath out slowly, then walked around the barrier.

A small Japanese woman in a crisp blue and white kimono was folding her scattered underwear. She had knelt before the futon to do it, with her feet tucked under her bottom. She didn't look up when Chloe appeared. Her movements were so sharp, her grey-streaked bun wiggled on her head. 'You shouldn't leave these out,' she said. 'The moths will get them.'

'They were only there for a little while. I wanted to see what sort of clothes I own.' She sat on the futon so she could see the woman's face. 'My husband must have told you I lost my memory. I'm afraid I don't remember your name.'

'Your husband,' said the woman, then muttered something foreign, something derogatory from the sound of it. Chloe didn't understand a word. Apparently, Japanese wasn't among the languages she knew.

'Excuse me?'

The woman snapped out a bra before folding it atop

the others. 'You may call me Auntie. Just like everyone else.'

Chloe touched her arm. 'Are you angry with me? Did I do something to you?'

'David-san says we must not answer your questions. He says you must find your memories yourself.'

'And you always do what David-san tells you?' She wasn't sure where her anger came from, but it was more than annoyance at being kept from her own past.

As Chloe's temper rose, the woman called Auntie calmed. She set down a pair of red silk panties and stroked them with crooked fingers. 'I owe ... your husband my life,' she said, then turned to Chloe with a smile that lifted all the lines of her weathered face. She had been a beauty once. Bone structure like that didn't lie. The glow in her eyes still charmed. 'Six years ago, I needed an operation no Japanese doctors were doing. David-san arranged for me to come to the US. He paid my bills. He flew specialists in on his jet. Every day, he came to visit and hold my hand, even though we had never met before I travelled to this country. When I recovered, I offered my humble services as the keeper of his house.'

'But you're his aunt.' Chloe was appalled by the idea of this elderly relative scrubbing his floors.

'To work is honourable, especially to work in payment for a debt.' She placed Chloe's underwear in the drawer and closed it gently. Without turning, she said, 'I must leave now. I have a meal to oversee. Please tell one of the servants if you need anything.'

Chloe was glad to hear she had help. Maybe David's aunt wasn't scrubbing floors. Then something else struck her. 'Auntie? If there are other servants, why were you folding my underwear?'

'I wanted to see if you truly had lost your memory.'

'And?' Chloe said, thinking she must be some piece of work if this woman thought she was faking her amnesia.

Auntie considered her, eyes narrow, mouth pursed. Chloe fought an urge to squirm under the examination. She couldn't help feeling this old woman saw straight to her soul – which was more than Chloe could do. After what seemed like an eternity, the housekeeper nodded. It was not precisely a nod of approval. 'You are different,' she said. 'But underneath you are what you always were.'

Her words bore the weight of a curse. Chloe resented the hell out of that, but she couldn't prove she didn't deserve it.

The chauffeur came to dinner. He was a personal friend of her husband, or so David claimed. They were awfully stiff for bosom buddies. David's aunt knelt in the doorway like a servant of the shogun. Every so often she would slide open the partitioned door and accept a covered dish from one of the other servants. When she placed it on the table, she would bow.

'Is she for real?' Chloe whispered.

'It's her way,' David said. 'She was trained as a geisha.'

'But she's not your geisha. She's your aunt, and she's eighty if she's a day. Good Lord, can you imagine what that does to her knees?'

'Her knees are probably stronger than yours,' said Sato, the first words he'd uttered beyond 'pass the fish'.

'Yes, well, I'm sure she's superior to me in every way. That doesn't mean she ought to kow-tow to her own nephew.'

David set his chopsticks down. 'The way she behaves satisfies her sense of honour, not mine. She takes pride in serving well.'

Chloe shook her head at her sauce-smeared plate. She

could see she wasn't going to earn any points with this argument. Honest to God, though, she couldn't stand to see a woman kiss a man's boots that way. She stabbed her fork at a little heap of shrimp. Servile women. The burn of anger told her she knew something about that, though not, perhaps, from personal experience. No. She was more the type to make a man bow down to her.

But anger wasn't going to get her anywhere. She reminded herself that being disliked made a person vulnerable. She forced herself to breathe more slowly, to pay attention to what she was eating. This food was good, she decided. The tastes were simple but fresh, and – really – who cared what she ate so long as she didn't have to cook it?

She waited until the rice was served – two big, steaming bowls of it – before she asked about The Seven Veils. 'I have a business, don't I?'

'Uh, yes,' said David, and spooned a small portion of rice into a clean dish.

Sato heaped a big, sticky mound on to his, as if he hadn't just eaten a six-course meal. 'You have a dinner theatre,' he said, his tone oddly insinuating.

'I guess that explains the entry in my account book for Performance Staff.'

Sato's snort changed abruptly to a grunt. Chloe suspected David had kicked him under the table. 'You don't have to worry about that,' David said. 'Your business will keep until you get back on your feet. I'll keep an eye on it for you.'

Chloe swallowed her ire and let him pat her hand. Don't worry your pretty little head, she thought. She was beginning to see a pattern here. First Auntie, and now Sato, and hadn't Dr Perkins mentioned that David wasn't 'forthcoming'? Chances seemed good the entire staff had been ordered not to talk about her past. Maybe David was following doctor's orders, but maybe, just maybe, he didn't want her to remember who she was.

David had calls to make after dinner, so Chloe wandered the house in search of clues to the time she'd spent here. Dr Perkins had said be patient, but she was too stubborn to let David have his way, assuming he did wish to keep her in ignorance. She didn't know why he'd want that unless he'd done her harm. Or perhaps she'd witnessed some shady business deal? Neither seemed likely on the surface, but she knew there were currents here she didn't understand.

She explored a long corridor on the second floor where exquisite Japanese dolls sat in spotless glass cases. Their porcelain faces stirred mixed emotions: delight and something that might have been envy. Clearly, David was fascinated by the geisha.

Was this what other wives felt on discovering their husbands' *Penthouse* stash? Was submission what David wanted in a partner? Was that what lay behind his apparent desire to keep her helpless?

Like a thief who fears discovery, she slipped past the open door to the library where David was making his calls. Her heart pounded as the stairs creaked under her feet. When she reached the third floor, she found a long bare room, empty of furnishings apart from an elaborate stereo system. Awareness quivered just out of reach. She'd done something here, something dangerous. Through the window at the end, she saw a dark gravel garden. Without knowing why, she hurried towards it, shoved up the heavy window, then strode past the moonlit boulders to a stucco wall. Knees shaking, she leaned out and sucked clean, cold air into her lungs. Her exhalations turned to ghostly curls of silver. Rather than go back inside, she shoved her hands under her arms.

A decorative garden spread out across the grounds below, ponds and pines and an arched wooden bridge like a postcard from Japan. None of it seemed familiar, not one stone, not one tree. Fine with me, she thought. Who wants to remember?

Then she shook her head. What was she so afraid of? Of what would happen if she didn't get her memories back? Or what would happen if she did? She set her jaw. She would get them back. She'd face whatever they were. She wasn't a coward.

At least, she didn't think she was.

'You'll catch your death,' said David's voice.

She spun around. He was a tall silhouette backlit by the room behind him. A wave of terror rolled through her, black and suffocating. On his hand a gold ring glistened. *Mary Alice isn't feeling well.* She cried out and closed her eyes. Whatever was coming, she didn't want to see.

'Hey,' he said. 'Hey.' He wrapped something around her, an afghan, the sort that always hangs in a triangle from the back of a couch. 'I didn't mean to scare you. Are you OK?' She nodded against his chest, curling close. He rubbed her through the blanket. 'You're freezing.'

But she wasn't shaking from the cold.

Without stopping to think, she wrapped her arms around his waist. His body was lean and hard, so hard there seemed nothing to him but sinew and bone. This shouldn't have been comforting, but he was warm and when he pressed his lips so gently to her hair she thought she never wanted to leave his side.

'Maybe I ought to scare you more often,' he teased, his lips wandering down to her ear.

Desire slammed through her as abruptly as fear had. The blanket slipped unheeded to the ground as she turned her face to catch the brushing journey of his mouth. He stiffened, then kissed her once, chaste and soft. 'It's too soon,' he said, his voice both tense and husky.

She slid her hands up the warm cotton back of his shirt, feeling muscle and spine and wonderfully broad shoulders. Her hands tingled with pleasure. She slid them down to cup the hard, narrow rounds of his buttocks. His breathing changed. She squeezed. Motion brushed her belly, his erection rising between them. Chloe smiled. This power was something she knew, something she was sure of. She drew a circle on his buttocks and felt his penis lurch. 'Maybe a kiss would help me remember.'

His answer was choked. 'I don't want to rush you until you're sure of what you feel.'

She pushed her hips closer, rocking them into his. Her body was ready to take him, more than ready. Everything between her legs was soft and wet and hot. She hooked her calf behind his and gave her clit the friction it was aching for. 'I'm sure I want you,' she purred.

For a moment he let her grind them together, his eyes closed, his breath coming in broken gasps. Then he stepped back. 'Wanting isn't enough,' he said. He pulled her hands from his backside and pressed a kiss to her knuckles. His expression conveyed regret, but it was also wary.

'You don't trust me,' she said, stunned and sick at heart.

His silence was more eloquent than words.

14

David woke at sunrise, miserably aroused from a dream of Chloe. He had no idea how to handle her. His path had seemed so simple in the hospital when he'd opened his mouth and the words 'you're my wife' fell out. He'd planned to court her, win her, and then – when she'd fallen in love – gently break the truth.

But she wasn't the blank slate he'd expected. True, she was different from before. She seemed less brittle, her vulnerability more in the open. But the old Chloe hadn't been erased, even if her memories had. He folded his hands over his belly. The warmth beating outwards from his sex tangled with his thoughts like vines.

The old Chloe had kissed him last night. When he'd hardened at her touch, triumph had flared in her eyes. She loved the power she had over him, over men. But he'd seen a new Chloe, too. That Chloe had betrayed an interest in his past; had worried whether she might have hurt her sisters. That Chloe told stories of long-ago trips to the library, of books too interesting to leave behind, and a mother who rewarded her for reading them. For the first time, he could imagine her as a child: fiercely curious, smart-mouthed, no doubt, but loved and loving. She seemed more connected to the girl she'd been, now that she'd forgotten her. The old Chloe had hidden that sweetness. The new Chloe set it free.

But which Chloe was real? More to the point, could he trust either one?

Too agitated to face his T'ai Chi Ch'uan exercise, he headed for the kitchen. Auntie was there before him, preparing tea. He kissed her good morning and cocked one eyebrow at the chef. The man was slicing bagels and bacon. 'A *gaijin* breakfast, Auntie?'

She pushed her lips out. 'Comfort food.'

'Why would you think I need comforting?'

'Hah. Maybe I want to comfort your "wife".'

'I'd be happy to believe that, but I don't, not with the way you've been acting since she returned.'

Auntie hung a teaball in a pot of scalding water, covered it, and turned over an egg timer. 'I'm ashamed of you,' she said. 'This is the kind of lie *she* would tell.'

He laid his hands on her tight, narrow shoulders. He didn't have to ask who 'she' was. 'It's just for a while, Auntie. I promise I'll tell her the truth when the time is right.'

'And when will that be? When she breaks your heart again?' She shoved the tin of tea back into its spot. 'I have seen you worrying over her. I know she did something cruel to Sato. He's been dragging his tail like a man who cannot find a second to hold his sword.'

David's face heated under a surge of guilt. He and Sato needed to talk about what had happened, but he simply couldn't face his friend until he'd unsnarled this muddle with Chloe. He smoothed a strand of Auntie's hair into her bun. 'Sato is not suicidal.'

'If he isn't, it's only because he is sticking around to see what that viper will do next.'

'Don't call her a viper, Auntie. Anyway –' he strove for lightness '– she can't do anything. She doesn't remember how.'

'Trust me, David-san. Some things a woman never forgets.'

Breakfast, at least, improved his mood. Cream cheese and bacon topped his bagel: not health food, perhaps, but food for the soul. He chomped through the crusty, creamy, salty combination and decided he'd found nirvana. As if in agreement, the sun shone through the slatted windows to beam a blessing on his face. Last night's frost rimed the gardens, but here in the dining room all was warm and well. For once, Auntie's infernal teapot was absent. An urn of coffee sat on a celadon trivet, accompanied by freshly squeezed orange juice and a basket of bagels the chef must have flown in from New York. Chloe sat around the corner from him, sipping coffee from a china cup. She looked sleepy but beautiful. He was pleased she'd woken early enough to join him. Her return might not be going as he'd expected, but her presence added savour to his morning.

With some amusement, he noticed she avoided the bacon. He'd watched her consume it many times before. Perhaps getting conked on the head had revivified her sense of what a nice Jewish girl ought to eat. Next time, he'd ask the chef to order lox.

He saw she'd nabbed another of his sweaters. Her small frame swam in it, but her skin glowed against the mossy green. This was an encouraging development. She wanted to be near to him, if only through his clothes.

She waited until he'd taken a second bite to shatter his optimism. 'I want to go to The Seven Veils,' she said.

His heart plummeted. 'I thought we decided –'

'No. You decided.' She set down her knife. He could see she was trying to keep her temper. 'I just want to walk around; see if anything looks familiar. I know the club was important to me. Maybe it will spark something the house hasn't.'

'All right, I'll go with you.'

'No!' Her voice was sharp, perhaps sharper than she wished because she reached out to squeeze his hand. 'I appreciate the gesture, but you'll only make me nervous. I need to stay calm if I'm going to get any good out of this.'

He swallowed what felt like a boulder-sized lump of bagel. Was his second chance going to fall apart so soon? She'd only been home a day.

His thoughts must have shown on his face, because hers twisted with sympathy. 'Oh, baby,' she said, the endearment startling him as much as the hand that cupped his cheek. 'Don't be hurt. I want to remember for your sake, too. You deserve to have your wife back.'

Don't do me any favours, he thought, but he was caught in a noose of his own making. All he could do was nod – and try to come up with damage control.

David wouldn't loan her a car without a driver. His protectiveness set her back up but, even with directions, she wasn't sure she could find the place. At least he didn't ask Sato to drive her, though the chauffeur she got grinned far too much for comfort. He spent half his time leering at her in the mirror as if they'd –

No. She pushed the suspicion away. Maybe she'd flirted with the man. Just because she wore dental floss for underwear didn't mean she slept around.

The drive was long and quiet. Snow had fallen in the mountains the night before, carpeting the woods on either side. She slipped into a daze as she watched the grey-white landscape form a rolling tunnel around the car. She remembered David's kiss, the tautness of his buttocks under her palms, his erection prodding her belly. Her flesh pulsed at the remembered sensations. Whatever had been wrong with their relationship, it wasn't sex. Her hand wandered to the skin above her cashmere scarf, fingers stroking her throat as her mind drifted to all the things she wanted David's soft, gentle mouth to do.

The driver glanced knowingly in the mirror. She responded with an icy stare. He flushed to the tips of his ears.

Now that was a useful skill. She pondered where she might have learned it until they reached their destination.

The Seven Veils inspired a smile. Her inn, a sprawling white structure with black keyhole shutters and snow-covered swings on the veranda, was as wholesome as a Norman Rockwell painting. As charmed as she was amused, she stepped from the car. A weathervane in the shape of a rooster spun lazily on the roof. Everything appeared well kept. The shrubs were clipped, the paint fresh. Obviously, she'd taken pride in this enterprise. Mine, she thought, wondering at it all. This place is mine.

She told the cheeky driver to wait in the car. The limo had a heater, after all, and he was getting paid to shuttle her around.

Her key slid neatly into the heavy black door. Inside was a bristly straw mat. The walks hadn't been shovelled so she stomped her boots free of snow. She'd worn jeans and another too-big sweater of David's. None of her clothes were as comfortable as his and she hadn't wanted to dress up. This was just a visit, not a working day. All the same, her skin tingled with adrenalin as she gazed around the empty lobby.

It was decorated for Christmas. A Douglas fir, complete with presents and angel, sat in the centre of the domed space. Pine boughs framed the doors. Nestled among the greenery were real oranges, their skins spiked with cloves. Their scent perfumed the air and her stomach rumbled, despite the breakfast she'd packed in. Had she missed the holiday, or was it still to come? Lord, now she knew how Rip Van Winkle felt.

A burst of laughter floated out from what appeared to be the dining room. People, she thought, people who'd expect her to know them. Hands suddenly cold, she followed the sound. I'm not a coward, she reminded herself. I'm not a –

Six young faces looked up in unison, three men and three women, all attractive.

The actors, she thought, noting their bohemian dress. They sat at a round table near the stage. Like the rest of the forty-odd tables, this was bare of linen. Forty tables, she mused, with an average of six guests per table. Figures danced through her mind, her account book coming alive. As if it were no more complicated than tying her shoes, she weighed the cost of laundry, catering, staff, insurance, mortgage and maintenance against the income from two performances, one weekend a month at five hundred bucks per head.

The totals were impressive. They told her The Seven Veils had drawn a full house for every show. What sort of dinner theatre delivered that kind of attendance? Or charged that much for tickets?

But there was no time to solve the mystery because one of the performers, a young man with sandy hair and a neat goatee, leaped from his seat and threw out his arms. His beret nearly fell off his head. 'Miss Chloe! Thank God you're back. Come help us brainstorm. We're trying to work up an idea for next month's show but it's really lame.'

'It is not lame,' said a stunning woman with bobbed black hair and cool grey eyes.

'Puh-lease,' said Mr Goatee. '"Cowboy Carmen"?'

As the two continued to argue, an elegant Latino pulled another chair into their circle. He offered it to Chloe. Before she could sit, the third man – a freckled redhead with arms like a lumberjack – took her coat. The courtesy brought a glow to her cheeks. At least she hadn't fouled this nest. Everyone seemed happy to see her. A tiny blonde with Dresden-blue eyes reached over to pat her knee. 'Welcome back,' she whispered under cover of the bickering.

'Thank you,' Chloe said. 'But I'm not sure you realise I don't –'

'Sure we do,' boomed Mr Goatee. 'This morning, Mr Imakita, your *husband*, broke the news of your unfortunate accident. Warned us not to shock you with too many lurid details from your past.' He planted his hands on his hips and played drag queen. 'You know, you might have told us you got married. We would have thrown a party.'

Annoyed by David's interference, Chloe tried to pull her thoughts together. She tugged the sleeves of his sweater farther down her wrists. 'Um, well, since I don't remember why I didn't tell you, I don't know if I should apologise.'

'Of course, you shouldn't,' said the Latino gentleman. 'Your private life is just that.' He flattened one brown hand across his chest. 'Please allow me to do the honours. I am Fernando. This adorable blonde is Sheryl. Lauren is our icy-eyed femme fatale.' The woman with the raven bob nodded. 'Here is Gina of the long brown hair, the freckle-faced farmboy is Chuck, and, loath as I am to introduce him, the oaf with the beard is Harry.'

'Thank you so much,' Harry lisped. He leaned across the table, his eyes bright, his ego uncrushed. 'Is it really true? You can't remember anything?'

'Bits and pieces, but not a clear picture, no.'

'So you don't, like, know who we are?'

'I'm afraid not.'

'Freaky,' Harry marvelled.

Chloe couldn't help but laugh. She might not remember these people, but she felt more at home than she had since leaving the hospital. The camaraderie wrapped her like an old pair of jeans. But maybe this was a form of remembering, emotion coming back minus the events that had inspired it. She wished she could call Dr Perkins and ask, but she didn't want the good doctor passing judgement on her. Actually, she didn't want anyone passing judgement on her.

'So.' She rubbed her hands together. 'Tell me about Cowboy Carmen. It sounds intriguing.'

Pale-eyed Lauren couldn't resist elbowing Harry's ribs. 'See,' she said, then turned to Chloe. 'The scene opens in a Texas honkytonk, Carmen's Place. She's a señorita from south of the border. All the men are in love with her, but she refuses to tie herself down.'

'Remind you of anyone?' Harry teased.

Fernando nabbed his beret and slapped his shoulder with it.

Lauren tipped up her nose and went on. 'Carmen's lovers have always accepted her independence, until she sleeps with the son of a local landowner. After one night together, he thinks he owns her. He sees her dancing with the ranch hands and is so enraged he throws her over his shoulder and carries her out.'

'That's the lame part,' laughed Gina of the long brown hair.

'That's the good part,' Harry insisted. 'Women love masterful men. So he sweeps her off to the ranch and ravishes her. And, of course, she loves it so much she swears to be true to him for ever.'

'Dream on,' Lauren scoffed. 'If you think you're going to ravish one of us, you're nuts.'

Harry folded his arms and grinned. 'You'll do it if Miss Chloe says you should.'

Chloe blinked. Suddenly the pieces were falling into place. This wasn't a cosy, Mousetrap-type theatre. This was a sex show. That's why the place was packed. That's why she got away with charging outrageous prices. These nice young people were copulating for an audience. She waited for disgust to swell inside her, but oddly enough it didn't. The whole thing made her laugh. Cowboy Carmen. How wonderfully silly it was, and how well it would play if she paired Harry and Lauren as the sparring couple. It would be hot as well as funny. The audience would eat it up.

'So what do you think?' asked Fernando, his dark eyes resting on her face with flattering warmth. Unlike the chauffeur, his expression made no claims to intimacy.

She tapped her fingers together. 'I think you need a new ending.'

'Told you!' Lauren gloated. This time Harry elbowed her.

Chloe smiled. 'I think Carmen should pretend she's going to let the cowboy ravish her. Then, at the last minute, she trips him up and ties him to the bedposts. Standing up, of course, so the audience can see.'

'Hm.' Gina warmed to the idea. 'Cowboy Carmen Bondage.'

'Then she can torment him,' Lauren said.

'Dance for him –'

'Remove her clothing piece by piece while he gets harder and harder –'

'Then she ravishes him?' Harry suggested.

Silent laughter lifted Chloe's chest. 'Then I think she gives him a taste of the whip.'

'Ooh.' Gina's eyes glowed. 'S&M Cowboy Carmen Bondage.'

Harry groaned.

Chuck slapped him on the back, his lumberjack's wallop driving the air from his lungs. 'Buck up, Harry. You have to admit it's kinkier this way.'

When Harry buried his face in his hands, Chloe reached across the table to tug his sandy forelock. 'What do you think, Harry? Could you get it up for the sting of leather, or are you strictly a vanilla sort of guy?'

'I don't know,' he muttered grudgingly. 'Maybe.'

Gina, who sat on the other side of him from Lauren, peered into his lap. 'Maybe, hell. He's splitting his seams just talking about it.'

A current flowed around the table as everyone registered what she'd said. Harry was aroused. Harry was secretly interested in having Lauren whip him. Chloe felt as if someone had slid a sleek, warm finger up her sex. She was wet, soft, and the sight of the lovely flushed faces that surrounded her only made her more so. This was the power they would share with the audience. This was the magic they could create.

She took Harry's hand between her own and gently stroked its palm. 'Don't worry, Lauren will make sure your initiation is a pleasant one.'

He looked up, his green eyes wide and vulnerable. 'Will you train her?'

The question took her by surprise. 'Me?'

'Oh, do!' Lauren agreed. 'I don't want to fake it. I want to know how a pro swings a whip. You can help me with the stripping part, too. I've done a little, but only for fun and, God, you were, like, a legend. My big brother used to drive to Atlantic City every summer to –'

Fernando cleared his throat.

'Oh, shit.' Lauren pressed her hands to her mouth. 'We weren't supposed to talk about that.'

Chloe's face went cold with shock. She'd been a stripper? A *legendary* stripper? That was why Harry wanted her to train Lauren? Oh, but it all made sense. She'd remembered the sensation of pole-dancing; the invisible, hard-breathing crowd; holding the audience in the palm of her hand. The power had been an aphrodisiac, the control – just like when she'd kissed David last night.

No wonder he'd been reluctant to have her come here. Obviously, he preferred she leave that life behind.

But what was the harm in what she was doing? Her

little troupe was happy, healthy, eager for a new challenge. If what they did was trash, then it was fun trash. She suspected that maybe, just maybe, it was something more. Why couldn't sex be art and art be fun? Sex was important. Sex had been affecting human affairs since there had been human affairs. Sex was mysterious and complicated and frightening. Sex was conflict and drama. Sex was a perfect subject for theatre.

David had no right to be ashamed of her, no right at all.

Fernando squeezed her rigid shoulder. 'Are you OK?'

She blinked back the sting of passion. 'Yes, it was just a surprise. I'd remembered a little, but...' Her voice trailed away.

'I am so sorry,' Lauren said. 'What an idiot!'

'No. No harm done.' She stood, suddenly feeling disconnected from the cosy group. 'I'm going to walk around the place; refamiliarise myself. You guys keep at it. You're doing fine.'

As she left, she heard them squabbling again but paid them little mind. A stripper. What else would her memories turn up? Her thoughts in turmoil, she wandered through a large, empty kitchen and down a long, dim hall. The wind whistled around the building. Now that she'd left the reach of her employees' voices, the place had an abandoned air. It needed people to bring it to life, food and drink and music.

A small brass plaque marked the door at the end of the hall. MANAGEMENT, it said. Well, that was her. Chloe pushed it open and squinted against the light pouring in the French windows. The sun had come out. Its effect on the inch of snow outside was blinding. Eyes watering, she hung her coat on the hook she found behind the door.

Once her vision adjusted, she took in the room. She didn't know what she'd expected after the revelations of the past half-hour, but not this. Her office boasted a mahogany desk a banker could have sat behind, a separate console for her computer, a contoured leather chair, and a row of three tall black filing cabinets. A single picture hung from the wall, a reproduction of Toulouse-Lautrec's *At the Moulin Rouge*. That alone marked this the office of an entertainer, though Elvis on velvet seemed more like what a topless dancer would choose.

Former topless dancer, she corrected, though she wasn't entirely sure that was the case.

She sank into the moulded chair and swivelled from side to side.

She'd bared her body for men, for the thrill of manipulating their emotions and, of course, their wallets. Clearly, she liked money. What she didn't know was why she liked it so much, to the point of obsession, really. She paged through a pile of receipts waiting to be filed, but found no answer there. She flipped on her computer and scrolled through a long guest list. It read like a politician's donor file. Someone had made notes beside the club members' names: their occupations, their preferences in drinks and seating. She found promotional copy she'd used for previous performances. The titles sparked nothing but curiosity. *The Pool Game. Busted. Big Man on Campus. The Chinaman's Folly.*

The scope of what she'd forgotten amazed her. She didn't look forward to learning it all again from scratch. Then she remembered the way she'd called up the figures from her account book. Evidently, she had a photographic memory. Lord. She was an amnesiac stripper with a university education and a mind like a steel trap. Could the irony get any thicker?

She spun her chair backwards, meaning to calm herself by gazing out the window. As she did, she caught sight of what the file cabinets hid: another door, a plain, new door without the handsome detailing that marked the club's original construction.

What now? she thought as she rose to investigate.

The door opened on to a long, narrow cell that ran parallel to her office. With arms outspread, she could touch both windowless walls. A bare sixty-watt bulb revealed a wooden table, a VCR and a small TV. Four tapes lay on the table, recordings of The Seven Veils' shows.

Chloe took the hard little chair and ignored her jumpy stomach. This was her chance to see how down and dirty her theatre got. She began to slide *Busted* into the VCR's maw. Then she noticed the tape that should have been labelled *The Chinaman's Folly*. It bore the name *Sato's Folly* instead.

Had she bullied the chauffeur into performing? Was that why he didn't like her? There was only one way to find out. She pushed the tape into the slot.

The drama that unfolded wasn't anything she'd imagined. Worse, the sick feeling in her gut told her the story held more than a kernel of truth. Sato had attended this performance, and David. She'd recorded their names on her guest list. 'Likes champagne,' she'd noted next to Sato.

'Hopelessly in love with employer,' she should have said.

'Shit.' She punched the rewind button. What a cruel thing to do, not only to Sato but to David. If she could trust the implications of the tape, David hadn't known his friend had a crush on him any more than he'd known his wife was sleeping around. No wonder those two were awkward around each other. No wonder Sato mistrusted her. He had every reason to.

She pressed her temples. She was a bitch, a calculating, coldhearted –

Her hands dropped as one more revelation pierced her agitated brain.

David had forgiven her, or – at the very least – he wanted to. He'd been patience itself with her, showing her nothing but kindness since the accident. When had he put his fury behind him? Before the accident? Because of the accident? Had she conned him into it somehow? Was he that stupid, or that saintly? And how in the world could she bring herself to ask?

The tape finished rewinding with a hiss. She pulled it out and tapped it against her palm.

In light of this discovery, her suspicions about David seemed ridiculous. As far as her marriage went, one thing was clear. David wasn't the villain of the piece. She was.

15

The housekeeper didn't want to tell her where Sato was. She actually pretended she didn't know.

Chloe put her smooth hand over the gnarled one that was polishing the kitchen counter. Auntie looked up, her expression managing to convey both innocence and ire. The latter Chloe was willing to believe. 'Auntie,' she chided. Apparently, the tone worked, because Auntie's glance cut guiltily away. 'I know you know where Sato is or, if you don't, you could find out in five minutes. I've been here long enough to know who's got her finger on this household's pulse.'

'I'm very busy,' Auntie said, going back to her scrubbing. 'I don't know when I will have five minutes.'

'It's come to my attention that I owe Sato an apology.'

Auntie rubbed harder at an invisible stain. 'Memory coming back, is it?'

'No. But this apology won't wait until it does.'

'Hmph.' Auntie threw the rag in the sink. 'You're right about one thing. I know the people of this house. I may not know how, but you hurt Sato. I'm not going to help you do it again.'

'I promise, Auntie, I only want to talk to him. I'll do my best not to hurt anyone.'

Auntie pinned her with button-bright eyes. As she had that day in her bedroom, Chloe felt as if her soul were being stripped. 'You fooled me once,' Auntie said.

'Look.' Chloe gripped the edge of the counter. 'I can't prove I'm on the level now, but Sato is a grown man, and as likely as you are to be on his guard. Please,

Auntie. Sato and I need to air this out, if only to give him a chance to yell at me.'

Auntie opened the refrigerator and pulled out a covered tray. Chloe thought she'd failed, that Auntie was dismissing her, but she pushed the tray into Chloe's hands. 'You may bring him his lunch. He is in the basement taking a shift with the security cameras.'

'Thank you,' Chloe said. Now all she had to do was keep her word.

The surveillance room was a windowless bunker with shiny navy walls. Sato sat in front of a semi-circular console that would have been at home on the bridge of a space ship. A computer monitor was recessed into its tilted, stainless steel surface, a touchscreen from the looks of it. Chloe goggled at the bank of televisions. They showed live images of the gates, the grounds, and various entries to the house. Every thirty seconds, the scenes changed.

She'd had no idea David was so security-conscious.

Sato crossed his arms. 'Are you going to give me my lunch or stand in the door gaping?'

She set the tray on a little table beside the console, her eyes still held by the monitors. 'Auntie said I could bring this.' She watched a groundsman raking leaf clutter from the garden, a good-looking young man, completely unaware he was being observed. Her thighs tightened. A trickle of warmth dampened her panties. This was turning her on. The question was on her lips before she could think better of it. 'Are there cameras in the bedrooms?'

'Why? So you can sneak down here and watch them?'

'Probably,' she said, then laughed. Everything considered, she shouldn't have found her answer funny. Sato certainly didn't. He glowered like a *kabuki* villain. She bit her lip, the imp still driving her. 'You didn't answer my question, Sato. Are there cameras in the bedrooms? As a resident, I think I have a right to know.'

His jaw tightened. 'Only in David's bedroom, and David has the ability to turn them off.'

Chloe didn't have to ask whether he'd spied on his employer. Could any human being resist watching his beloved sleep? A flush crawled up Sato's bullish neck and over his smooth, round face. He knew she'd guessed. Her gaze drifted down his shirt and found a thickness behind the zip of his slacks. It pushed up beneath his belt, moving the buckle out of line.

'Damn you,' he said, a growl forced through teeth.

She closed her eyes, too aware of the hot, quick pulse between her legs, the heaviness, the dark temptation. This was familiar. She'd tormented him this way before, and she'd enjoyed it. 'I'm sorry,' she said, and opened her eyes.

He had braced his arms on either side of the console. His head was bowed as if he hadn't the strength to hold it up. 'It does not matter. Nothing can change what happened. Nothing can make it any worse.' He turned to her, one shoulder supporting the side of his head. Seeing the lines of sorrow in his face, lines she'd engraved, she felt such contempt for herself it was almost a pleasure to find an answering hatred in his eyes.

No. It *was* a pleasure. Some corner of her soul hungered to be hated as much as it hungered to be loved. A sliver of compassion cut through her self-disgust. Why would anyone want to be hated? But her arousal bled over the question, muddying her thoughts. When she'd watched the tape at the club, she'd condemned what she'd done, but it hadn't seemed real. Now she knew, bone deep, that she and this man had been intimate, and that desire as well as cruelty had ruled it. Their history was written in the hard, resentful glare of his eyes.

He still wanted her, in spite of everything. She had joined David as his object of desire.

Trembling at the flare of lust this inspired, she pressed her thighs together and reached behind her for the tape she'd tucked in the back of her jeans. 'I came to give you this,' she said, her voice husky despite all she did to firm it. 'I want to apologise. I don't remember why I staged this, but whatever the reason, I shouldn't have betrayed your secret. It was wrong of me and I'm very sorry. As far as I can tell, it's the only copy. You can destroy it if you want.'

He looked at the tape; ran his thumb over the neatly lettered label. '*Sato's Folly*. That is appropriate.'

She wanted to lay her hand on his shoulder. Instead, she stroked the rounded corner of the console. 'Maybe you should leave this job. Give yourself a chance to get over him.'

'Oh, you'd like that, wouldn't you?'

'I don't know. Did I try to push you out before I lost my memory?'

'No.' Confusion had replaced most of the anger in his eyes. 'I do not understand you. Not before and not now.'

'That makes two of us.'

Her rueful admission did not appease him. Swivelling his chair to face her, he reached out with both hands and pinched the hardened points of her nipples. She jerked, but he didn't release her, merely squeezed a little tighter. Two hot spears of sensation streaked through her body, spreading and tingling as they went. Her sex released a rush of fluid.

'You still want me,' he said.

She grit her teeth against her arousal. 'I don't have to do anything about it, though, do I?'

His arms fell. She staggered back until she hit the bunker's door.

'No,' he said. 'You don't.'

His face was calmer, his spine straighter. She didn't need a blow-by-blow memory of their relationship to know he'd won this round. He'd earned it, though, hadn't he? She owed him a victory. Probably a few. She shouldn't begrudge him this one. As she let herself out, however, she knew she did begrudge him. Chloe Dubois didn't like to lose, not ever, not to anyone.

David had meant to see Chloe as soon as she returned from the club, but the complications of doing business long-distance prevented it. The inconvenience couldn't be helped. His alternative was to return to New York and commute back on evenings and weekends. That he refused to do. Their situation was delicate enough without leaving Chloe alone all day.

All the same, he felt bad about missing her return, and worse when neither she nor Sato showed for dinner. Stomach tight, he took two bites of *chanko-nabe*, the famous sumo-wrestler's stew Auntie had made to cheer the absent head of security. Unable to swallow, he laid his chopsticks down. 'I'm sorry, Auntie. I'm afraid I'm not hungry tonight.'

Auntie removed the dishes without a word. Apparently, her spirits were no higher than his. He put his head in his hands, his neck aching with fatigue.

Auntie patted his hair. 'I'll wrap these up, David-san. You'll be hungry later.'

Later. He rose and smoothed his navy pullover down his chest. Later wouldn't improve until he straightened out his now.

He found Chloe in her room. She was lying fully clothed on top of the futon, her hands folded on her stomach, her wine-struck hair spread in a fan across the pillows. David sat beside her hip and stroked the silky strands. She didn't move. 'I found something at the club,' she said. 'A tape of our last performance. It was cruel of me to make you and Sato watch that.'

Her chin quivered. He drew a slow line around her forehead, peace seeping through him at this evidence of remorse. She had changed. She wasn't the same woman she'd been before. 'It wasn't the nicest thing you've done,' he said. 'But if you set your mind to it, you don't have to do anything like that again.'

Her eyes turned to his, their lids puckered with confusion. 'How could you forgive me? How could anyone be that good?'

'It's nothing to do with being good. I love you.'

She sat up and gripped his shoulders. 'You shouldn't forgive something like that. No one should.'

'I love you,' he said again.

She searched his eyes, but he could not give a more sensible answer. He pulled her closer, cradling her head and rubbing the tense muscles between her shoulder blades. Her arms crept around his back, first just matching his embrace, then tightening it. Desire welled inside him, a glow of warmth that soon turned to grinding hunger. It had been so long. His control hung by a thread. He dragged his lips up the side of her face and kissed her temple. He mustn't push her. He mustn't rush this.

Her hands kneaded his shoulders, then slid down his back to his buttocks. He exhaled hard to forestall a groan.

'I need you,' she said.

He wasn't sure how she meant it. He wasn't sure he cared. Unable to hold off a second longer, he pushed her back on the bed and slid his hands under her sweater, his sweater. Bare, warm flesh met his cupping palms. Her nipples were hard. This time he couldn't hold his groan inside. 'I love this,' he said, squeezing her flesh between his fingers. 'I love you being naked, under my clothes.'

She pulled him down for a juicy kiss. The feel of her was heaven. He notched her mons with his erection and ground them together as if he could push through to the other side.

'I need you,' she said, trying to wedge her hand between their groins. 'I'm burning up.'

'No.' He pulled her hand away from his zip. 'You never let me do for you. Let me tonight.'

She moistened her upper lip, nervousness showing.

He was afraid he'd ruined the moment, but then her hips squirmed against his, a hungry squirm, a let-me-get-closer-to-this-nice-hard-cock squirm. He hid his smile against the bend of her jaw. 'What's the matter?' he said, and tongued her galloping pulse. She wriggled again. He bit her earlobe, then sucked it into his mouth. 'Don't you want me to take care of you?'

Her head rolled from side to side. 'I don't deserve it.'

'But I deserve it,' he said. 'It's what I want.' He rocked their hips together, hard, the way he knew she craved. Her breath rushed out. He pulled her sweater over her head. When the hem cleared her face, something made him stop. Her arms were stretched over her head, trapped by the moss-green wool.

'What?' she said, clearly impatient.

A pulse beat harder in his groin.

'I want you like this,' he said, not quite believing he was saying it, but not wanting to take it back. 'I don't want you to be able to touch me.'

Her lips moved in a second, silent query.

'Hush. Don't move.' He kissed her lightly and pulled one of the pillowcases loose. She watched, wide-eyed, as he wrapped it around her wrists, binding them even tighter.

'You haven't done this before, have you?' she said.

He loved the wildness in her voice, the tremor that shook the hard, flushed points of her breasts. 'Hush,' he said again. 'Trust me.'

He stripped off her jeans and panties and socks, baring everything but her bound arms. Her belly rose and fell, her navel a flickering shadow at its centre. His blood moved like molasses through his veins, thick and dark. It all seemed to be going to the rock-hard pole inside his trousers. 'You forgot your ring,' he said, his voice so hoarse he wondered if she could hear him.

'My ring?'

He retrieved it from the keepsake box on her dresser. He straddled her hips, pushing her knees down when they rose.

'Be still,' he ordered, his own words like a hand squeezing his shaft. He wanted to control her, to force her to take everything he had. He worked the little loop through the slit in her navel, fumbling over the fastening before it caught. The silver gleamed. He flicked it with his finger. She shuddered. Her lips were parted in surprise, but she did not speak. The sight of her own piercing had struck her dumb. He'd always thought that ornament dangerous: wild woman's jewellery. Tonight it seemed the mark of slave.

He drew his fingers down the neatly groomed curls of her mons. She made a little noise, a back-of-the-throat whimper. He looked down. The lips of her pussy glistened with arousal. He curled his thumbs inside and found her drenched. Pinching the folds between finger and thumb, he spread them apart. He had never stared at her sex this way; had never seen its vulnerabilities as clearly as she could see his. Her little bud was berry-red and hard, its tip peeping from the hood. He massaged her labia where they met above the inspiring display.

'Maybe you should get a ring for these, too,' he said.

She moaned. A drop of oiled desire slid from the mouth of her sex.

He thought he would explode. He bent, pressing his mouth to her opened secrets. She was soft, tart against his tongue, spicy to his nose. He reached into her, tasting the evidence of his power, exploring her, owning her. When she strained closer, victory sang in his veins. She was his, at his mercy. A muscle quivered in her thigh.

'Please,' she said, the sound choked.

She'd never begged him before. His cock twanged like a tuning fork, juice seeping from its slit to soak his cotton briefs. He didn't care. She was all that mattered: her desire, her sticky desperation. He weighted her hip-bones with his hands, his thumbs reaching into the bend of her thighs to keep her spread.

'Please,' she said.

The word was a drug. He wanted more. He wanted her to weep. He drew her clit into his mouth, sucking it, rubbing it gently with his tongue. She sighed, long and grateful. Her buttocks clenched, lifting her sex as far as she could beneath his hands. He would feed this impatience. He would grow it. He brought her to the edge in waves, ebbing and flowing, winding her tighter until her sighs turned to growls and her legs jerked with frustration.

'David!' she said. She was begging with his name but not begging him to stop.

He pulled his hands down her long, lean legs, drawing them apart, drawing his mouth from her sex. 'David,' she whimpered. He looked at her. She was a different woman, a helpless woman. Her body was flushed from breast to thigh. Her bound hands clenched above her head. Her muscles rippled with restless motion. He desired her with an urgency that wasn't quite sane. I'm going to fuck you, he thought. I'm going to fuck you so hard you'll scream.

Any second he'd be saying it. Any second he'd be doing it. He pulled off his sweater. He undid the first two buttons of his shirt and ripped it over his head. Her gaze fastened on his chest. Heat swept his face. He knew his nipples were hard. He touched the tiny beads; rubbed them between two fingers. He'd never flaunted himself like this, but tonight he couldn't resist. Look, he thought, look what I've got for you. His body hummed with need, but he felt incredibly strong, incredibly male. Chloe bit her lower lip. 'I need you,' she said, a small, girlish plaint.

His cock was an iron pain between his legs. Just a little longer, he told it. Just a little. This was too delicious to rush. He lifted her foot and kissed its toes. They curled against his mouth.

'What do you need?' he said. 'I want to hear it from your lips.'

Her body twisted on the futon. 'I need you.'

He scraped his nails down the arch of her foot. She cried out, her back arching off the bed. He lifted the other foot. 'Oh, God,' she said, but he had no mercy.

'What do you need me to do?'

'I need you to fuck me. Please, David. Do it now. Jam your cock inside me.'

He released her foot and dragged down his zip. Air rushed from his lungs. The easing of the pressure on his cock allowed fresh, hot blood to surge into the rigid flesh. He stood and shoved his trousers to his feet. He kicked them away. He would take her naked. Nothing would come between them tonight. Her eyes glittered at the strength of his erection. He stroked it for her, fisting it once, down and then up. Pre-come oiled the reddened skin. With the middle finger of his right hand, he spread the moisture that seeped uncontrollably from his slit. She licked her lips and the skin beneath his finger stung.

'Come to me,' she said, lying as he'd left her. Her knees didn't move, still spread and bent, as if his will had bound her in place. 'Come to me, David. I'll go mad if you don't.'

Power pounded through him. He knelt between her

legs. He caught her wrists in one hand and a knee in the other. He levered her right thigh over his chest.

'Hot,' she gasped. 'Oh, God. Your skin.'

They were both all over sweat. He manoeuvred the swollen tip of his penis between her lips. He hit higher than he expected. The firm little rod of her arousal slipped beneath his glans. He rubbed the two nerve-rich surfaces together, loving her clit's hard, slippery evasion. Chloe whined in her throat, a panicked sound, her pre-orgasmic sound. He clutched her wrists tighter and bit her neck, fighting the urge to drive himself inward with all his strength. 'Do you want me inside you?' he demanded. 'Do you want my cock inside your pussy when you come?'

'Yes,' she groaned. 'Yes!'

His thrust shocked them both with its force. For a moment, he feared he would come. He hadn't made love to her since Japan; hadn't got off since she blew him in the garden. Now entering her was almost enough to break him. He gasped for control. She was so close, so warm and wet. The intimacy of their joining awed him. Her skin pulsed next to his. Her womb hugged his tip. Waves of heat rippled down his cock. She was coming.

She laughed at the orgasm, a startled, happy sound. Something snapped inside him. She shouldn't laugh at him. She shouldn't. He tightened his hold on her wrists and began to fuck her, punishing half-thrusts, hard and deep, pushing her thigh even higher. She came again, more strongly, and he pumped faster yet, racing the lightning that was streaking down his spine. She dug her heels into the bed to meet his thrusts. Their rhythm was perfectly matched. They were working together now. They would crash and burn as one.

Sweat poured down his face. His breath whistled through his teeth. Her expression tightened yet again. She was almost there. He could bring her with him. He could – her thighs clamped his hips. He ground deeper, gulping for air, the agony of almost coming too sharp to bear.

Then the world turned inside out for both of them.

Sensation burst, squeezing through his cock like white-gold fire. She spasmed around him as he poured himself into her: the love, the pain, the incredible pleasure that felt like his heart ripping in two. The flood of emotion overwhelmed him. He collapsed under it, on to her, his hold on himself shattering. To his horror, he began to weep. He tried to pull away, but she had freed her arms. She stroked his back and head, trapping him in her gentle prison.

'Oh, baby, don't,' she said. The endearment tightened his throat. If she discovered his lie, would she ever call him baby again? She kissed his sweaty temple. 'It's all right. We'll work it out.'

In spite of his embarrassment, her caresses soothed him. His eyelids drooped. 'That's right,' she said, easing to the side until his head was cradled on her breast. 'Sleep, baby, sleep.'

He wanted to ask if she loved him but, when it came right down to it, he didn't dare.

David's side of the bed was empty, the sheets cold under her searching hand. What sort of husband didn't want to spend the night with his own wife? The answer was all too clear: one who didn't trust her enough to share the intimacy of sleep. Her throat convulsed on a cry she didn't know how to release. Rather than try, she rolled out of bed and padded to the window. She touched the glass. The moon was huge and white, the landscape empty. Winter-thin grass rolled to a distant neighbour's stubbled fields.

What a lonely fucking sight, she thought, eyes burning with more hurts than she could remember.

He'd been crying for her. That broken heart was her doing.

But what of her? The tightness in her chest told her she loved him. This was different than what she'd felt for Sato. This went deeper than the body. This was a cure for a sickness of the soul. She pressed the heels of her hands over her eyes. Was finding her past the answer? If she knew all the wounds she'd inflicted, could she heal them? Or would she stop wanting to?

He's my last chance, she thought, though for what she couldn't have said.

16

The cowboy was too quick on the draw.

Chloe's scenario demanded he not become erect until Lauren, in her role as Carmen, began her striptease. Unfortunately, Harry found being handcuffed to the bedposts so stimulating they'd had to give up the start limp, get hard idea. Now he was having trouble with the whip. He called a halt for the second time in ten minutes.

Lauren groaned dramatically. 'She hasn't touched you yet, Harry. How can you be worried about coming?'

Chloe relaxed her whip arm and let the tip trail on the stage. They'd spent four days practising with a dummy for a target. Lauren had a good eye and a steady arm. Now all she had to do was get a feel for the difference between a swing that left a mark and one that raised a welt. Chloe wouldn't permit the latter even if Harry agreed. She was beginning to suspect he would.

The extent of his enthusiasm had taken everyone by surprise, Harry included. Now his face glowed with a combination of arousal and embarrassment. He'd shaved his goatee to get into character and was naked except for a pair of fringed buckskin chaps. The leather covered the inside of his legs, but not the outside. His genitals were bare. She doubted his cock could get any harder. It jutted up from his sandy blond thatch, trembling with the energy of high desire. Chloe had offered to let him wear a cup until he was sure of his whip-mistresses. He'd declined. She'd thought he was being macho. Silly her.

He sucked in a breath and blew it out. 'Sorry,' he said. 'I think I'm OK. You can continue.'

Fernando and Chuck were watching him squirm from the pit in front of the stage. Chuck rested his hefty arms on the apron. 'You know,' he said. 'You're not gonna be able to call a halt in the middle of a performance.'

'I know,' Harry sighed. 'She's just so ... commanding. I'm sure I'll learn to handle the excitement once I get more practice.'

'You're dripping,' Lauren accused, and stomped the spot of pre-come that glistened between his feet. Her cowboy boot rang against the wood. 'You haven't lost your hard-on since we started. You're never going to make it through the whole scene.'

'Maybe you should let him come,' Fernando said. 'Take the edge off. From the looks of things he'll be able to get it up again without much trouble.'

Chloe crossed her arms. The whip trailed over her shoulder. 'Would you prefer that, Harry? We can uncuff you and you can go, well, take care of yourself.'

Harry's face contorted. 'Actually, um ...'

Lauren knew what he was getting at. 'Shit,' she said. 'He wants you to whip him until he shoots.' She smacked Harry's breastbone with the back of her hand. 'She's a married woman, peabrain.'

'Well, it's not like having sex.'

'It's just like having sex. It's an incredibly intimate exchange of trust and power, and you shouldn't be asking somebody to do it just because you want to get off.'

'Hey, I'd let you do it if you had more practice.'

'Pig.'

'That means she likes you,' Fernando teased.

Lauren glared at them both before stomping off.

'What did I say?' Harry pleaded. 'Don't go. You're the best, Lauren. You're the only one I want whipping me.

Oh, hell.' He sagged in the handcuffs, his erection finally fading.

Chloe struggled not to laugh. Once they pulled this show together, Harry and Lauren were going to set the stage on fire. Hiding her smile, she dug the key to the cuffs from her pocket. When she'd freed one arm, Harry draped it around her neck. 'Think it'll help if I apologise?'

'Maybe. But I'd appreciate it if you didn't apologise too well until after the performance.'

Harry gaped at her, then laughed. 'You are bad. You want her mad at me.'

'Just call me a method director.' She reached across him for the second set of cuffs. One of the main doors swung open. Thinking Lauren had returned, she and Harry looked up. But it wasn't Lauren. It was David.

Chloe jerked, alarm washing over her in waves. This did not look good. Here she stood, embracing a half-naked, handcuffed man with a serious whip stowed in the back of her jeans. The term 'smoking gun' did not begin to cover this.

David's expression was stiff. 'I'm sorry,' he said. 'I didn't realise you were rehearsing.'

'We're not. I mean, I'm not. I'm not planning to – Oh, fuck.' He didn't give her a chance to finish. He'd already left the room. Panicked, she vaulted off the stage and ran. 'David, wait!' She caught him at the front door with his hand on the gleaming brass handle. 'I'm not performing. I was just teaching one of the women to use the whip.'

He didn't take his hand from the door. 'What difference does it make? I wouldn't have any say if you did want to perform.'

'Of course you would.' She wrapped herself around his back, her cheek pressed to his clean-smelling neck. 'You're my husband. Don't you think I'd ask you before I took my clothes off for a bunch of strangers?'

She felt more than heard his sigh. 'Would you?' he said. 'Would you even care what it would do to me?'

'Jesus.' She blinked hard to clear the sting of tears from her eyes. 'I know I've hurt you in the past, but believe me, I'd care.'

He turned and took her hands between his own. 'You don't know how much I want to believe that.'

'Then do believe it. I may not have my memory, but I know how I feel. I care about you, David. I do not want to hurt you.'

He nodded and kissed her knuckles, but his eyes did not drop their guard.

There had to be a way to convince him she'd changed – a way to convince herself, for that matter. She paced the veranda in the icy twilight, the house a cage too small to contain her. She'd felt this way before, she knew: the need to run, to escape the confines of her skin. The old Chloe pressed against her awareness like a demon. Screw David, she said. He must have known what you were before he married you. If it bothers him now, he's got no one to blame but himself.

He probably thought he could save her.

He must have believed he could change her.

She leaned on the wall that surrounded the gravel garden, her hands clasped so tightly her wedding ring threatened to split her glove. What had the old Chloe got except a husband who feared her, sisters she didn't speak to, no close friends, no safety for her heart, no peace for her mind. Screw the old Chloe, she thought. Screw waiting for her memories to come back. Now was the time to start pushing her life in the direction *she* wanted it to go. She loved David. Whatever had been true in the past, this was true today. She wouldn't let the old Chloe lose him.

All she had to do was find a way to win his trust.

She strode to her room and threw off her coat. She stared around her, at the tea-green futon where David had held her captive, at the painted screen that hid her desk, at the beautiful kimono that hung from the wall that faced her bed. Emotion stirred like a sleeping dragon: hurt, anger. *Why should I change when he* – Then the memory stopped. Maybe she stopped it. Her mind slid sideways. She remembered his hall of dolls, each perfectly attired creation protected by its own glass case. The dolls' beautiful white faces were etched in her memory. With their tiny red lips and demurely lowered eyes, they were the image of feminine surrender.

Was that the sacrifice she needed to make: to surrender her will to his, to prove she could?

Warmth spread through her chest, easing its tightness. Yes. This made sense. She dragged her desk chair to the kimono's niche and climbed on to the seat. Gently, she pulled each sleeve from the pole that held it. The cloth was cool and smooth, like water to wash a sin. It pooled over her arms as she stepped to the floor.

She knew just who to turn for help: Auntie. Her presence in the house seemed fated. She'd been born in Japan; had lived as a geisha. She'd built her life around service. Convincing the older woman to teach her wouldn't be easy, but Chloe would do what it took.

Auntie's rooms were a taste of old Japan. Rice-paper screens divided the space into sections and tatami mats covered the floor. One long window overlooked the back garden. The walls were white plaster with dark wooden beams. From them scrolls hung, unframed, yellowed with age. They showed pictures of the Floating World: geisha strolling down the streets of old Kyoto, *kabuki* actors in costume, cherry blossoms, young men drinking sake. A lacquered black cabinet stood opposite the door.

On its shining front, a bamboo design was picked out in gold. Chloe imagined it held a shrine.

'I'm sure you have not come to admire my humble furnishings,' Auntie said, her head still bowed from ushering her in.

'I've come to ask for help.' She lifted her armload of kimono. Auntie took it from her and spread it across a rice-paper divider, her competent hands smoothing out the wrinkles.

'You wish to play dress-up.' The stiffness of her shoulders said she disapproved.

'No.' Chloe released her pent-up breath. Her cheeks were hot, but she had to make Auntie understand. 'I wish to make a symbolic gesture of submission to show my husband I'm not the woman I was, to prove I love him.'

Auntie shook a sleeve straighter. She stroked the embroidered water lily that floated up its length. 'You think being geisha is about submission?'

'I think it's about putting another person's interest before your own.'

To Chloe's surprise, Auntie chuckled, a soft, rusty sound. 'Being geisha is the art of making a man *believe* his interest comes before your own. Behind the mask, the geisha belongs to herself. She is paid well for the illusion she creates. In many ways, she is more independent than the Japanese wife. True submission, the kind you speak of, comes only from love. It, too, is an art, one that grows not from self-denial but from pride in one's ability to serve gracefully. One serves the self by serving the beloved.'

Auntie glanced back over her shoulder, her wrinkles lifted by an elfin smile. 'But perhaps David-san's view of geisha is the only one that concerns you?'

'Yes,' Chloe said, relieved she didn't have to engage in

a philosophical debate. 'I wish to make a gesture that will be meaningful for him.'

Auntie pursed her lips. 'Come. I have tea brewing. I will tell you a story about your husband.'

She led Chloe around the rice-paper wall to a table where a homely brown teapot sat on a trivet. She gestured for her to sit on a cushion, then drew two small cups from a cabinet, this piece intricately carved in dark, polished cedar. With some difficulty, Chloe crossed her legs and wedged them under the low table. Auntie assumed the cushion opposite her and tucked her feet under her bottom. Though her kimono was plain grey cotton, she sat as regally as a queen.

'When I first came to this country,' she began, 'I stayed with David's mother, Helen. She lives in Minnesota, near the famous Mayo clinic, where I was to receive treatments for my condition. Helen's mother was my cousin. We had been playmates in Japan and Helen had heard many stories of Michiko, the toast of Kyoto.

'I suppose the stories intimidated her. She thought I must be a grand Japanese lady. She didn't realise I was in so much pain, it was difficult for me to be friendly. In any case, to make up for her feelings of insecurity, she began to brag about her wonderful son. How successful he was. How respectful. How generous to his beloved mother.

'All this praise made me wonder. I watched them together and saw he was everything she claimed: smart, polite, and as careful of her as a china doll. Too careful. He loved her, I thought, but he did not trust her. When he looked at her, his eyes held a wound she had inflicted.

'Anyone who knows me will tell you I am a busybody. Already, I liked this serious young man who had gone to so much trouble to help a relative he had never met. I wanted to know what had hurt him. We spent much time together during my treatments. First we talked only of me, my life in Japan, my memories of Kyoto. Slowly, though, he began to tell me the story of his youth.'

Auntie lifted the teapot and poured a gold-green stream into Chloe's cup. The motion of her arms, even the fall of the tea, seemed choreographed. She returned the pot to its trivet and laid her palms on her thighs.

'When David's mother was a little girl, she was taken with her parents to Manzanar, an internment camp in California. This was during World War II, soon after the attack on Pearl Harbor. It was thought by the US government that Japanese-Americans might try to hamper the war effort. To prevent this, they were taken to these camps where the danger they posed could be contained.'

Though Chloe knew this part of the story, she remained quiet. Auntie blew on the surface of her tea. 'I suppose the camps could have been worse. The people were not tortured or starved. Schools were established, silly things like cheerleading and beauty shops. But it was still a prison. For three years, more than a hundred thousand citizens were kept under guard. They were forced from their homes to live in cramped communal barracks, without privacy, without dignity – without any Japanese-American anywhere having been proven to have committed an act of disloyalty. Innocent people were treated like criminals because of this baseless suspicion. Do you know what it's like not to feel safe from your own government, to be hated by your neighbours and friends?'

Chloe shook her head, though her words stirred a formless dread. She swallowed a sip of bitter tea.

'The feeling never goes away,' Auntie said. 'Not completely. Certainly, it never went away for David's mother. Her husband died in an accident when they'd been married two years. There was no one to protect David but her. Because of this, Helen vowed her son would be more American than the Americans. His countrymen would never have an excuse to treat him as less. He would study harder. He would be obedient and polite and honest. He would play the right games and make the right friends. He would be the perfect American son.'

Auntie freshened Chloe's tea, her face creased by a rueful smile. 'Helen didn't realise the perfect American son didn't exist. Poor David stood out like a sore thumb with his perfectly pressed clothes and his dutiful manners and his Japanese face no amount of apple pie could erase.'

Chloe played her fingers over the rim of her cup. Steam filled her palm. Her throat felt just as hot. 'He was lonely.'

'Yes,' Auntie agreed. 'He was lonely and curious. He wanted to learn more about this country his mother never spoke of. He began in secret to study *ikebana* –'

'Flower-arranging.'

'*Hai.* Yes. And also to read about the Floating World.' Auntie's eyes slanted in amusement. 'You see, he had heard his aunt was a famous geisha.

'One day, while David was at school, Helen found these books about Japan hidden in his room. Sadly for him, this was also the day his report card arrived in the mail. He had received a "C" in what you call physical education.' Auntie smiled. 'David never did like baseball.

'Helen had all afternoon to fume about the failings of her son, all afternoon to mutter to herself and grow more and more angry. When he finally arrived, she was cooking dinner, stirring meat in a pan of boiling oil. So strong was her anger that, on seeing him, she lashed out with the metal utensil and struck him beside the eye.'

Chloe pressed her hands to her mouth. 'His scar!'

'Yes. The spoon was so hot, it stuck to his skin. He had to be rushed to the emergency room to treat the burns.

'Helen was horrified by what she'd done. She shed many tears and begged her son's forgiveness. Naturally,

David gave it, but he could not forget. The memory of his mother striking him was always in his mind, reminding him he would never be as perfect as she wished.'

Chloe looked down at her tea. 'You're saying he'll never forget what I did, either.'

Auntie squeezed her knee, her hand strong and warm. 'I'm saying it's not enough to beg forgiveness, to put on a kimono for one night and pretend to be humble. You must change the pattern of your actions and you must be patient. You are not the first to leave scars on his heart.'

'So you won't help me?'

'I'll help you,' Auntie said. 'But you are the one who will have to make my help work.'

David left her a note. Chloe found it at the breakfast table, folded in half beside her plate. Her hands shook as she opened it, but it only said he had to go into the city for business. He'd be back that evening, and Auntie shouldn't wait dinner. The note wasn't signed. Perhaps he didn't know how to close it. 'Sincerely, your husband'? With a wry smile, Chloe handed the missive to Auntie.

Auntie hmphed over it, then sat at the head of the table. 'Tonight, then. You will give him his present tonight.'

'But I've hardly practised.'

Auntie waved away her doubt. 'You are a quick student. You move like a real geisha now. It must be the dancing you do. Tell me –' She grinned and leaned closer. 'Can you really make tassels twirl around your nipples?'

Chloe almost spat out her coffee. She hoped Auntie wouldn't ask to trade lessons.

She waited for David in whiteface and kimono, with her tray and cups and her kettle of sake. The kettle was snuggled like a baby in a special warmer, the sort that heats in a microwave and cools over the course of hours.

Auntie swore this was the only legitimate use for the contraption.

She waited through sunset and star-rise. She wandered through her husband's rooms, touching his clothes, sniffing his bay rum soap, studying each picture that hung from the slate blue walls. He owned a number of antique *shunga*, erotic woodblock prints. All the men had enormous phalluses, all the women cherry mouths. Gods and geisha. Their clothes were as beautiful as their faces. Their genitals met through the flowing folds.

It disturbed her to find no evidence of her own presence, not so much as a toothbrush in the bathroom, as if he'd exiled her.

Flashes of resentment warred with fears that her marriage was too broken to fix. She found a stack of wrapped Christmas presents in the back of his walk-in closet. One with her name on it had the shape of a jeweller's box. No doubt the old Chloe would sell whatever was in it to buy a few more Krugerrands for her stash.

She shuffled back to the bedroom. It was hard to walk without tripping on the kimono; hard to breathe through the *obi* Auntie had wound around her ribs and breasts. She stared at herself in the mirror over David's writing desk. The *obi*, white with pink cherry blossoms, glowed against the flowing green kimono. Her hair was swept into a bouffant bun, her face obliterated with white pancake, then redrawn in the image of the Orient. The transformation was startling. She did not recognise herself. She looked Japanese. Even the curves of her figure had been camouflaged into something more demure.

Was this the kind of woman David wanted? Was this the kind of woman she could be?

The clock said eight. She decided to sit. She needed

the practice. Kneeling with her legs tucked under her was, to her, the greatest challenge. Even with the cushion, ten minutes later, needles of pain were shooting through her folded calves. She wriggled to the side but didn't rise. This was her penance. If she could pay it without complaint, tonight would go well.

Superstitious idiot, she mocked, but she remained as she was. At eight thirty she heard David's footsteps in the hall. Quickly, she composed herself, hands laid neatly on her thighs, head bent, heels tucked.

'What in the world?' he said when he saw her.

She ordered her eyes to remain lowered. 'I have arranged a present for my master after his long day at work.'

'Christ.'

She flinched at the anger in his voice. 'Is my master not pleased?'

He hunkered down beside her in his suit, one knee popping as he did. He lifted her face on the side of his hand. 'You really don't remember, do you?'

Had she done this before and made a joke of it? Lord, she had a genius for self-sabotage. But there was nothing for it except to forge ahead. 'I'm sorry, master. Have I done something wrong?'

He shook his head, visibly throwing off his suspicion. He touched her white cheek with the tip of his finger. 'You look pretty. Let me wash the day off my face and I'll come sit with you.'

She waited while he used the bathroom, her nervousness doubled by his unexpected reaction. Calm, she thought, forcing her breath out in an even stream. I'm calm. All I have to do is pour a little sake and tell my husband I love him. No big deal.

He came back barefoot, his shirtsleeves rolled to his elbows, his tie a memory. He lowered himself cross-legged to the cushion opposite hers. Between them and to one side stood a lacquered stand in sapphire blue. Atop it sat a stack of three nested cups. The porcelain was sealing-wax red with a patterned gold leaf rim. All were loans from Auntie: prized possessions, she suspected. Once convinced, Auntie had entered fully into the scheme.

David fingered the smallest of the nested cups. 'Why don't you tell me what this is about?'

She'd been afraid he'd want explanations. Rather than answer, she removed the smallest cup and offered it to him. Without being told, he took it in the proper manner, holding it in the fingertips of both hands. She lifted the sake kettle from its cosy and poured a steaming stream of wine. David stared at it, then at her. His brow furrowed.

'This is about *en musubi*,' she said. 'A connection between two people which is not easily loosened.'

'*En musubi*,' he repeated. The crease in his forehead deepened. He lifted the cup to his lips, still holding it with that trademark delicacy.

'You must finish it in three sips,' she said.

He took the first sip, then blinked and lowered the cup. 'Chloe, this is *sansan-kudo*, the exchange of nuptial cups. This is not a game.'

She wished he didn't sound so stunned. 'I'm not playing,' she said. She set the kettle back. 'I want you to think of me as your wife again. I want us to wake in the same bed. I want you to trust me.'

Still, he did not drink. 'This is a serious commitment.'

'I'm ready for one.' She lifted her eyes and filled her lungs with air. 'I love you, David.'

'Chloe.' He smoothed her hair around the curve of her ear, his expression sad and gentle. 'Without your memories, you can't be sure of that.'

'I can be sure of what's in my heart. This love feels

like it's been there a long time. The strength of it hurts me. The distance between us hurts me.'

'Chloe.' This time her name was a low murmur of sound. His eyes glittered as they searched hers. 'You put me to shame.'

She could not hold his diamond gaze. 'If you don't want to tie our destinies together...'

'No.' He covered the hand that lay across her thigh. 'I'm sure they're tied already, but I would be honoured to share the ritual sake with you. If you're sure that's what you want.'

'I'm sure,' she said. It might have been all she was sure of, but she was sure.

She watched him finish the cup in two more sips. He handed it back without speaking and poured the sake for her. His motions were almost as graceful as Auntie's. She loved his hands, their colour and their shape, their self-conscious gentleness. When the little cup was full, she closed her eyes and inhaled the rich, sweet fumes. This is my promise, she thought. To keep trying even when trying is hard. She drained the wine in three slow swallows. She handed him the middle cup and filled it.

'Thank you,' he said, and he, too, closed his eyes as he drank. He passed the cup to her. His hand trembled when he poured.

The three sips slid warm and sharp down her throat. This is my promise, she thought. To give way sometimes, even when I don't want to.

She poured the third, largest cup, lingering over the task, hearing the bell-like tinkle as the hot rice wine struck the porcelain. The ritual stilled her deep inside. So many husbands and wives must have shared this cup. So many must have come through the darkness with this taste on their tongues. David waited for the wine to cool, the steam wavering her view of his beautiful face.

His eyes smiled, fine lines etching the delicate skin at their corners.

'You are my wife,' he said, and drank.

He poured for her as she held the cup between her fingers. Her head was spinning. She was going to be drunk. She hoped she could finish this cup the way she must.

She took the first swallow, then stopped.

'This is my promise,' she said. 'To do my best not to hurt you or those you love.'

'That includes you.' His voice was warmer than the wine. 'You must promise not to hurt yourself.'

She nodded, heart swelling, and let the last two mouthfuls run down her throat. The smell was like new grass, the taste heavy. He laughed when the sting of it made her cough, slapping her back and tugging her to her feet. She immediately fell over, her legs completely asleep. Still laughing, he carried her to the futon and chafed her calves. The pain of returning circulation made her wince. She was on his bed, though, and his eyes were shining with love.

'My God,' he said, 'how long were you sitting like that?'

'Just half an hour.'

'Half an hour! You're lucky you don't have gangrene.' He tumbled her backwards, his weight easing over hers, his chafing turning to long, sensual strokes. The kimono pooled around her knees, but his hand roved even higher. He nuzzled the shell of her ear. 'Can we wash off this make-up so I can kiss you?'

'I don't think I can wait that long,' she said, and wound her arms around his neck.

Like oiled ivory, David slid into her sex. He felt as if this were the first time they'd made love, as if he'd been waiting to do this since they'd met. Maybe he had.

Tonight, they fitted like lock and key, softness embracing hardness; no struggles, no conflict, just two bodies that were meant to join. Each impact of his hips was gentle, waves lapping their chosen shore. Chloe's kimono and *obi* lay in careful folds across a chair but her face and shoulders were white as snow. Her smile was barely recognisable beneath the tiny, painted mouth.

'I love you,' he said, the words rolling out on a tide of joy.

Her knees rose and she arched closer, drawing him deep inside her warmth. Her fingers trailed lightly up his back. He couldn't suppress a shiver.

'Show me.' Her eyes glowed gold within their rim of sable lashes. 'Show me you love me.'

He showed her, and she showed him, her caresses speaking as sweetly as her words. Whether she knew it or not, she was taking back that night in Tokyo, putting herself in the geisha's place, washing both their sins. She said she loved him. When she touched him this way, he believed her. They came together, deep and slow, his groans mingling with hers. She held him until he softened, then led him to the bath for a good, long scrubbing.

They christened the tub, wet skin sliding as he bent her backwards over the rim. His thrusts were leisurely, decadent, giving him time to admire each sleek response. She hummed with appreciation as her fingers slipped down his spine. 'I love your butt,' she said. 'It is so adorable.'

He laughed when she squeezed a double handful, then gasped when one finger began to probe. 'What are you doing?'

Her tongue curled over her upper lip. 'I'm loving your adorable butt.'

Her finger pressed inwards, eased by the soap that had started their play. He couldn't breathe. No one had touched him there before. More intense than the unfamiliar pleasure was the incredible sense of acceptance. She wanted every part of him, every part.

'Like that?' she whispered.

He closed his eyes and rested his forehead on hers. 'Yes,' he said. 'Yes.'

She began to rub him deep inside. 'Don't stop moving,' she said. 'You've got to feel it at both ends to get the full effect.'

He did as she advised and immediately lost his ability to speak. Tingles of pleasure rebounded between her penetration and his. She found his prostate and his cock nearly purred. Ooh, this was good, unutterably good. He thrust slower, not wanting the delirium to end. For long minutes, he floated on a heady edge. His eyes only opened when Chloe squirmed a hand between their hips. Her finger began to circle her clit. 'I can do that,' he said.

She shook her head and smiled. 'I can pace myself this way. You just enjoy.'

He couldn't argue, not when his cock was wallowing in bliss, not when her hand felt so intimate between them. When she finally came, her contractions drew his so closely after, they seemed to be experiencing the same peak. He groaned into her hair, feeling his seed wrench from him in delicious, lazy throbs.

Chloe took a moment to catch her breath. 'You are good,' she said. 'If I've ever had better, I sure don't remember it now.'

Her humour surprised him into laughing. It was a hopeful sign, he thought, for both of them.

They slept together and woke in each other's arms. The clock read eleven twenty-five. He'd missed an important meeting, but he didn't give a damn.

Chloe smiled like a satisfied cat. 'I love you,' she said, her voice thick with sleep. He knew those words would never pall.

Feeling like a new man, he slipped out of bed and drew on his robe. Chloe pushed up on her elbows to watch. 'It's occurred to me I'm running out of time,' she said. 'What do you want for Christmas?'

He gave her bottom a playful smack. 'I've already got it.'

But that was before Auntie announced their visitor.

17

Auntie gripped his forearm with both hands, as worried as he'd ever seen her. 'I wasn't sure what to do. She asked if Chloe was here. She says she's her sister.'

They stood alone on the second-floor landing. Auntie had whispered her news. Clearly, she could guess what this meant as well as David could. His anxiety rose, but he patted her shoulder. 'Don't worry, Auntie. I'll take care of it.'

He saw the woman before she saw him. She waited on the sectional couch in the lowest level of the living room. Her hands were knotted in her lap and she perched on the edge of the cushion with her knees pressed together. A grey pleated skirt brushed her sensible shoes. She was a careworn version of Chloe, a little plump, not so stylish. She had the same straight dark hair, though, and her lips held a hint of Chloe's provocative pout.

David's heart knocked his ribs. Pull yourself together, he thought. See what she wants. Maybe whatever it was could wait. He didn't need much more time. He and Chloe were almost there. Smoothing his shirt down his chest, he stepped into the light-filled room.

'Hello,' he said.

Chloe's sister jumped from the couch as if he'd set off a firecracker. 'Oh! Mr Imakita.' She pulled the edges of her pastel pink cardigan over her breasts, then remembered her manners. She offered her hand. 'I'm Beth Quinlan. Beth Cohen, I used to be. I'm sorry for disturbing you at home, but I—' Her cheeks turned pinker than her sweater. 'I found your address in my father's desk and I was hoping you could tell me where my sister Sam is. She's probably calling herself Chloe now, Chloe Dubois. I really need to speak to her. If you know anything . . .'

'Why?' he said.

'Why?' She stroked her throat, turning Chloe's seductive habit into a nervous one. 'Well, our father died. He left her some money, though I don't imagine she'll care about that.'

An odd swooping sensation rolled through David's belly. 'The judge is dead?'

'Yes, a brain aneurysm. No one knew. It was quite a surprise. Look.' She pressed a thumbnail to her teeth. 'You seem to know where she is. There are things I need to – I don't know what she told you about our family, but there are things I need to tell her, to explain.' Her eyes filled. 'I need to make peace with her, and she probably needs it, too.'

David looked down. He hadn't pulled socks on and his feet were bare: freezing, actually. He curled his toes against the Bokhara rug, reining his mind back to where it didn't want to be. He knew there was a strong chance that seeing her sister would revive Chloe's memories. This blurred reflection of her face had to be so much more deeply engraved than his own, so much more firmly bound into the emotions of her life. But there was no choice to make. He couldn't keep this from her, no matter what the cost to either of them.

'Stay here,' he said, his voice gruff. 'I'll bring her to you.'

'Oh.' The woman fell back a step. All the blood had drained from her face. 'She's here?'

'Yes.' He hesitated, wondering how to explain Chloe's amnesia, or his lies. 'She's had an accident. If she seems different, that's why.'

'An accident.' The woman sat, her hand pressed to her bosom. 'She wasn't ... She wasn't badly hurt, was she?'

'No,' he said, and left before he lost his nerve.

David said her sister was here; said she had something important to tell her.

Chloe couldn't think. Where were her clothes? Her sister was here, now, in the house. The kimono was folded over an armchair. No. She couldn't wear that. Her sister would think she'd lost her mind. 'God, I can't even remember her name.'

'Beth,' David said. 'Her married name is Beth Quinlan.'

Was that the middle sister then? Or the youngest? She pawed the covers in search of her panties. Then she remembered. She hadn't worn any under the kimono. Auntie had said it wasn't done. She clapped both hands to her head. Where was her brain?

'Sit.' David pushed her into a chair. 'I'll bring clothes from your room.'

She should have gone herself but she couldn't seem to ... Her gaze caught on David's bureau. A moment later, she was tearing through his sweater drawer. Here. The periwinkle V-neck with the heather specks. This was her favourite. She pulled it on and rolled up the sleeves.

She was waiting in the chair, hands gripping the arms, when David returned with her clothes. He smiled at the sight of her wearing his sweater. 'I'll have to buy more of those if we're going to keep sharing this way.'

Too nervous to respond, she stabbed her feet into the jeans he handed her. She almost tripped putting on her split-toed, Japanese-style socks. They were white. Auntie said they had to be new and white.

'Hey,' he said. 'C'mere.'

She shuffled to him, hugged his waist and buried her nose in the open neck of his shirt. He hadn't showered since last night. He smelled even better than the sweater did. 'I love you,' he said, rubbing her back in slow, comforting sweeps. 'Whatever happens, remember that.'

'You make me feel as if I'm going off to war.'

He laughed and pushed her gently towards the door, swatting her bottom when she faltered. 'I'll wait here. Come back when you're done.'

Her cotton *tabi* whispered on the stairs, much quieter than the beating of her heart. God, she was terrified. She felt as if a million moths were beating at her skin, at her brain, darkness beating on darkness, beating at the wall she'd built to keep herself safe. She had to stop at the bottom to calm her ragged breathing. She closed her eyes and pressed her hand to her breast. It was too soon. She wasn't ready to face this. How could she possibly explain that she'd forgotten –

A scent drifted into the entryway: Emeraude, the perfume her mother wore. She plunged backwards in time and saw herself watching Mummy's nightly ritual at the marble-topped vanity: the powder and the cream and the silky pink robe with the lace around the collar. Oh, how she'd coveted that robe. One night, though, she'd wanted something else. 'Could I have a cross?' she'd asked. 'Just a little one, like Mary Alice had.' Her memory was a ragged ghost, lingering in shreds: Mary Alice fighting Daddy on the couch the night Mummy stayed late at the Mucniks'; Mary Alice, whose bright red curls had spilled to her shoulders. Daddy had to push them aside when he – *When my father hears about this, he'll kill you.* But Mary Alice never got the chance to tell. Daddy had put his hands around her soft white throat. Daddy had squeezed and twisted until her neck made that terrible, terrible noise.

She could see the black, wiry hair on the back of his hands; could feel the choking panic in her throat. *Don't make a sound. Don't make a sound.* But Beth had whimpered and he saw where they huddled behind the couch.

She'd wanted to be sick. She'd wanted to close her eyes and scream. 'Mary Alice isn't feeling well,' he said, 'and you three ought to be in bed.'

Her mother didn't understand. Her mother thought Mary Alice was a nightmare the family needed to put behind them. 'No, you can't have a cross,' she said, her lips angry-thin. 'Why don't you wear that nice Jewish star Nana bought you?' But it wasn't that she wanted a *cross*. It was that she wanted to feel closer to Mary Alice, who she'd loved, who she hadn't said a word to save, not even when the police asked if their babysitter had seemed frightened that night. 'No, Officer,' she'd said. 'Mary Alice seemed like always.'

She had betrayed Mary Alice worse than her sisters ever betrayed her. Beth and Sharon had really forgotten. Samantha had known the truth.

Gasping, Chloe sat on the bottom step. Her memories flooded back, not just her childhood, but her dancing and Sato and David and the way the Tokyo geisha had taken him in her little red mouth until his back arched off the hotel bed. She remembered everything, as if the memory of her father murdering Mary Alice had been a dam holding it back.

She remembered the years a man's touch had stirred nothing but an eerie calm, and the gusto with which she'd reclaimed her sexuality once it had woken up. She'd wanted more and more, until that became a burden, too. She'd almost been ready to throw it off before the accident, though the prospect had scared her. Committing herself to one man, to David, would have made her vulnerable. She hadn't guessed her own hand would strike the fatal blow.

David. She stretched her hands out before her. The big marquis-cut diamond winked in the wintry sun. They weren't married. David wasn't her husband. She couldn't take it all in. She wiped cold sweat from her face with the hem of his sweater. She wrapped her arms around her knees and shook. She didn't want to get up. She wanted to crawl back to her room and hide beneath the covers.

But her sister was waiting, her little sister Beth who had something important to tell her and probably was just as scared as she was. Chloe couldn't let her down.

She pushed to her feet and took four shaky steps into the front room. Beth was standing by the far window, her arms clutching her waist, her long hair falling straight from a simple gold barrette. Chloe remembered she'd worn it that way when they were kids. 'Hello, Beth,' she said.

Beth turned. She made a sound that could have been her childhood name. Her face crumpled. Chloe crossed the room and offered her arms. Beth fell into them.

'Daddy's dead,' she choked against her shoulder. Chloe stopped breathing. Dead? Her father was dead? Then Beth pushed back and wiped her cheeks. 'I'm sorry. I shouldn't cry. I shouldn't even care.' She sniffed and pulled herself together, her expression so reminiscent of their mother's Chloe felt like a time traveller. 'He died two weeks ago. A brain aneurysm. I found your address in his things. It took me all this time to work up the nerve to see you.'

Her expression was shy, unsure of its welcome. Chloe clasped her sister's upper arms. 'I'm glad you did. Are you OK? Are Mom and Sharon holding up?'

'Yes. You shouldn't worry about us.' She wiped her nose on the back of her hand, an angry, impatient gesture. 'I didn't come to cry on your shoulder. I came – I came to ask your forgiveness for letting you stand alone. We were cowards, all of us, me and Sharon and Mother.'

Chloe's face tingled with shock. Beth remembered the murder? When? How? But her sister was crying again, fat tears trickling down her soft, PTA-mother's cheeks.

Chloe grabbed a tissue from the nearest end table. 'Here. Blow.'

Her sister laughed weakly. 'Just like Mom. God, you must hate us.'

'No.' She pulled her sister into the shelter of her arm. 'I don't hate any of you.'

It was true. Her rage was gone, swept away by the relief of seeing Beth again, by everything she'd been through. God knew she'd seen first hand the mind's power to forget. She squeezed her sister closer. 'You honestly didn't remember what he'd done. I know that now.'

Beth dabbed her nose with the tissue. 'I did a little. Pieces of memories. Things that didn't make sense. I forced them out of my head. I wanted –'

'You wanted to love your daddy. You wanted him to love you.'

'But we betrayed you!'

Chloe released her and leaned against the window. Beyond the winter-bare trees, the roof of their neighbour's barn shone red and white, high on a hill, so small and perfect it seemed like a child's toy. 'I have my own sins, Beth.'

'No.' Beth's denial was staunch. 'You were the strong one. You tried to tell the truth.'

'Too little, too late, I think, and when I saw I couldn't beat him, I ran. I ran more out of anger than fear, Beth, and I left you alone with a monster.'

'You were a kid yourself.'

'Maybe.' Chloe stroked the image of the barn through the glass. 'But I liked being his favourite, Beth. I liked the outings only I got to go on. I liked the special presents. You and Sharon were Mummy's pets. I told myself I deserved what he gave me. But when I found Mary Alice's necklace in his desk, I knew they were only bribes.

Worse: he made me his accomplice. He liked having me know.'

Beth caught the hand she'd curled into a claw. 'Don't put that on yourself. Mother did treat us better. Even before you told what Daddy did, you talked about Mary Alice. You mourned her. You reminded Mummy there was a reason to doubt her husband's word. She couldn't face that. But I think, in her heart, she knew. When you called her that first time, after you started stripping, she never told him what you'd been doing. I think she was afraid he'd track you down.' She covered her mouth with a fist, forcing back another spate of tears. 'Rachel, my eldest, looks just like you did at her age. One day I looked at her and saw you staring at Daddy. I saw you not believing Daddy's lies. Oh, I just want to die when I think of all those years you spent alone with nobody to look out for you! I wish I'd tried to find you as soon as I remembered. I shouldn't have waited a day. I shouldn't have let my shame stand in the way.'

'Don't.' Chloe cupped her sister's anguished face, remembering the girl she'd been, remembering stories whispered under bedsheet tents and holding hands for the walk to school. Despite everything, there had been love between them, more than enough to compensate for moments of weakness Chloe had known herself. 'Don't be ashamed,' she said. 'You're here now. The things he did can't keep us apart any more. We can be sisters again, if we want to.'

Beth squared her shoulders. 'I want that, Sam. I want that more than anything.'

From his bedroom window, he watched them amble through the garden. Chloe was taller than her sister. She had her hands shoved in her coat pockets. Beth gestured as she talked, the motions familiar; family traits, he

245

supposed. Both their heads were bowed but they brushed shoulders as they walked. They were twining the threads that bound them back together. He could see that from here.

God keep her, he thought. Lead her down the right path, even if it leads away from me.

He reached the entryway just as Chloe was saying goodbye.

'New Year,' she said, kissing her sister's cheek. 'If you think Mom and Sharon can handle it.'

Her sister hugged her back. 'Promise you'll come see me even if they can't. I told Terry, my husband. He wants to meet you, too.'

'I'll try.'

Beth shook her finger. 'Try hard, Sis. I don't want to start another year without you.'

She waved past Chloe's shoulder at him, and then they were alone. Chloe shut the door and rested her forehead against it. David stayed where he was. 'Do you want to talk?' he said.

She shook her head. 'I need to think. It's so much to take in.'

'Your memory came back, didn't it?'

She turned. Her face was different. Her expression had a depth he'd never seen in it before. She looked both older and more beautiful. With her thumb she turned the ring he'd given her back and forth. He supposed he should be glad she hadn't removed it.

'Yes,' she said. 'I remember everything.'

'I'm sorry I lied to you about being married. I –'

'No.' She held up her hand. 'Don't explain. I can't handle any more right now. I'm not angry. I just ... can't handle it.'

'I understand.' He retreated one step upwards, his face stiff from trying to hide his hurt. 'I'll be in the library if you change your mind. I have some work to catch up on.'

She nodded, but he wasn't entirely certain she'd heard.

The kitchen was empty. Chloe wasn't sure why she'd come here. To find Auntie, perhaps, to prove she was worth forgiving by someone who didn't love her.

Someone like herself.

She prepared a serving of green tea, stirring a teaspoon of the bitter powder into a soup-bowl-sized dish. The drink needed honey, but she let it be. The sorrows of life were in that brew. All she needed was a bit of salt and she could drink a cup of tears.

She gazed at the array of pots on the wall. Auntie and the kitchen staff had scrubbed them so well she could see her reflection in their copper bottoms. Spoons hung from a line of hooks next to the huge stainless steel stove. She thought of David's scar. When she'd asked about it the first time, he'd said a cinder leapt out of a fire. They'd both lied to protect their parents.

She propped her elbows on the counter and lifted the dish of tea, gripping it Western-style, taking the warmth in through her palms. David could have told the truth. She'd bet his love for his mother made more sense than the corner of her soul that mourned the judge. That was some irony. She, who'd been living as if she'd forgotten how to love, still felt something for the one person who'd done the most to destroy her capacity for it. Her heart must not be as cold as she'd thought.

And it had only taken being flattened by a truck to make her believe it.

Getting her memory back hadn't been what she'd expected. She wasn't the woman she'd been before the accident, or the woman she'd come to think herself after it. She'd thought the amnesia had provided her first true vision of herself, from the outside. What a monster, she'd thought, and thank God that part of her had been erased. But the outside was only half the story. There weren't two women: a good Chloe and a bad Chloe. There was only her, one woman, in whom the bitter and the sweet mixed inextricably.

Smiling wryly, Chloe reached for a tin of almond biscuits. She pried off the lid and dunked one in her tea. She took an emphatic bite. There. The bitter and the sweet in one mouthful. It wasn't bad. In fact, it was pretty damn good.

Her hatred for herself had been leading her around by the nose, sabotaging every relationship that looked as if it might reward her with more happiness than she deserved. She'd had to prove to herself how bad she was. Obviously, the job she'd done was flawed. David loved her anyway. And maybe, just maybe, she loved herself. She'd saved herself, hadn't she? Whatever the world might think of the means, she'd put her all into her stripping. She'd taken pride in it, just as she now took pride in The Seven Veils.

She barked out a laugh and popped the rest of the tea-soaked biscuit in her mouth. Even with half her brain cells on sabbatical, she'd taken care of her precious club. She'd made a silk purse from a sow's ear. If she chose, she could do the same with the rest of her life.

She wiggled her bogus wedding ring, a two-carat glitter of unmet dreams. 'How' was the question; 'how' and 'how well'.

18

He lifted the note from the centre of his bed. Was it a goodbye note? He hadn't seen Chloe since he'd left her in the entryway that morning. Now it was past sunset. Had she used the intervening hours to pack her things and leave? Fingers stiff with dread, he unfolded the plain white paper.

'Come to the practice room,' it said. 'I'm ready to talk.'

He pressed the note to his chest. Was this a good sign or a bad one? She was still here at least. But what if she wanted to go? After all he'd done to keep them together, could he really let her leave? For that matter, did he have what it took to stop her?

All he knew for certain was that he'd need his wits about him. He contemplated a head-clearing shower, then settled on a quick shave. He nicked himself twice, worrying that he'd kept her waiting too long. Finally, he filled the sink with cold water and dunked his head. Enough was enough. If she wouldn't wait five minutes for him to pull himself together, they hadn't come far enough for it to matter. He couldn't spend his life walking on eggshells.

He dried his stinging face and studied his reflection. He looked pale and stern, not what he wanted, but the best he could manage. Nerves had robbed him of the power to smile.

When Chloe first came with David to Vermont, she'd hidden her chain in a gym bag, muffled in a towel. She used the same method to carry it to his practice room.

She'd bought the thing for a former lover, a congress-man's aide who grumbled every time she dragged it out, but brayed with pleasure when she bound him. The links were heavy stainless steel, two fingers thick, and long enough to wrap a straining male body like a string of Christmas lights.

This would be the first time the chain had wrapped her.

She shut the door, lit three votive candles, and stripped off her clothes. A low, electric hum flowed through her naked limbs. She remembered the sensation from her performing days. In a way, this was a perform-ance, too, but a performance for someone she loved. That made it different. Her anticipation ran deeper tonight. A pulse settled between her legs like tom-toms pounding out a call.

She spread the towel and knelt. The geisha pose came easier now. With a soft clink, she draped a loop of chain behind her neck. The steel was cold. Her nipples shrank at the chill. She let one end dangle to the 'Y' where her abdomen met her thighs, then crossed the other beneath one breast, behind her back and around her front again. The arrangement lifted her breasts in offering. She cir-cled her waist three times. The last loop bound her hips. A few feet of chain remained, twinkling silver in the candlelight. She arranged the final length across her thighs, her pleasure at its shiny sleekness both childish and adult. The combination lock was huge, bigger than her fist. She set it, shank open, on the towel in front of her knees. She folded her hands.

She was trembling. This time, though, as she waited for her lover, her emotions were not at war. She wanted this, not merely for David, but for herself. Beneath the warming, snakelike weight of the chain, her sex was wet and yielding. She closed her eyes and imagined him inside her, over her, his body pressing the metal into her tender skin. She began to breathe harder, her belly moving in and out beneath its self-imposed constraints. She hadn't known just thinking about submission could excite her. When her fantasy appeared in the flesh, she'd have to be careful not to lose herself

A rush of cold air brought her eyes open. David was entering through the tea garden, ducking under the sliding door. A shiver that was more than a chill swept her skin. She remembered the night she'd let him watch her dance. Then, she'd revelled in her power. Then, she'd been in control. Tonight she'd taste the opposite thrill. Her trepidation was so like arousal she wasn't sure she knew the difference.

He walked forwards until his stockinged feet touched her knees. His khaki trousers still held the morning's knife-like crease. He brushed a lock of hair from her face. 'What's all this?' he said.

She squeezed her hands together in her lap. 'I want you to know I can surrender to you. Even with my memories back, I can do it.'

'Is that what you think I need? You, on your knees, chained like a slave?' When she didn't respond, he hunkered before her, haunches on heels, knees spread so that the warmth of his body beat towards her. The lock lay between his feet. 'Chloe, I've always enjoyed our lovemaking, no matter who led the way. You don't have to do something you're not comfortable with just to please me.'

'That's not what this is about.'

'Isn't it?' He touched her cheek. 'Aren't you afraid I can't love you as you are?'

'I think you can love me. I'm just not sure you can live with me.' She fiddled with the end of the chain, unable to lift her gaze. This was not going as she'd expected. 'Maybe you should consider this a compromise.'

His hand withdrew. 'What are we compromising?'

The caution in his voice cut her. But maybe it was warranted. She doubted he'd like this bargain. Her hands tightened on each other. She couldn't back down. Not on this.

'I can't give up the club,' she said, the words rushing out. 'I want us to be together, to be married for real if you'll have me. I know a shrink would have a field day over why I'm drawn to it, but I'm proud of what I've accomplished at The Seven Veils.' David opened his mouth to speak but she stilled him by touching his knee. She lifted her eyes, letting him see she meant every word. 'I'm not a healer, David. I'm not a computer genius or a cordon bleu chef. I'm not even a great dancer. I'm a spinner of sexual fantasies. That's my one true gift. If you ask me to give it up, you ask me to be less than I can be. I won't let you do that. I wouldn't let anyone.'

He was the first to break eye contact. Some strong emotion had him in its grip. He braced his fingers against the towel to steady his balance.

'Say something,' she said.

He shook his head. 'You shame me.'

'No.' She clasped his wrist where tendons tensed under his weight. 'That's not what I mean to do. I understand how hard this is for you. You're a public figure. You have a position to maintain. People would snicker if they knew your wife ran a sex show.'

'If I love you, I shouldn't give a damn.'

'You're only human.'

'Too human.' Half his mouth curved in a smile. 'I've been foolish, Chloe. All my life I've wanted to be respected, to fit in. But I never will: not here, not in Japan. I'll always be different.'

'Different isn't bad. You made your fortune by being a maverick.'

'Yes, I did. You'd think I'd have stopped wanting to be anything else a long time ago.'

'David, I understand why you need to –'

'No, you don't, because you don't understand the other David Imakita, the David Imakita who fell in love with a wild woman because he wished he could be wild himself.' He raked his hair back with a sigh. 'I haven't been fair. I wanted it both ways. I still do. I can't bear to think of you dancing for strangers, and I'd never agree to share you. But if you gave up who you are, if you became a demure, respectable woman . . .'

His voice trailed away, the conflict in his eyes now. Somewhere deep inside her a smile began to warm. He was saying her badness excited him. He was admitting that no matter what she did, she'd always have the power to make him want her.

She'd have to be very careful not to abuse the weapon he'd laid in her hands.

'You're a brave man,' she said.

He touched the chain that circled her waist. 'No braver than you. You make me proud, Chloe.'

She watched his eyes, measuring his sincerity. Was he proud of her? Was it possible? But she had to believe him. She had to take this leap or there was no going forwards from here. She drew a deep breath and let it out and knocked a hole in the wall she'd built between herself and every man who'd ever loved her. David was welcome inside. However this ended, she promised herself she'd never be sorry she'd let him in. This was the risk with which she reclaimed her soul.

'You'll be the only one I sleep with,' she said. 'The only one I love. No matter who I dance for, no matter who I tease, I'll always come home to you.'

'And you won't give up being wild?' He stroked her breasts between the chains, the back of his fingers skimming their peaks. 'You won't let me change you too much?'

She laughed, suddenly seeing the humour in her position. 'Really, David, I wouldn't say wrapping my naked body in chains is a sign of creeping conservatism. Think of it as an invitation for you to be wild with me. You know I like seeing you let your hair down, and I know you like taking charge.'

His eyes glowed, then shuttered. 'Sometimes,' he said. 'But not tonight.' Scooting closer, he took the chain that looped her neck and lifted it over his head. 'Come on. Let's be slaves together.'

The suggestion turned to honey between her legs. She smoothed her hands up his chest. 'If we're slaves, baby, this shirt has got to go.'

He smiled quite wickedly for a corporate stiff. 'No one's stopping you from taking it off.'

He nuzzled her neck as she undid the buttons, sucking her skin between his teeth and pricking it with tiny bites. She shivered, but did not falter at her task. His breathing grew quicker. She shoved his shirt over his shoulders, glorying in their fine, lean width. Hands were not enough. Helpless to resist, she dragged her teeth across the muscle, nipping him as he'd nipped her. He yanked his arms free of the cuffs and set his hands on her waist. His fingers slipped between the metal links.

'Take off my trousers,' he said, a whispered order. No, she thought. She didn't have to obey. Not yet.

She cupped his erection through the khaki and kneaded him: deep, ball-compressing squeezes. When his chest was as red as his cheeks, she let go. The candles threw shadows over the creases at his crotch. She scratched them with her nails. 'Say the magic word, David-san.'

'Please,' he whispered, and licked the bite he'd placed at the crook of her neck. 'Please undo my trousers.'

She released the catch, then dragged down the straining zip. His cotton briefs swelled through the opening. His hips rolled in silent plea. But silence wasn't good enough, not tonight, not with all the dreams she'd been dreaming. 'Shall I lift you out?'

'Yes,' he said, his voice like strong black coffee.

She lowered his waistband, not rushing the unveiling, watching new skin emerge a fraction at a time. Hipbones appeared, then the concave sweep of his abdomen, and an arrow of tangled hair. His cock bobbed as if yearning towards her touch. Its head was caught beneath the waist of his briefs. He looked down at himself, at her hands so close to his pulsing sex. His fingers dug into her buttocks. His forehead grazed her brow. Heat poured through Chloe's veins. She knew what he wanted. She knew what she wanted. The suspense was thick enough to eat. She pulled the elastic free and he sprung upward, his cap dewed with a single tear. She'd never seen him so hard. She reached deeper and pulled his balls into the open as well. Their wrinkled skin tightened as she handled it, the weight convulsing with excitement in her palm.

'I want you,' he said. 'I don't think I can wait.'

She swept both thumbs up the rigid girder of his cock. 'You aren't the only one, baby.'

He started to smile, but she covered it with a kiss. He moaned and increased the pressure until the edge of his teeth bruised her lips. Gasping, he broke free. 'I'm taking you,' he said. 'Right now.'

He lifted her on to his lap, on to the hot, smooth curve of his glans. Her pussy contracted as he found her quivering entry. He was there, right there, blazing silk pushing up through her cream, past her aching, swollen walls. He was thick and perfect and strong. With a throaty sigh, she sank to his root. Chains clinked, then scored her flesh as he embraced her. 'Wrap the end around me,' he said. 'I want us chained together.'

She passed the last length behind him, her hands shaking with excitement. All of her shook, inside and out. This was so good. This was nothing she'd ever dreamt. He seemed to know what she was thinking. He seemed to love it. He drew circles on her back as if drinking her tremors through his skin. 'Tighter,' he demanded in a new, harsh voice. 'And lock it.'

She pushed the big lock between two links and snapped it shut. It hung between her right hip and his left, a cold, solid weight. The feel of it made her clench around him, then soften with a liquid rush. They were bound together. Nothing could tear them apart.

'You like this,' he growled. 'You're dripping down my cock.'

She couldn't deny it. She didn't want to. Lost in the thrill, she began to rock. The chains raked each other, one loop holding his head, the other his waist. They were a fulcrum to guide her strokes, to deepen them, strengthen them. The metal bit her skin but she didn't care. She clutched his shoulders, a child on a rope, giving herself to the joy of swinging high. She loved him. She didn't care how far she fell.

He caught the back of her neck and kissed her, groaning into her mouth, trying to cram his cock further in. 'Deeper,' he said. 'Take it all.'

She took him. Her muscles strained. Her heart exulted. They strove together in the chains, slipping out of sync as they both began to lose control. Her skin grew slippery, his hold unsure. He gripped the links that crossed her back and pulled her harder yet. Her thighs ached, a strangely sensual pain. She was strong enough to take it; brave enough to take it. Feeling built between her legs, rising hammer blows of pleasure. Impact. Withdrawal. Shove. And pull. Heat swelled. She was thick inside: tight. A thousand nerves compressed with every thrust. He was stronger than she was. She gave the rhythm over to him; let him control each stab of bliss. Finally, he battered the crucial barrier between striving to come and not being able to stop it.

'Now,' she begged against his panting mouth. 'Let it go.'

He pulled in a breath. He drove deep, then threw his head back against the chain. He groaned. The sound slammed her into orgasm. She felt his penis shoot and a second wave of rapture drowned her first. Her sex throbbed around his, soft walls tensing, draining every spasm. She could not let go. She clutched him with all her might. Then he moaned her name and she relaxed, completely, every muscle. An incredible sense of wellness filled her being. Her cheek dropped to his shoulder, his to her head. They sighed in unison at the utter heaven of release.

'God,' he breathed. 'That was good.'

She began to chuckle, then to laugh.

'What?' He rubbed his cheek across her hair.

'I'm happy,' she said, 'and I don't feel guilty at all.'

David skipped down the stairs whistling a passage from Rimsky-Korsakov's *Scheherazade*. Chloe was hugging the pillow. If getting her memory back reminded her she wasn't a morning person, making up had robbed her of any desire to fake it. David was too happy to complain. Anyway, he had to fly to Seattle today, to meet one of Imakita's manufacturers.

When he hit the first floor, he noticed Auntie overseeing a handful of staff who were carrying boxes up from the basement. Her expression was fierce, but her eyes sparkled. David peered past a cardboard flap. Christmas ornaments. Apparently, Auntie had decided the holidays were coming this year. None too soon, either. Christmas Eve was – good Lord – two days from now.

He kissed the housekeeper's cheek. 'Save the tree for me.'

Auntie hmphed. 'Don't I always?'

'Yes, you always. You're a gem among gems.'

He wondered if Chloe would help. She'd decorated her precious club, after all. She couldn't be too uptight about the trappings of Christian holidays. Just in case, though, he'd see if he could find a menorah in Seattle.

The smell of eggs and sausage wafted out from the dining room. Mm. He was starving. He swung into the room and stopped. Sato sat before a loaded plate, eating with slow deliberation. A bright red napkin covered his tie and shirtfront. David couldn't recall the last time he'd seen him at a meal. His mood sobered. His happiness had come at a cost to his oldest friend.

'Morning,' he said, and turned to the sideboard where the chafing dishes sat.

Sato returned the greeting with an unintelligible grunt. He gave David a few minutes to eat before pulling the napkin from his collar. He wiped his mouth. 'I have news, master.'

David winced at the title. He set down his fork. 'Yes?'

'It's from the private firm I hired to watch Chloe's father.' His face stiffened. 'I'm afraid it is not very timely. I did not keep up with that correspondence as I should have.'

'I know her father's dead, if that's what you mean. Her sister showed up yesterday looking for her.'

Sato's neck bowed another inch. 'Then I am doubly sorry not to have prepared you.'

'Sato.' David laid his hand on his friend's sloping shoulder. 'There's no harm done. Everything turned out for the best.'

'Chloe's memory –?'

'Has returned. But it's not a problem. We've reached an agreement.' He turned his cup in its saucer. Sato might not enjoy hearing the rest, but it didn't seem fair to keep him in the dark. 'I think we're getting married for real.'

'You have asked her?'

'More or less.'

Sato nodded as if he'd been expecting this. He pushed to his feet. The only sign of his agitation was his napkin falling to the floor. 'Congratulations,' he said. 'Let me know the date and I will arrange security.'

He left, ignoring David's attempt to call him back. David sighed into the dregs of his coffee. He had to do something about Sato, for Sato. But God only knew what.

The big evergreen twinkled in the corner of the living room, draped with lights and balls and tiny straw dolls in traditional Japanese costume. David considered himself no more Christian than he was Shinto or Buddhist, but he had to admit he had a soft spot for the rituals of Christmas. Happily, Chloe didn't mind. She sat on the step-ladder, gazing at the garish Laura Fleet doll that served as this year's angel. Laura's silver derringer glinted in the tiny lights. With her hands on her hips, she looked as if she were daring them not to have a merry Christmas.

David smoothed her hair over her shoulder and kissed her cheek. 'Happy?'

'Very.' She wrapped one arm around his waist. 'But I have a confession to make.'

'A confession?'

'I'd forgotten until now. I'm afraid I'm blackmailing your company.' His jaw dropped and she burst out laughing. 'It's true. The fellow who used me as the model for Laura Fleet tried to squirm out of paying me. I got angry and went to the company lawyers. I told them if they didn't agree to pay me a percentage of the take, I'd pose for *Penthouse* and tell the world I was the real Laura Fleet.' She rubbed the side of her nose, sheepishly amused. 'I guess they didn't want that kind of publicity for a family game.'

David pinched the bridge of his nose. 'I can't believe none of my employees saw fit to tell me this.'

'Don't be mad. They argued me down to a small percentage, virtually minuscule. Nobody knew those games would be so popular. Afterwards, I think they were too embarrassed to admit they'd been out-bargained by a stripper.'

'They'll be more than embarrassed when I get through with them.'

She tugged his tie. 'Don't make a fuss. I can give the money back. I've socked it away.' She grinned. 'I've got a secret Swiss bank account.'

He couldn't resist her childish glee. He pulled her off the ladder and into his arms. 'You don't need to give it back. We're paying for the use of your image. That's not blackmail. It's unusual, maybe, but not blackmail.' He rested his cheek against her hair. 'I presume the lawyers got it in writing that you won't pose nude for publication.'

'I knew you'd like that part.'

'I admit I don't hate it.'

'You,' she said, 'are not completely reformed.'

'And you are?'

Her eyes slanted, cat-like. 'Think how dull your life would be if I were.'

He kissed the tip of her nose. 'I can stand a little dullness.'

'Well,' she said airily, 'maybe I can, too.'

He knew she meant it, for all her teasing tone. He hugged her closer and they swayed before the glittering tree. Like newlyweds, he thought, though of course they weren't. She snuggled her nose into the crook of his neck, inhaling his scent with a relish he found incredibly endearing. Her next words, however, were not so sweet. 'I think we should wait a year.'

'You mean, before we get married?'

'We've been through so much. We need time to get to know each other, to be sure.'

He thought this over. 'Six months.'

'Six months isn't very long.'

He teased his tongue around the shell of her ear. She shivered. He decided he liked this negotiation method. 'In six months you could be a June bride.'

'Ugh.'

'OK, I could be a June groom.'

She scrunched her shoulder to evade his mouth. 'I refuse to wear white.'

He laughed silently to himself. She was giving in. They really were going to be married. 'You can wear any colour you want as long as the important parts are covered.'

'Ho ho. Which are the important parts?'

He lifted her off her feet and kissed her breathless. 'Come to my room and I'll show you.'

'Fine,' she said.

'Fine,' he answered, and they both ran up the stairs.

Chloe trailed her hand down the centre of his ribs until her palm lay on the warm, heaving hollow beneath. He'd really gone the distance for her, actually *shtupped* her to the point of screaming. Now his cock lay limp and heavy across his thigh. She followed its curving line with the tip of one finger. 'Happy?' she said, echoing his own question.

He smiled like a sated tiger and stretched against the rumpled covers. She had put that smug expression on his face. It pleased her more than she would have dreamed possible.

She ran her finger back to his navel. 'Have you told Sato about us getting married?'

His smile faded. 'Yes,' he said, and she knew he wouldn't truly be happy until his friend was.

'Do you want me to talk to him?' she offered.

'No.' He petted her hair over her breasts. 'This is something I need to handle myself.'

David set the weekly security report aside. He rested his hips on the front edge of his desk, his ankles crossed, his ribs a vice around his heart. Sato waited, stiff and flushed. Hard as he tried to hide it, the pain in his eyes was like the spark at the end of a live wire. David could almost hear it buzzing. 'We need to talk, old friend,' he said.

Sato's jaw tightened. 'I am sorry, master. I have ruined our friendship.'

David cursed and led him to the library's sofa. He pushed Sato down, then took a seat beside him. 'Listen,' he said. 'You haven't ruined anything. You felt what you felt. You're human. I'm sorry I didn't see it sooner.'

Sato swallowed. 'I treasure every day you spent in ignorance. At least then we were friends.'

'We're still friends, damn it. No one knows me better than you.'

'I betrayed you.'

David raked his hair back and looked to the ceiling for inspiration. He didn't know which offence to address: Sato's sleeping with Chloe, or his supposedly repulsive infatuation with him. Chloe first, he thought. Even Sato had to admit there were extenuating circumstances there.

He propped his forearms on his knees, mimicking Sato's pose. 'Chloe and I had no promises between us, not then, and I know she pursued you. You only betrayed your sense of what was due me for offering you a chance to succeed outside the sumo ring. But you've done a great job for me. I've always owed you as much as you owe me. Anyway, that's done. Let's put it behind us.' He pressed folded hands to his mouth. 'I have something difficult to tell you.'

'If it's about the wedding . . .'

'No. It's about you.' He squeezed his fingers tighter. 'I'm firing you.'

Sato's whole body jerked. David had to grab his arm to keep him from rising. 'It's nothing to do with your performance. I have no complaints on that score. But I know you won't leave unless I make you. You think I need protecting, someone to pick up the pieces when Chloe and I break up. I don't think that's going to happen, but if it does, I'm strong enough to survive it. You need to worry about you for a while. You need to get away.' He met Sato's stricken gaze. 'I'm giving you a year's severance pay.'

'A year's!' This time Sato did jump to his feet.

'Say another word and I'll make it two.' David chose to take Sato's grimace as a smile. He stood and gripped his shoulder. 'I hope you'll spend the money serving no one but yourself.'

Sato stared at the polished black tips of his shoes. 'It has been my honour to serve you.'

David didn't know what he'd done to earn this devotion, much less how to repay it. Words failing, he cupped the side of Sato's face. What he saw there humbled him: such pain, such love. For the first time, Sato's feelings became real to him, to heart as well as head. Sato loved him, not as David loved Sato, but as David loved Chloe. A wave of pity swamped his chest.

'Master,' said Sato, his voice all misery.

David pressed his lips to his forehead, but it seemed a

Judas kiss, not nearly enough to prove he thought no less of his friend because he loved where David couldn't. He lowered his mouth to Sato's.

Sato stiffened in shock. For a moment, neither moved. David could hear their watches ticking. He wondered if he should pull back, if he had done the wrong thing, but then Sato opened the kiss and closed him in his arms. The hardness of his mouth was strange, the weight and breadth of his body. He stood quiet under the strangeness, accepting what Sato needed to give, returning what he could. He stroked Sato's hair, the first time he could recall doing so. Its surface was as sleek as a seal's. He was not aroused, but there was pleasure in this caress, perhaps the simple pleasure of giving comfort.

It wasn't long before Sato pulled back, his face flushed but calm. 'Thank you,' he said. 'Now I know.'

David wasn't sure what he knew, but if Sato was more at peace, so was David – despite feeling terribly embarrassed now that the kiss was over.

'I will leave before the week is out,' Sato said.

'There's no rush.'

'It is better if I go soon.'

'I'll miss you,' David said, then wondered if he should have.

Sato smiled like a temple Buddha. 'Good,' he said. 'I will miss you, too.'

They exchanged their presents in private, in bed. The jewellery box she'd found in his closet turned out to contain an uncut ruby as big as her thumbnail. Wow, she thought, admiring its blood-red glow.

'I thought you could have it set in a ring,' he said.

She flashed her diamond. 'You already gave me a ring.'

He cleared his throat. 'A more private sort of ring.'

'I see.' Her chest shook with the laugh she was holding

inside. She should have known. Her proper American lover had a piercing fetish. 'Any suggestions as to where I might wear the ring?'

'It's totally up to you,' he said, but she could hear his erotic gears turn. He had a preference all right, a deep, dark fantasy. She knew she'd enjoy coaxing the secret loose.

Fighting a grin, she handed him her own package, gaily wrapped in the Hanukkah paper he'd brought back from Seattle. The festival of lights wasn't actually burning today, but his consideration meant the world.

He began easing the paper loose. 'You've got this taped good,' he laughed.

She started to say she hoped he liked it, then wiped sweaty palms down her thighs. She'd braved the last-minute crowds to shop for the rest of the household, but for David she'd found nothing nearly good enough. His gift had to be special. His gift had to say something. In the end, she'd boxed up her chain and taped the combination to the lock.

She held her breath as he pried off the lid. He stared. He reached inside and stroked the shiny metal. The chain clinked. His lips moved as he read the combination. A wine-red flush spread upward from his chest.

'We'll share this,' he said, his voice thick.

She knew she had done the right thing.

19

Sato descended the steps from the boardwalk and crossed the sand to the edge of the Atlantic. A beach at daybreak: what more could a lonely man want? The breeze was brisk, the waves capped with foam. The air smelled of salt and fish and, very faintly, yesterday's suntan lotion. An old man with a baseball cap and a metal detector nodded as he passed on his search for buried treasure. Two hotels down, a woman and a young child fought with a recalcitrant kite. The wind carried their shrieks of laughter. Other than that, Sato had the beach to himself.

He still felt self-conscious. His bathing suit had not seemed so small in the shop. With an effort, he shrugged off his embarrassment. His body would never be less than solid, but he was leaner than he'd been in some time. He had been training his staff to function without him, training them hard for the last six months.

It felt like six days.

He had meant to leave at once; truly he had, but David had not pushed and somehow there was always one more thing to do. Finally, Chloe had come to him with a gentle smile and a set of plane tickets. 'A friend of mine owns a hotel in Atlantic City,' she said. 'He'll make sure you're comfortable. The day after the wedding, you go.'

Then she had hugged him, quickly, as if she were embarrassed to be caught doing him a kindness.

She had also asked for the name of the private detective he had engaged to follow her father. 'My family and I have decided to hire him,' she said. 'If we put our heads together, we're hoping we can figure out what he did with Mary Alice's body. After all these years, her family deserves to know what really happened. They deserve to bury their daughter.' Her eyes had gleamed with determination. He could only imagine what it had cost her family to face that old tragedy, and what it had cost her to make them do so. But they had come through it. Ever since Beth's visit, one or the other of her sisters called her every week.

He had stopped worrying about her and David. Even if he had not, he would have when he saw her at the wedding in her gold satin gown, beaming at her husband-to-be. A thousand stars had shone from her face. No one could doubt her love was real.

Lips twitching with a reluctant smile, Sato moved to the dry part of the beach and sat. The wedding had begun with disaster. Chloe's youngest sister accidentally set fire to her veil, the limo service drove some of the guests to the wrong hotel, and the band leader had shown up deeply in his cups. He had pulled himself together, but never had 'Blue Moon' sounded so dazed.

Sato dug his toes into the cool, powdery sand. The guest list had been mixed, to say the least. The Seven Veils' staff had rubbed elbows with its customers, who bumped along beside David's colleagues from Asia, who stared wide-eyed at everyone else. Imakita's American employees spent most of their time tugging at their ties or slipping off their heels. Apparently, computer geeks did not enjoy dressing up. They gazed at Chloe's glamourous friends almost as wide-eyed as the foreigners. If David had ever hoped to keep his business associates separate from Chloe's, he had burned that bridge by inviting them all.

Sato approved of the decision. Better to declare these things than to live in fear of having them discovered. At any rate, the differences between the factions dissolved as soon as the bottomless bar opened. From what he could see, the guests had a wonderful time, even the mothers of Chloe and David. Though they had begun by circling each other like wary dogs, the two widows had ended up commiserating over champagne.

'She doesn't want children,' Chloe's mother had complained.

'And he says he doesn't mind!' David's wailed.

Sato had chuckled at that. Mothers. The world over they were the same. He braced his arms on the sand behind him, relishing the wind in his face. The ceremony itself had been simple. At its conclusion, David had smashed a wine glass under his heel and all Chloe's relatives shouted '*mazel tov!*' This was not half as startling as when they put the bridal couple in chairs and carried them, shoulder-high, around the room. Everyone had caught the spirit of it, even the Japanese. 'Higher,' Auntie had cried. 'Carry them to the moon!' Sato could still see his friends bobbing above the sea of joyous faces, laughing themselves and hanging on for dear life.

Later, Sato had let Chloe drag him into that exuberant Jewish circle dance, that *hora*. He had kicked with the best of them, roaring out the *Hava Nagila*. For a while, he even forgot his broken heart.

David had glowed like he'd had a visit from the Buddha. Sato had never seen him so content. He knew it was time he admitted it. Chloe was good for his old master. Chloe made David happy.

And wasn't that what every man should wish for the person he loved?

With that thought foremost, he had stiffened his spine to dance with the bride. Chloe rewarded his diplomacy by making fun of his date, a sweet Hungarian without a thought in her head beyond what she could do to please him. 'You can do better than that,' she said as they waltzed around the glittering ballroom. 'David's lead programmer, for instance. Sure, he's a geek, but he's got a good body and he was definitely giving you the eye.'

If he was, Sato had not noticed. Then again, he had not noticed much lately. Even last night when he picked up that boy at the casino bar, he had not bothered to remember his name.

He narrowed his eyes at the sparkling horizon. The sex had been fantastic. The first time they had not even removed their clothes. The boy merely fell to his knees behind the door, dragged down Sato's zip and sucked his raging erection into his mouth. Ah, the pleasures of a male mouth, so warm and strong and fearless! He brought Sato to the edge in minutes, but Sato had not wanted to come that way, not the first time. He lifted the boy up, watching his eyes widen as his feet left the floor, as his jeans were torn down his legs. Sato had pinned him to the wall with his shoulders, hiked his legs around his hips, and ripped the condom open with his teeth. With one thrust, he buried six months of longing between the firm pink cheeks of his arse.

'Wow,' the boy had said. 'You are hot.'

He had masturbated himself while Sato fucked him, his hand a blur between their bellies, spitting in his palm when the friction grew too hot, moving the loose, flushed skin up and down the rigid spike. Sato had never seen a man do that before, not in front of him, not so openly. His skin had prickled all over with awe. He had not been able to look away. He came much more quickly than he intended, but his eyes remained open. When the boy reached his crisis a moment later, Sato wrenched one hand from his buttocks to cover the spurting head.

'Oh, yeah,' groaned the boy, squeezing Sato's palm so close it must have hurt. 'That's the stuff.'

Sato had not even softened when he pulled out. He was ready to go again before the boy had caught his breath. It had been a long time since he had slept with anyone, man or woman. He was sure this explained why he was so potent with his partner, why they had exhausted two boxes of condoms and a whole bottle of lubricant. Sato's organ was still a little sore, and he might have pulled a calf muscle when he bent the boy over the bureau and took him 'doggy' style. The boy had claimed he wanted to watch Sato in the mirror. He himself had been an inspiring sight, a beautiful, healthy, milk-fed specimen of American male. A true blond. Sato had fallen asleep running his fingers through his golden thatch. No doubt, Chloe would have made fun of that, too.

Since they had spent so little time talking, Sato could not say if the boy was smart. He had been sweet, though, and – like the Hungarian – eager to please. Unlike the Hungarian, however, he had interested Sato enough to take to bed. He might be worth seeing again, as long as he was here. He found himself hoping the boy would still be in the room when he returned.

The pad of sandy footfalls made Sato turn. As if his thoughts had conjured him up, the boy approached in all his fair, athletic glory. His abs were so tight Sato could count each muscle. He held two lidded cups of designer coffee from one of the chains his countrymen loved. 'I don't know if you drink this stuff,' he said, 'but it's strong and black.'

'I drink it,' Sato said and took both cups while the boy plunked down beside him.

They sipped in silence, watching waves curl and foam across the pearly sand. An unexpected peace swelled in Sato's breast. Life went on, just like the ocean. At least his body was ready to move on. As the Americans liked to say, that was nothing to sneeze at.

The boy drained the last of his coffee and planted the cup in the soft, pale sand between his feet. He looked at Sato from the corner of his eye. 'You're an interesting man,' he said. 'You have an intensity a person doesn't see very often, and I don't just mean in bed.' He screwed the empty cup in a circle. 'I'd like to see you again, Sato, but I need to tell you something first.'

'Yes?' Sato said, flattered and a little curious.

The boy blew out his breath, perhaps for courage. 'I like women,' he said, 'and I won't pretend I don't.'

Sato began to laugh. He laughed until his belly shook, until tears ran down his cheeks. He had not laughed this hard in years. The young man stared at him as if he did not know whether to get angry or join in. 'Forgive me,' Sato gasped, giving the young man's arm a squeeze. 'I am not laughing at you. I know some gay men do not feel comfortable with bisexuals. This, however, is not a problem. You see, I like women myself.'

'Oh,' said the young man. 'But you like men, too, right? I mean, I couldn't have been your first.'

Sato coughed back another laugh. 'No. You were not my first. Merely my first in a long time.'

'Yeah, well, I could tell you'd been, uh, storing it up. You were pretty awesome.'

Sato could not resist teasing. 'You mean for an old man.'

Beneath his golden tan, the young man's face turned the colour of a brick. 'No, no. I think you're just right. Guys my age, well, sometimes they don't have much to talk about afterwards. Just cars and shit, you know, or working out.' He grimaced in disgust.

'Physical fitness is important.'

'Well, sure.' The young man waved his hands. 'I go to the gym, but I don't want to talk about it. I just want to do it. Do you like opera?'

Sato blinked to follow this shift of subject. He answered slowly. 'I like *kabuki*.'

The young man nodded. 'I saw some *kabuki* once in San Francisco. It was about these forty-seven masterless samurai. *Ronin*, they called them. It was pretty cool: the costumes and the way the actors made the speeches sound so dramatic. I gotta tell you, though, I didn't understand what was so honourable about everybody killing themselves at the end.'

'No,' Sato agreed. 'Living is more difficult than dying.'

'Amen.' The young man's voice held such fervour Sato thought he might not be so young after all.

But he seemed to have run out of conversation. He squirmed in the sand, his taut buttocks digging out a seat like a boy with ants in his pants. Then he forced himself to stop. The part of Sato that had trained David's security staff approved his effort at self-control. The young man moistened his lips. 'So,' he said. 'Would you like to get together again and, you know, see what happens?'

The young man's bravery touched him. Sato gathered his long, tanned hand into his own and gently rubbed its back. With some astonishment, he realised he had never made this kind of gesture in public before. Unaware of this, the boy's eyes sparked with a return of arousal. Sato felt his cheeks warm, among other things.

'Yes,' Sato said. 'I would like to see you again.'

'Good.' His companion's smile flashed like sunshine. ''Cause you are the hottest thing I've tumbled across in years.'

They both laughed, their hands linked tight with the kind of tension that would soon dictate a return to the hotel. Enjoying the rising urgency, now that he knew it would be met, Sato lifted his face and watched a trio of gulls wheel over a jetty.

'I am ashamed to admit this,' he said with a rumbling chuckle. 'But you will have to tell me your name . . .'

Visit the Black Lace website at
www.black-lace-books.com

LOOK OUT FOR THE ALL-NEW BLACK LACE BOOKS – AVAILABLE NOW!

All books priced £7.99 in the UK. Please note publication dates apply to the UK only. For other territories, please contact your retailer.

SUITE SEVENTEEN
Portia Da Costa
ISBN 978 0 352 34109 9

When vibrant, forty-something widow Annie Conroy spies her new neighbours having kinky sex in their back garden, she decides it's time that she too woke up and smelt the erotic roses. And where better to begin her daring adventures than the luxurious Waverley Grange Country Hotel, and its hidden den of iniquity, the chintz-clad but wickedly pervy Suite Seventeen? Under the stern but playful eye of exotic master Valentino, Annie quickly discovers the shocking hidden depths of her own sensuality, and surrenders herself body and soul to his outrageous games of power. But when the Waverley's entire future hangs in the balance, and Annie has the means to help save it, dare she gamble on going one step further . . . and giving her heart to the mysterious man who's come to control her?

Coming in July 2007

THE TEN VISIONS
Olivia Knight
ISBN 978 0 352 34119 8

The moment she starts her doctorate in Oxford, Sarah is beset with mysteries. An old portrait in her rented house bears an uncanny resemblance to her. Her new lover insists he's a ghost. Her attractive, sinister supervisor refuses to let her see manuscripts on witchcraft. An ordinary hill on the meadow fills her with fear – and not just her, but also the man with whom she falls in love. Every time she has sex, she hallucinates strange places and other times.

   Through sex magic and orgasmic visions, she must fight betrayal to learn the truth behind the secrets.

LEARNING TO LOVE IT
Alison Tyler
ISBN 978 0 352 33535 7

Art historian Lissa and doctor Colin meet at the Frankfurt Book Fair, where they are both promoting their latest books. At the fair, and then through Europe, the two lovers embark on an exploration of their sexual fantasies, playing intense games of bondage, spanking and dressing up. Lissa loves humiliation, and Colin is just the man to provide her with the pleasure she craves. Unbeknown to Lissa, their meeting was not accidental, but planned ahead by a mysterious patron of the erotic arts.

Coming in August 2007

THE BLUE GUIDE
Carrie Williams
ISBN 978 0 352 34131 0

Cocktails, room service, spa treatments: Alicia Shaw is a girl who just can't say no to the little perks of being a private tour guide in London. Whether it's the Hollywood producer with whom she romps in the private screening room of one of London's most luxurious hotels, or the Australian pilot whose exhibitionist fantasies reach a new height on the London Eye, Alicia finds that flirtation – and more – is part of the territory.

But when internationally renowned flamenco dancer and heartthrob Paco Manchega, and his lovely young wife Carlotta, take her on as their guide, Alicia begins to wonder if she has bitten off more than she can chew. As the couple unleash curious appetites in Alicia, taking her to places more darkly beautiful than she has ever known, she begins to suspect she is being used as the pawn in some strange marital game.

DIVINE TORMENT
Janine Ashbless
ISBN 978 0 352 33719 1

In the ancient temple city of Mulhanabin, the voluptuous Malia Shai awaits her destiny. Millions of people worship her, believing her to be a goddess incarnate. She is, however, very human and consumed by erotic passions that have no outlet. Into this sacred city comes General Verlaine – the rugged gladiatorial leader of the occupying army. Intimate contact between Veraine and Malia Shai is forbidden by every law of their hostile peoples. But she is the only thing he wants – and he will risk everything to have her.

Black Lace Booklist

Information is correct at time of printing. To avoid disappointment, check availability before ordering. Go to www.black-lace-books.com. All books are priced £7.99 unless another price is given.

BLACK LACE BOOKS WITH A CONTEMPORARY SETTING

☐ ALWAYS THE BRIDEGROOM Tesni Morgan	ISBN 978 0 352 33855 6	£6.99
☐ THE ANGELS' SHARE Maya Hess	ISBN 978 0 352 34043 6	
☐ ARIA APPASSIONATA Julie Hastings	ISBN 978 0 352 33056 7	£6.99
☐ ASKING FOR TROUBLE Kristina Lloyd	ISBN 978 0 352 33362 9	
☐ BLACK LIPSTICK KISSES Monica Belle	ISBN 978 0 352 33885 3	£6.99
☐ BONDED Fleur Reynolds	ISBN 978 0 352 33192 2	£6.99
☐ THE BOSS Monica Belle	ISBN 978 0 352 34088 7	
☐ BOUND IN BLUE Monica Belle	ISBN 978 0 352 34012 2	
☐ CAMPAIGN HEAT Gabrielle Marcola	ISBN 978 0 352 33941 6	
☐ CAT SCRATCH FEVER Sophie Mouette	ISBN 978 0 352 34021 4	
☐ CIRCUS EXCITE Nikki Magennis	ISBN 978 0 352 34033 7	
☐ CLUB CRÈME Primula Bond	ISBN 978 0 352 33907 2	£6.99
☐ COMING ROUND THE MOUNTAIN Tabitha Flyte	ISBN 978 0 352 33873 0	£6.99
☐ CONFESSIONAL Judith Roycroft	ISBN 978 0 352 33421 3	
☐ CONTINUUM Portia Da Costa	ISBN 978 0 352 33120 5	
☐ COOKING UP A STORM Emma Holly	ISBN 978 0 352 34114 3	
☐ DANGEROUS CONSEQUENCES Pamela Rochford	ISBN 978 0 352 33185 4	
☐ DARK DESIGNS Madelynne Ellis	ISBN 978 0 352 34075 7	
☐ THE DEVIL INSIDE Portia Da Costa	ISBN 978 0 352 32993 6	
☐ EDEN'S FLESH Robyn Russell	ISBN 978 0 352 33923 2	£6.99
☐ ENTERTAINING MR STONE Portia Da Costa	ISBN 978 0 352 34029 0	
☐ EQUAL OPPORTUNITIES Mathilde Madden	ISBN 978 0 352 34070 2	
☐ FEMININE WILES Karina Moore	ISBN 978 0 352 33874 7	
☐ FIRE AND ICE Laura Hamilton	ISBN 978 0 352 33486 2	
☐ GOING DEEP Kimberly Dean	ISBN 978 0 352 33876 1	£6.99
☐ GOING TOO FAR Laura Hamilton	ISBN 978 0 352 33657 6	£6.99
☐ GONE WILD Maria Eppie	ISBN 978 0 352 33670 5	

BLACK LACE BOOKS WITH AN HISTORICAL SETTING

- [ ] THE AMULET Lisette Allen — ISBN 978 0 352 33019 2 £6.99
- [ ] THE BARBARIAN GEISHA Charlotte Royal — ISBN 978 0 352 33267 7
- [ ] BARBARIAN PRIZE Deanna Ashford — ISBN 978 0 352 34017 7
- [ ] DANCE OF OBSESSION Olivia Christie — ISBN 978 0 352 33101 4
- [ ] DARKER THAN LOVE Kristina Lloyd — ISBN 978 0 352 33279 0
- [ ] ELENA'S DESTINY Lisette Allen — ISBN 978 0 352 33218 9
- [ ] FRENCH MANNERS Olivia Christie — ISBN 978 0 352 33214 1
- [ ] LORD WRAXALL'S FANCY Anna Lieff Saxby — ISBN 978 0 352 33080 2
- [ ] NICOLE'S REVENGE Lisette Allen — ISBN 978 0 352 32984 4
- [ ] THE SENSES BEJEWELLED Cleo Cordell — ISBN 978 0 352 32904 2 £6.99
- [ ] THE SOCIETY OF SIN Sian Lacey Taylder — ISBN 978 0 352 34080 1
- [ ] UNDRESSING THE DEVIL Angel Strand — ISBN 978 0 352 33938 6
- [ ] WHITE ROSE ENSNARED Juliet Hastings — ISBN 978 0 352 33052 9 £6.99

BLACK LACE BOOKS WITH A PARANORMAL THEME

- [ ] BRIGHT FIRE Maya Hess — ISBN 978 0 352 34104 4
- [ ] BURNING BRIGHT Janine Ashbless — ISBN 978 0 352 34085 6
- [ ] CRUEL ENCHANTMENT Janine Ashbless — ISBN 978 0 352 33483 1
- [ ] FLOOD Anna Clare — ISBN 978 0 352 34094 8
- [ ] GOTHIC BLUE Portia Da Costa — ISBN 978 0 352 33075 8
- [ ] THE PRIDE Edie Bingham — ISBN 978 0 352 33997 3

BLACK LACE ANTHOLOGIES

- [ ] BLACK LACE QUICKIES 1 Various — ISBN 978 0 352 34126 6 £2.99
- [ ] BLACK LACE QUICKIES 2 Various — ISBN 978 0 352 34127 3 £2.99
- [ ] BLACK LACE QUICKIES 3 Various — ISBN 978 0 352 34128 0 £2.99
- [ ] BLACK LACE QUICKIES 4 Various — ISBN 978 0 352 34129 7 £2.99
- [ ] MORE WICKED WORDS Various — ISBN 978 0 352 33487 9 £6.99
- [ ] WICKED WORDS 3 Various — ISBN 978 0 352 33522 7 £6.99
- [ ] WICKED WORDS 4 Various — ISBN 978 0 352 33603 3 £6.99
- [ ] WICKED WORDS 5 Various — ISBN 978 0 352 33642 2 £6.99
- [ ] WICKED WORDS 6 Various — ISBN 978 0 352 33690 3 £6.99
- [ ] WICKED WORDS 7 Various — ISBN 978 0 352 33743 6 £6.99
- [ ] WICKED WORDS 8 Various — ISBN 978 0 352 33787 0 £6.99
- [ ] WICKED WORDS 9 Various — ISBN 978 0 352 33860 0
- [ ] WICKED WORDS 10 Various — ISBN 978 0 352 33893 8

To find out the latest information about Black Lace titles, check out the website: www.black-lace-books.com or send for a booklist with complete synopses by writing to:

> Black Lace Booklist, Virgin Books Ltd
> Thames Wharf Studios
> Rainville Road
> London W6 9HA

Please include an SAE of decent size. Please note only British stamps are valid.

Our privacy policy
We will not disclose information you supply us to any other parties. We will not disclose any information which identifies you personally to any person without your express consent.

From time to time we may send out information about Black Lace books and special offers. Please tick here if you do <u>not</u> wish to receive Black Lace information.   ☐

Please send me the books I have ticked above.

Name ....

Address ....

....

....

....

Post Code ....

Send to: Virgin Books Cash Sales, Thames Wharf Studios, Rainville Road, London W6 9HA.

US customers: for prices and details of how to order books for delivery by mail, call 888-330-8477.

Please enclose a cheque or postal order, made payable to Virgin Books Ltd, to the value of the books you have ordered plus postage and packing costs as follows:

UK and BFPO – £1.00 for the first book, 50p for each subsequent book.

Overseas (including Republic of Ireland) – £2.00 for the first book, £1.00 for each subsequent book.

If you would prefer to pay by VISA, ACCESS/MASTERCARD, DINERS CLUB, AMEX or SWITCH, please write your card number and expiry date here:

....

Signature ....

Please allow up to 28 days for delivery.

floor. 'Congratulations,' he said. 'Let me
and I will arrange security